BEYOND the GAME

NEW YORK TIMES BESTSELLING AUTHOR

KAYLEE RYAN

Beyond the Game

Cover Design by Sommer Stein, Perfect Pear Creative Covers
Cover Photography by Sara Eirew
Edited by Hot Tree Editing
Proofreading: Deaton Author Services & Editing 4 Indies
Paperback formatted by Jersey Girl Design

Other Titles by Kaylee Ryan

With You Series
Anywhere with You | More with You | Everything with You

Soul Serenade Series
Emphatic | Assured | Definite | Insistent

Southern Heart Series
Southern Pleasure | Southern Desire | Southern Attraction | Southern Devotion

Unexpected Arrivals Series
Unexpected Reality | Unexpected Fight | Unexpected Fall | Unexpected Bond
Unexpected Odds

Riggins Brothers Series
Play by Play | Layer by Layer
Piece by Piece | Kiss by Kiss | Touch by Touch

Out of Reach Series
Beyond the Bases | Beyond the Game

Standalone Titles
Tempting Tatum | Unwrapping Tatum | Levitate
Just Say When | I Just Want You
Reminding Avery | Hey, Whiskey | Pull You Through | Remedy | The Difference
Trust the Push

Entangled Hearts Duet
Agony | Bliss

Cocky Hero Club
Lucky Bastard

Box Sets
Series Starter - Kaylee Ryan

Co-written with Lacey Black
Fair Lakes Series
It's Not Over | Just Getting Started
Can't Fight It

Standalone Titles
Boy Trouble | Home to You

Chapter One

PAISLEY

THERE IS NOTHING LIKE THE SMELL OF THE BLAZE STADIUM ON GAME DAY. THE OVERPRICED stale beer that permeates the air, freshly popped popcorn, hot dogs, and dirt. *It smells like home.* I grew up here watching my dad and honorary uncles play for the Blaze. As the family of the starting first baseman, we had the option to sit in the suites, but my mom, sisters, and I loved being in the center of the action. Seats right behind the dugout where Dad could say hi to us, and we could yell back and know that he could hear us.

I have so many childhood memories from this stadium, and I missed it while I was away at college.

Playing for my college team, a pitcher like my grandpa Monroe, I've played in a lot of stadiums. Sure, most were college, but none of them, even my home team stadium, ever felt like this. My home away from home.

"Earth to Paisley," my best friend, Willow, says, waving her hand in front of my face. "Are you in there?" She laughs.

"Stop." I swat at her hand while grinning. "It's been a while since I've been here. I'm just taking it all in."

"You grew up here. What could possibly be new for you?"

Willow and I have been best friends since day one of kindergarten. She and

I played T-ball together. She liked it but never had the strong love for it that I did. She stopped playing around the fifth grade, but she has always been one of my biggest cheerleaders. She and I attended the same college and roomed together all four years. We actually still live together today. After graduation, we rented a condo not far from my parents' place. Dad, of course, helped us find it. Even though I'm twenty-two, he likes to have me close. Who am I kidding? He likes to have all four of his girls close—his words, not mine. Regardless that my mom is his wife, he includes her as one of his girls with me and my sisters.

"It's not new," I finally answer. "It's the familiarity, like coming home."

"Girl, you and your baseball." She links her arm through mine. "Don't get me wrong, I'm all for some hotties in baseball pants. We better grab our snacks and find our seats, or I'm going to miss the stretches. That's one of the best parts of the game."

She's not wrong. While I love the sport, no, it's more than that. Baseball and softball are a part of me. There isn't a single solitary thing I don't love. Even watching the players in their uniforms. I even like to tease my dad about it. It's fun to see him get all wound up about me dating. He claims I'm not old enough. At twenty-two, I know different, and so does Mom. The truth of the matter is I don't know if I'll ever meet a man who my dad thinks is good enough for me. His words, not mine, but I believe them. It's not just me. It's my two younger sisters, Parker and Peyton, too. We're all three daddy's girls.

We make our way to the concession stand and order our first round of snacks. We both get a large drink and a hot dog, which we smother in ketchup and mustard. This is just the first round. We're seasoned pros at pacing ourselves.

"Ready?" Willow asks.

"Yes. I just need to grab some napkins." I grab a pretty large stack and shove them into my small crossbody purse. Stadium hot dogs are messy. Well, all the ketchup and mustard I added is messy. I need to be prepared, which is something I've learned over the years. With my hot dog in one hand and my drink in the other, I lead us to our seats.

My family has sat in these seats for as long as I can remember. It's a Monroe family tradition that I plan to keep alive.

"Damn, number thirty is looking fine today," Willow says dramatically before taking a huge bite of her hot dog.

"Mm-hmm," I agree before taking my own bite. Nothing is better than a man in baseball pants.

"Is anyone else in your family coming today? Whose ticket am I stealing?" Willow asks.

"Nobody's that I'm aware of. Parker had a game. It started about thirty minutes ago," I explain. My sisters, like me, followed in our dad's footsteps. All three of us fell in love with the game and play softball.

"Good. I don't have to censor myself." She laughs.

"When have you ever censored yourself?" I fire back.

"When your parents are here, and Peyton. Parker's old enough to enjoy my commentary." She grins, and I can't help but return it. My best friend is what my grandma calls boy crazy. She's not one to sleep around, but she loves to flirt, and she's made looking at the players its own sport. She blames me for dragging her to so many games over the years.

All I can do is shake my head and smile. Willow has been my person since I was a little girl, and I wouldn't change her for the world. When we're asked to stand for the national anthem, we turn to face the flag. Chills race down my spine as the stadium grows quiet, and nothing can be heard but the sultry voice of a local high school student singing our country's anthem.

When it's over, I move to sit and bump into someone. I turn to look over my shoulder and apologize, but my breath stalls in my lungs. The most gorgeous guy I've ever seen in my entire life is standing behind me, holding his hand up in apology.

"Sorry about that," he says in his deep sexy voice, as he takes the seat next to mine.

I open my mouth to reply, and nothing comes out. I feel an elbow dig into my side as Willow leans around me. "Hi."

Our sexy neighbor grins, and the dimple in his cheek pops out. His brown eyes sparkle. "Nice to meet you, ladies. I apologize." He nods toward me.

"I should have been paying attention," I say, finally finding my words. "I didn't know anyone was sitting there." He's sitting in seats I know the team owns. He must be related to one of the players, or maybe he's a friend. Either way, it's going to be hard for me to focus on the game, and for me, that's saying a lot.

"Yeah, I'm running late. Traffic." He shrugs. "I don't usually wait until the middle of the national anthem to show up at a ball game."

"You should take some pointers from my girl here," Willow says as I turn to look at her. She's being her usual outgoing self, but as always, she has my back. "We always leave early. No way are we missing warm-ups." She wiggles her eyebrows, and I can feel my face heat.

"Warm-ups." He nods, a grin playing on his lips. "That's the best part, is it?" His voice is teasing.

"Well, if you play for our team, it is." Willow laughs. "I mean, hot guys in tight pants. We. Are. Here. For. It." She nods, returning his smile.

"What about you?" the sexy guy asks.

"Me?"

"You digging the tight pants too?"

He's teasing, and I feel myself relax a little. "That's part of it," I admit.

"And the other part?"

"There are lots of them. The smell of the dirt, the food, the crack of the bat... hell, even the wave is essential to the experience."

"Uh-oh," Willow says with an eye roll, "now you've done it. You got my girl here talking about baseball, and now we're doomed to hear all about it the entire game."

"Stop." I laugh, which earns me a smile from both the sexy guy and my best friend. "I love the game. Baseball was a major part of my household growing up." I don't tell him that Easton Monroe is my dad. I also don't tell him that my uncle Drew, who is not my uncle but one of my dad's best friends, is the general manager of the Blaze. He retired from playing for the team and took over when the current GM retired. Baseball was more than just a big part of my life growing up. It was my life.

Still is.

"What about you?" Willow asks him.

"I'm a fan," he says, lifting his hat from his head, and running his hands through his hair.

"If you're not a Blaze fan, don't tell us. Well, don't tell her." Willow points toward me. "She's a ride or die."

Our sexy seat neighbor raises his eyebrows in question. "She's not wrong." I shrug unapologetically.

The crowd roars as the Blaze team takes the field, and I turn my attention to the game. Mindlessly, I take my seat, watching as the game starts to unfold. We have a great team this year, and our chances of going all the way are high. "Hell yeah!" I cheer when the Blaze strikes out the Tomahawks.

Willow leans around me to talk to our sexy neighbor. "Told you so." She laughs. "By the way, I'm Willow, and this is Paisley," she introduces us.

He offers Willow his hand, which crosses over in front of me. "Cameron," he says. His voice is deep and husky, and the ink covering his arms has me squirming in my seat. What is it about this man that has me reacting like I've never been in the presence of a hot guy? He's hands down the hottest, so I'm guessing that's my hang-up.

I feel another elbow, and my head whips around to glare at Willow, who nods toward Cameron. His lip is tilted up in a grin, his dimple playing peekaboo. His eyes flash to his hand that's just hanging out there, waiting for me to accept his handshake. My face heats, and it's not from the sun.

"Sorry," I say sheepishly. "Paisley." I offer my name even though Willow already told him as I slide my hand into his. His hands are so much larger than mine, and they're rough and calloused, which makes me wonder what he does for a living. However, I can't seem to form the words to ask him from the spark that's shooting up my arm. It's as if I've been zapped with electricity. My eyes widen, and if I hadn't been watching, I would have missed the slight widening of his eyes.

Does he feel it too?

"Pleasure to meet you, Paisley." His voice drops to a low octave that's even sexier. I don't remember him saying something similar to Willow. Then again, I was zoning out too. Willow clears her throat, and I snap out of my Cameron trance and realize I'm still holding his hand as I stare at him.

"So hot," Willow whispers. I hear Cameron's low chuckle, which tells me he heard her.

"Stop," I reply to my best friend under my breath.

"I'm just saying," she replies. This time, she doesn't even bother to try to lower her voice.

I've never been embarrassed and turned on all at the same time. This is most definitely a first for me. What's also a first? Me being at a game and not being able to focus. It's usually the other way around. I tune out the world as I let myself get lost in the game and the happenings on the field. Today, that's not the case. I'm hyperaware of every move Cameron makes. A shift of his legs, the stretch of his arms, and the way he's constantly stealing glances my way.

I feel it all.

Every movement.

It's driving me insane.

Normally, I'm glued to my seat, and it's Willow or my sisters who bring me more snacks. On the rare occasion that I do leave my seat, it's for a run to the bathroom. Not today. Today, I need a break. I stand abruptly and turn toward Willow. "I'm going for more snacks. Do you want anything?"

"Oh! Cracker Jacks." She grins. "Hey, Cameron, do you need anything?" she asks. I shoot her a warning glare, but she pretends not to notice.

"You making a run?" he asks, standing and stretching his arms over his head.

My eyes go to his waist, where his shirt rides up, and I can see just a sliver of his toned abs, and oh, God, is that a V I see? Just when I thought he couldn't be any more attractive.

"Paisley?" He bends down, his eyes capturing my attention.

"Yeah." I nod. I think he asked me if I was going to get snacks, but I can't be sure. My answer seems to be the right one when he gives me a nod of his own.

"I'll come with. I need to stretch my legs anyway."

It's on the tip of my tongue to refuse, but Willow speaks up before I can. "In that case, a refill, please?" she asks sweetly. She can pretend to be sweet and innocent all she wants. I know what she's doing. She's playing matchmaker. She's always after me to date more. I don't know how many times I've heard her tell me that there is more to life than baseball, and well, softball by default. If my college would have let me play with the guys, I would have. It's bullshit if you ask me.

"I can get whatever you need," I tell Cameron.

"It will be good to stretch out. Come on." He offers me his hand, and I stare at it for three heartbeats before he takes the decision away from me. He reaches for my hand and laces his fingers through mine as he guides me up the steps.

My heart pounds against my chest, and my ears ring. My palm is sweating, and that just causes me to be embarrassed all over again. Sweaty palms when you're holding the hand of the sexiest man on earth is not my idea of a good time.

When we reach the top of the stairs, he drops my hand and places his own on the small of my back. He's walking close, too close, and I'm sure he can hear the rapid stutter of my heart inside my chest.

I expect him to drop his hand when we reach the concession stand, but he does the opposite. When someone needs to cross through since the line is long, he pulls me into his side, wrapping his arm around my waist.

"Excuse me," the woman with two small kids complaining they have to potty says as she walks in front of us, cutting through to the long line for the bathrooms.

"What are you getting?" Cameron asks. His lips are right next to my ear, his arm still around my waist.

"Uh…a pretzel," I say lamely. I've never been speechless in front of a man before. My dad is Easton Monroe. He was the starting first baseman for the Tennessee Blaze the majority of my life. I've met a lot of famous athletes—very attractive famous athletes—and I've never had this reaction before. I've never been breathless, with sweaty palms and the inability to speak coherently.

"Cheese or mustard?" Cameron asks. If he senses my inability to act like a normal human being around him, he doesn't show it.

"Both."

"My kinda girl," he says, and I can hear the smile in his voice. I don't dare look to test my theory. Instead, I stare straight ahead and focus on my breathing. He's just a guy. A ridiculously sexy guy.

"Next!" the concession stand attendant calls.

"Hi," Cameron greets her. "We need two soft pretzels, with both cheese and mustard, a box of Cracker Jacks, a bottle of water, a large Coke, and Paisley?" He peers down at me. "What do you want to drink?"

"Gatorade. Blue."

He nods. "And one blue Gatorade." He releases his hold on me, allowing me to close my eyes and pull in a deep breath. When I open them, he's passing money to the attendant.

"Cameron, no." I place my hand on his arm. "You don't have to do that."

He smiles at me. "I wanted to. What kind of guy am I if I don't pay for a beautiful woman's snacks?" He winks and turns back to accept his change.

"Thank you," I mumble as he hands me my Gatorade and Willow's Coke.

"Ready?" he asks.

All I can do is nod and follow along behind him. When we reach the steps, he moves to the side and motions for me to go ahead of him. I do, not because he told me to, but because I need my seat. Any other time, it would be for fear of missing the game. Today, however, it's because of the man walking along behind me, making my knees weak.

Chapter Two

CAMERON

IS THERE ANYTHING HOTTER THAN A WOMAN WHO LOVES BASEBALL? THE ANSWER IS NO. A few hours ago, I wouldn't have been able to answer that question. However, sitting next to Paisley during the Blaze game has me definite in my answer.

She doesn't just love the game. She gets it.

She understands the plays, the calls, and she's not invested because she's hoping to land a player. You can see it in her eyes. She truly loves the sport. Luck was on my side today when I was seated next to her. I make a mental note to thank the front office for the connection. Not the seat, but my seatmate.

"Time for some nachos," Willow announces as she stands and stretches. She's cute, but she's not Paisley. "Anyone want anything?"

"I'm good. Thanks, though," I tell her.

"P?" she asks.

"Popcorn," she says, reaching into her purse for money.

"You got the last round."

"Actually, it was Cameron."

Willow grins. "Interesting." She smiles at her friend before turning her gaze on me. "Thank you, Cameron. Are you sure I can't get you anything?"

Your friend's number? "Nah, I'm good. Thanks."

"You two kids behave." Willow points at each of us with a sassy grin before rushing up the steps.

"Damn," Paisley mutters as Marty Harris gets struck out. "We needed that hit," she mumbles.

I missed it because I was looking at her. How can I not? Her hair is pulled up in some kind of knot sticking out the back of her Blaze hat. She has on short cutoffs and a Blaze tank top. Her feet are in flip-flops, and her toes are painted a bright pink. She's understatedly sexy, and I'm having a hard time concentrating on anything but her.

I love baseball. I have since I was a toddler. I live for the game. No woman has ever been able to pull my attention from the game, well, unless you count my mom. I'm man enough to admit I'm a momma's boy. I have a soft spot where she's concerned. But she's the only one.

Until today.

Until Paisley.

"I've never seen you here before," she comments, never taking her eyes off the field. That's fine because that allows me to not take mine off her.

"It's been a long time since I've watched a game from the stands."

She slowly turns her head to look at me. Her eyes are now covered with sunglasses, but that's okay. I already have their dark brown color memorized. The color reminds me of my old baseball glove. "It's been a while for me too," she admits.

I want to ask her why, but Willow appears next to her friend, handing over her popcorn. "Thanks, Wil," Paisley says, taking the offered snack.

That's something else. She's not one of those women who are afraid to eat in front of the opposite sex. She's enjoying her snacks, and I never realized how much of a turn-on that could be. A woman who is unapologetically who she wants to be. It's endearing and sexy as fuck.

Glancing at the scoreboard, I see we're already in the sixth inning, and I will time to slow down. Not just because of my love of the game, it's the company as well. I haven't had the chance to find out all I need to know about her. Where is she from? What does she do? Does she have a boyfriend? There's no ring on her finger, and I'd like to think any man with a brain who would be lucky enough to call this woman his would be right here by her side. I know I would be.

"So, Cameron, do you have any cute friends?" Willow asks before shoving a chip into her mouth.

"I feel like this is a trick question." I laugh.

"Nope. I'm just not looking forward to being the third wheel."

"Willow!" Paisley hisses.

Willow shrugs. "I'm just saying, P." She's not the least bit sorry for her words.

"I have lots of friends." I'm already mentally scrolling through which of the guys I could set up with Willow. Talk about putting the cart before the horse.

She points at the field. "Do they look like that in baseball pants?" She wags her eyebrows.

"I don't really make it a habit to check out my friends' asses."

"Fair point," she agrees. "What about this? Do the ladies flock to them?"

"You could say that."

"Perfect. I'll take one of those, please." She wags her eyebrows again before shoving another chip into her mouth.

Paisley turns to face me. "I'm sorry. She's lost her mind apparently," she mumbles.

"I don't know. I think her idea has merit." I give her my most charming smile. The one my mom claims could charm any woman with a pulse. I'm leaning into her, and if I'm not mistaken, her posture shifts to lean in just a little closer to me as well.

"I'm sure you're busy doing… whatever it is that you do."

I should tell her what I do, but I like the mystery. Sitting next to Paisley has been the most fun I've had with a woman in longer than I can remember. "I can make the time," I assure her.

The crack of the bat echoes throughout the stadium, pulling her attention.

Jeffrey Jennings just hit a home run for the Blaze. This has Paisley jumping out of her seat and thrusting her hands in the air as she cheers. She begins to high-five the people sitting in front of us and behind us. They're all talking and celebrating like they're old friends, and I can't help but be envious. I want to be the one celebrating with her.

She takes her seat, and our arms brush each other on the armrest. She's quick to pull away, and I have to force myself not to reach over into her lap and lace her fingers with mine. With the softness of her skin against the roughness of mine, she's a perfect fit. I bite back a laugh. I'm being ridiculous. It's as if one look from this beauty and my world has been tipped upside down.

"Come on!" Paisley calls out.

My eyes travel to the screen to watch the replay. The first baseman, a veteran, John Hastings, missed a line drive that should have landed straight in his glove. Instead, the ball bounced off his glove and rolled right, and all three runners advanced. It was a play he should have had in the bag, but he's getting slower. If I'm being honest, he's been slow for a while. That's a part of the reason I'm here today. To take a look at the team, and first base in particular. It's a position that the Blaze needs to fill. In fact, since losing All-Star first baseman Easton Monroe, the Blaze has been lacking in that position.

"He should have had that," Paisley mutters, crossing her arms over her chest.

"Just ignore her," Willow says, leaning over Paisley to talk to me. "She takes her baseball seriously."

"Nothing wrong with being passionate about something," I reply. Both women turn to look at me, and I shrug. I have a passion for baseball as well. I also have a passion for the brown-eyed beauty sitting next to me.

Speaking of those brown eyes, I need to see them. Reaching over, I push her sunglasses down on her nose. "There they are," I say, my voice soft.

"What are you doing?"

"I needed to see your eyes." She meets my stare for several heartbeats. It's not until Willow interrupts does she break our connection and look away.

"Look!" Willow points at the jumbo-sized screen closest to our seats.

I don't want to pull my gaze away from Paisley, but I don't want to be a dick to her best friend, either. Not if I plan on seeing her again. My eyes follow to where Willow is pointing. I glance at the screen and see that we're on the kiss cam. I can't stop the grin that tilts my lips when I look back at Paisley. "What do you say?" I ask her. My voice is light, hiding the fact that I want to kiss her.

"Oh." Her cheeks pinken. "We don't have to. I mean, we don't know each other." The rise and fall of her chest and the way that she licks her lips tells me she's just being polite. She wants to kiss me as badly as I want to kiss her.

"P, it's the kiss cam, and you would literally be kissing Cam," Willow points out.

"She has a point. My friends do call me Cam." My smile grows.

"We don't have to," she says again. She says the words, but she leans in, just a fraction of an inch, but I see it, and I plan to give us both what we want.

I lean in close, blocking out the world around us. "What do you say, Paisley? Can I kiss you?" She swallows hard and gives me a subtle nod. That's the only invitation I need. Turning my ball cap backward, I slide my hand behind her neck and move her mouth closer to mine. Her breath hitches just before my lips touch hers, and I feel that sound all the way to my cock.

I take my time, softly pressing my lips against hers. They're softer than I imagined them to be. I nip at her bottom lip, and she gasps, opening for me. All bets are off when I slide my tongue past her lips, tasting her for the first time.

My free hand cradles her cheek as I allow myself to get lost in her. I kiss her slow and deep, taking my time. I have no idea if I'll ever get this chance again, and I'm taking it. What's that saying you miss 100 percent of the shots you never take? No way do I want to leave this stadium today with regrets, and not kissing Paisley would be the biggest of my life to date.

When I start to hear clapping and yells of encouragement, I know I have to pull away from her, but I don't know if I can. I kiss her a few more times, soft pecks against her lips, before drawing my head back to look at her. Her sunglasses are once again covering her eyes, but I can see the tint to her cheeks and the way she seems to be struggling to take a deep breath. I recognize the signs because I'm a victim of the same symptoms.

"Wow!" Willow says, breaking our trance.

Paisley sits back in her seat and stares out onto the field. I can't get a read on her. I don't know what she's thinking. "Hey." I lean in close and whisper in her ear, "You okay?"

"Sure," she says, not bothering to look at me.

"Sure" from a woman means the exact opposite. "Paisley?" I wait for her to look at me, but she never does. Something that feels a lot like panic rises in my chest. The last thing I want is for her to be pissed at me. She kissed me back. We were both willing participants.

"Oh, look at that replay." Willow points at the screen once again.

I can't resist as I turn my head and watch as my lips mold with hers. She pulls on my shirt, something I missed during the actual event. Reaching over, I lace her fingers with mine, giving them a gentle squeeze as I keep my eyes focused on the screen. The person running the camera nailed it. They caught the most passionate kiss of my life. I give myself a mental pat on the back that I am recording the game at home. This way, I can watch it over and over and over again. Not that I won't be able to remember it vividly. A kiss like that, with the buzz around the stadium, I'm sure we'll make the blogs and even YouTube before we make it out of the parking lot.

For the remainder of the game, the three of us are quiet. Unless it's to yell about a play or cheer on the Blaze, none of us says a word. She lets me hold her hand the entire time. I can only imagine what my mom is thinking. I know she's at home watching. She wanted to see if they would show me on camera in the stands. She's going to see the kiss and me holding this beautiful woman's hand and think that I've been hiding her away.

The truth is, if Paisley were mine, I'd never hide her away. I'd scream it from the fucking rooftops that she was my girl. That's saying something because I haven't had a girlfriend since high school. Not once I figured out every girl I dated was using me as a ticket out of our small-town Georgia life. College was the same, but I was smarter about it. I didn't date, and I still don't. You know, keeping your eye on the prize and all that. The prize being my career.

At the bottom of the ninth, the Blaze are up by two, and the bases are loaded. Paisley squeezes my hand, and the Tomahawks hitter steps up to the plate for his final hit. One more strike, and he's out, leaving the Blaze the victors. The pitch is thrown, and the umpire calls out strike again. Paisley jumps from her seat, as does Willow, and they dance around. I watch in fascination as she high-fives everyone around us again. I stand to join them in their celebration, and I'm not disappointed when she turns to face me and launches herself into my arms for a hug.

"We did it!" she cheers. All too quickly, she's leaving my embrace, but that's okay. I got to hold her for just the smallest amount of time, which was more than I needed to know that I need to see her again. I open my mouth to tell her that exact thing when an older gentleman sitting behind us commands her attention. I step up close, and it takes everything I have in the way of willpower not to place my hands on her hips and pull her close.

Finally, they end their conversation, and she and Willow both begin to gather their trash. "Thank you for the snacks and the company," Paisley says politely.

"And the kiss," Willow adds, with a wicked grin.

"That too." Paisley nods.

"I'll walk you out," I tell them.

"No. That's okay. It was nice meeting you, Cameron."

"Hey." I reach out and grab her arm gently. "Can I see you again?" I sound desperate even to my own ears, and maybe I am.

"Do you believe in fate, Cameron?"

"Never really thought about it," I admit.

"Not many do."

"Do you believe in fate, Paisley?" I shoot her question back to her.

"Not so much, but Willow here, she's a firm believer that everything happens for a reason."

"Okay?" I'm not really sure what she's getting at here.

"If we meet again, it was meant to be." She shocks the hell out of me when she goes up on her tiptoes and presses a kiss on my cheek. "Thanks again," she says before rushing up the steps.

Like the fool that I am, I stand here and watch her go. By the time I realize I'm letting her just walk away from me without a last name or even her phone number, I jump into action and sprint up the steps, stepping around everyone who happens to be in my way. I reach the top, and my eyes skim everywhere, but there is no sign of her.

"Fuck," I mumble under my breath.

"You never should have let her walk away," a gravelly voice says from behind me. It's the old man she was talking to.

"Do you know her last name?" I ask.

"I do."

"What do I need to do to get that information from you?"

"Nothing. I'm not giving it to you. If she wanted you to have it, she would have told you."

"Come on. I'm one of the good guys, I promise." I say the words and realize I sound like a creeper.

The old man chuckles and runs his hands over his graying beard. "I'm sure you are, but I've watched that girl grow up. She's no relation, but she feels like family. So, I'm sorry to say I can't help you. I heard her mention something about fate. All you can do, son, is hope and pray that fate is on your side and you see her again."

With that sage advice, he walks away. I'm left standing here like a fool as I mentally kick my own ass for letting her go—the best kiss of my entire life. The best day I've had with a woman to date, and I just let her go. What if she was my future wife? Pissed at myself, I make my way out to the parking lot. Every woman I pass with a ball cap and Blaze tank gets an extra careful look as I hope to find her in the sea of people.

It turns out luck isn't on my side.

Chapter Three

PAISLEY

IT'S BEEN TWO FULL WEEKS SINCE THE BLAZE GAME THAT ROCKED MY UNIVERSE ON ITS axis. It's also been two weeks that I've been able to avoid my dad. My excuse was work. As the new athletic trainer for the Tennessee Blaze, it was believable. However, my luck has run out as I stare down at the text message I just received.

Mom: Dinner at our place tonight.

Me: What if I had plans?

Mom: You can't avoid your father forever, Paisley.

Me: Fine. I'm bringing Willow.

Mom: She's always welcome.

Me: What time?

Mom: I'll have dinner ready at six.

Me: Okay.

There is no use in arguing with her because I know she's right. Dad has been calling me, and I've used the excuse that either I'm too busy or too exhausted to talk. I know he can see right through me, but it's bought me some time. It's bad enough that I know he's calling to talk about the guy I was, in his words, "all over at that game," two weeks ago. I already can't stop thinking about Cameron and that kiss. The way he held my face as if I was important to him—the soft yet firm press of his lips. And then there's the hand holding. I didn't know that it was possible to fantasize about holding someone's hand. Not even in my younger years did that happen.

It's not just that. It's the deep timbre of his voice, the way he filled out that T-shirt, the muscles, and his tattoos. Cameron Taylor is the total package and kisses like he's been trained to do so. I can't tell you how many nights in the past two weeks I've fallen asleep thinking about him and waking up the same way. Actually, that's not true. I can tell you. Every damn night he's with me.

I admit not getting his last name for myself or his phone number was a stupid mistake on my part. I've heard Willow talk about fate and how that's her plan to find the love of her life. Her plan is to shamelessly flirt until then. Not that I think Cameron is the love of my life. I mean, I guess he could have been, but my dumbass walked away without a way to get ahold of him. Not my best decision.

However, as it turns out, the media found him for me. He's a player for the Tennessee Outlaws, the Blaze farm team. I have the connections and the resources to find him, to reach out to him, but something is holding me back. I almost want to leave it in fate's hands. If we meet again, then maybe we'll see if something is there. And if not? Well, we will always have our day at the game and the kiss that rocked my world.

After cleaning up the training room, I make my way to my small office, grab my purse, and head out. As soon as I'm in my car and headed toward our condo, I dial Willow.

"Hey. Are you on your way home?"

"Yeah, but I have bad news."

"What? Are you okay?" I can hear the concern in her voice.

"No. We have to have dinner with my parents tonight." Willow's reply is to laugh raucously in my ear. "It's not funny, Wil," I whine.

"Yes, it is. Your dad has been after you for two weeks. Let me guess, the invitation came from your mom?" she asks, hitting the nail on the head.

"Yep."

"What time do we need to be there? No way am I missing this," she says, still sputtering with laughter.

"Traitor. I changed my mind. You can't come."

"Oh, that's fine. I'll just call Larissa. You know as well as I do, she's going to extend the invitation."

"Brat." I stick my tongue out for good measure even though she can't see me.

"You know it. See you soon," she says and ends the call.

For the remainder of my drive home, I'm thinking of how to divert my dad's attention toward my new job and away from Cameron. No matter what angle I think of, I know well enough that it won't work. I'm going to have to face the music. In this case, Easton Monroe. He's always been fiercely protective of his girls. That includes Mom, me, and my two younger sisters. I knew this was coming. I just hoped I could avoid it a little longer.

When I pull into our condo complex, Willow is sitting on the bench outside. She rushes toward the car, pulling open the passenger door. "What if I needed to go inside?" I ask her once she shuts the door.

"The only reason you need to go inside is to stall."

"Traitor," I grumble again, making her laugh.

"Seriously, Paisley, just woman up and face him. You're an adult."

"This is my dad we're talking about. He's going to want to know who Cameron is, and I have to tell him that he's just some guy I was sitting next to at the game and had the hottest kiss of my life with."

"I'd leave that last part out. And you don't have to tell him he was a stranger. Just tell him his name is Cameron, and it was for the kiss cam."

"Like Dad is going to let it go after that. I'm screwed. I'm going to have to sit through him lecturing me about safety and how dangerous it was." What's worse is that he's right. It was dangerous, but I had no control over the effect that Cameron had on me. I still don't. It's been two weeks, and he's commandeered every waking moment of my thoughts.

"I get his point, but we were in public, and it was being taped. You were fine. Not to mention that everyone in that stadium knows who you are, well, aside from Cameron. Wait. You don't think he knows that you're Easton Monroe's daughter and the new athletic trainer for the Blaze, do you?"

"No. I don't think he's aware of either." At least, I don't think he is. If so, he didn't let on at all that he knew who my dad or I was.

"It will be fine. He loves you. You know he might lecture you, but you have him wrapped around your little finger. Hell, your mom and sisters do too." She chuckles.

"I know it's out of love, but I hate disappointing him," I say as I pull into their driveway. I see my youngest sister, Peyton, pull back the curtain, and then she's gone, and the door is being thrown open.

"Paisley!" she calls out, making me smile.

Peyton is twelve going on eighteen and wise beyond her years. She's always smiling and happy to see me. As she jumps off the front porch and makes a beeline for me, I brace myself for her hug. When she wraps her arms around me and tells me that she missed me, I give myself a moment to hug my baby sister and pretend my dad isn't inside, waiting to grill me.

"Why has it been so long since you've been to see us?" Peyton asks once she's released her hold on me. I look down at my baby sister, who stares right back with her hands on her hips. I can't help but smile. She looks like Mom when she's scolding us.

"I started a new job," I explain.

"Yeah, but do you work all the time?" She tilts her head to the side, and I have to bite my cheek to keep from laughing at her and all of her twelve-year-old sass.

"You plan on standing out in the driveway all night?" My dad's voice meets my ears.

Looking up, I find him standing on the front porch. He's leaning against the post with his arms crossed over his chest and his legs crossed at his ankles. He's going for casual, but I know he's hurt and pissed that I've been avoiding him.

"Just saying hello, that's all," I call back. Reaching into my car, I grab my phone and shut the door. Peyton takes my hand and Willow's once we join her, and the three of us walk to the front porch in solidarity.

"Willow, it's nice to see you." Dad greets her with a hug and a smile. "Lady," he says, referring to the nickname he gave Peyton the day she was born. "Why don't you take Willow inside so I can talk to your sister."

"I already yelled at her for being gone so long," Peyton announces proudly.

Dad pulls her into a hug and kisses the top of her head. "Thank you, sweetheart," he says softly before releasing her. I stand frozen as my best friend, who I hoped would be a shield, and my little sister disappear into the house. "Sit with me." Dad holds out his hand, and I take it without hesitation.

He might be angry and disappointed with me, but my father would never hurt me. I'm not afraid of him, but I hate knowing that I hurt him and disappointed him. He takes a seat on the front porch swing and pulls me down next to him, wrapping his arm around my shoulders and hugging me close.

"I missed you, princess," he says, placing a kiss on the top of my head.

My shoulders deflate. "I missed you too, Dad."

We're both quiet for a few minutes when he finally asks. "So, who's the guy?"

"I don't know him," I tell him honestly. "He was sitting next to our seats. His name is Cameron. He plays for the Outlaws."

"Do you make it a habit of kissing strangers like that?"

"Like what?" I ask, feigning innocence when we both know that it's complete bullshit.

"Like he's your air."

I pull away so I can get a good look at him. "I wasn't," I defend.

"Paisley," he says in his dad voice. "I've watched that replay more times than I care to admit. I know what I saw."

"You may need to have your eyesight checked, old man," I tease in an attempt to lighten the mood.

"Who are you calling old man?" He chuckles.

"I mean, if the shoe fits," I taunt.

He brings me back to his chest, and his lips once again press against the top of my head. "I love you, Paisley. If anything were to ever happen to you, I don't know what I would do with myself. I just want you safe."

"I know that. I'm a big girl, and regardless of what you might think, I don't just randomly hook up with strangers. The kiss with Cameron was for the kiss cam. Yes, maybe we let it get a little out of hand, but I promise you it was an isolated event." I pause, collecting my thoughts. "You've set the bar high, Dad. I've watched you love Mom, Parker, Peyton, and me, and I won't settle for a man who won't love me the same way."

"There's my girl," he says approvingly. "Now, we better get in there before your mom comes out and yells at us for missing dinner."

Together, we stand from the swing. Dad tugs me into a tight hug. "I love you, princess."

"I love you too, Daddy."

"You barely made it," Parker, my middle sister, says when we walk into the kitchen. "Mom was ready to come and save you and then gripe at you for letting dinner get cold."

"Duchess, you let me worry about your mom." Dad winks at Parker, making her stick her tongue out at him.

"You do know that you two are nauseating, right? I mean, none of my friends' parents carry on like you two," Parker tells him.

Dad shrugs. "Sorry, kiddo. I love your mother, and I'm going to make sure I show her that every single day. You should remember that," he says, tapping the tip of her nose with his index finger.

I lean into Dad and whisper, "Like I said, you set the bar high."

"Are you two good?" Mom asks.

"Yes," Dad and I reply at the same time.

"Good. Let's eat."

We all grab a plate and fill it before going to the dining room to sit. I sigh in relief as I dig into my mashed potatoes. I was expecting this night to go much differently.

"So, Paisley," Mom says.

"Yeah?"

"Good choice." She winks at me.

"Good choice of what?"

"Cameron."

"He's hot!" Parker blurts.

"Lord, help me." Dad laughs and shoves a huge bite of roll into his mouth. He's definitely outnumbered with four women in his life, but I know he wouldn't want it any other way.

The rest of the night is like any other night at the house I grew up in. It's full of laughter and love. I meant what I told my dad. Watching the way he loves my mom, I want what they have. I want a man who has to kiss me as soon as he walks in the door from a long day because he's missed me so much he can't think of anything else. I want a man who will run to the store for tampons and chocolate for his wife or daughters and not blink an eye. I want a man who wants to be my partner and stand beside me in life. I might have let my hormones get the best of me at the game, but it was just a kiss. I'm far more selective when it comes to men and intimacy.

Cameron was a fun experience, but I doubt I'll ever see him again. There's a nagging in the back of my mind that tells me I'm lying to myself. I know there is a chance, but I can keep it professional. It was one ball game. It was one kiss. Besides, I need to focus on my career. Uncle Drew gave me a shot as the new athletic trainer for the Blaze, and I don't want to let him down. He claims I earned the position, that he just signed off on it, but I'm not naïve enough to think that my dad being Easton Monroe and Drew being my honorary uncle didn't influence that position in some way.

It's my time to prove myself. I have plenty of time to fall in love.

Chapter Four

CAMERON

I ALWAYS THOUGHT THAT WHEN THIS DAY FINALLY CAME, I'D BE CALM. I WAS CERTAIN that all I would feel was immense joy for all of the hard work I've put in over the years. I was wrong. As I pull open the doors to the stadium, there is a slight tremble in my hand. I've been playing for the Tennessee Outlaws for three years now. I played ball all four years of college, which my buddies thought was crazy. I made a promise to my mom that I would finish college and have a solid fallback plan, so that's what I did.

For three years, I've played hard and practiced harder. I've spent countless hours at the gym, and I treat my body like a temple. No drinking, and I eat only foods that are on the recommended list from our trainers. I've followed every rule and every guideline to the letter.

I wanted this.

Now here I am.

Walking through the doors of the stadium that is now my new home away from home, I keep my head held high and my shoulders straight as I make my way upstairs to the offices. Stepping onto the glass elevator, I look out over the field, and memories assault me. You would think it would be baseball, but instead, it's the only other thing in my life that can take my mind off the sport I love.

Paisley Monroe.

It didn't take the news outlets long to identify my kissing partner. It turns out she's the daughter of Easton Monroe, a retired first baseman for the Blaze. Her name was everywhere as they replayed that kiss. It took them a little longer to identify me. I get it. I play for the Outlaws, and not many people follow the farm teams. That's okay. I don't need my name out there. They gave me hers.

I've considered looking her up multiple times, but with games, practice, and time in the gym, I just didn't have the opportunity. Now, here I am getting called up. My dream is finally coming true.

Even still, as I walk into the stadium, I can't help but remember her. She was a breath of fresh air and that kiss. My cock twitches behind the zipper of my dress pants. I need to derail this train of thought fast. I'm about to meet with the GM, and I don't need that kind of embarrassment before he's even given me a chance to step onto the field.

The elevator door opens, and I take in a deep breath and slowly exhale as I exit.

"May I help you?" the receptionist asks.

"Cameron Taylor, here for Drew Milton."

"Of course, Mr. Taylor." She bats her eyelashes at me. You can tell they're fake, and I can't help but compare her to Paisley. She doesn't need that shit to be beautiful. She's already naturally so. "Right this way. Mr. Milton is expecting you."

I fall into step behind her and wait as she knocks on the doorframe, announcing our arrival. "Send him in." I hear a deep voice reply. The receptionist steps back and allows me to pass before shutting the door behind me.

"Mr. Taylor, welcome to the Blaze." Drew Milton, the general manager, stands to shake my hand. "Please have a seat."

"Thank you, sir."

"So, are you ready for this?" he asks, taking his seat once again.

"I was born ready," I reply, causing him to chuckle.

"I've been where you are, and I know the feeling all too well."

"Yes, sir."

"Call me Drew," he says, and I nod. "So, Cameron, I have to tell you that you already have quite the following."

"I don't understand?"

"That kiss of yours has been all over the sports networks."

I nod. "She's a beautiful woman," I remind him. I'm suddenly nervous that this may hurt me as being a part of the team.

"This is true." He leans back in his chair and steeples his hands together. "Did you also realize that the woman you were kissing was my niece?"

Oh, fuck!

"N-No, sir."

"Drew." He flashes me a smile. "She's not my niece by blood, but her dad and I have been best friends for years. I've known Paisley since she was little."

"It was the kiss cam," I tell him lamely.

"Uh-huh." He smirks. He stares at me for a few long heartbeats before guiding the conversation in a new direction. "Well, your contract has already been signed, so now all that's left is to give you a tour of the facility and show you your locker. We have a home game tomorrow that you'll need to be suited up for. Have you found living arrangements?"

"Yes. I'm renting a condo not far from here. Baseline Condominiums."

His grin grows wider. "I know the area. Nice place."

"It is. I was lucky to find one available."

"Almost sounds like fate."

"Yes."

"Well, let's take a tour."

"Um, before we go, can I ask you something?"

"Sure. What's up?"

"Can I have Paisley's number?" The question is out of my mouth before I can think better of it. My voice is strong, but my insides are quivering. I could have just fucked up my chance to play for the Blaze, but the thought of seeing her again pushed me to take the risk.

"That's rather bold of you, don't you think?" Drew raises his eyebrows, challenging me.

"Maybe." I shrug. "But it could also be fate that I got called up and that you're her uncle." I can't seem to keep my fucking mouth shut. I could be single-handedly ruining my career.

"Tell me, Cameron. Why do you want my niece's number?"

"I want to ask her out on a date."

He nods. "She spends a lot of time here," he says cryptically. "I have no doubt that you'll run into her again. I won't give you her number. You're going to have to ask her for it yourself."

"Is that an issue? If I were to date her?" I'm trying to keep the excitement out of my voice, knowing that she's hangs out at the stadium. I'm bound to run into her. Even if he won't give me her number, I can ask her for it myself. I know our interaction was brief, but I can't get her out of my head.

"No. As long as you're good to her, that's all I care about. Her dad, on the other hand, is going to be harder to win over. Let's just say he wasn't even a little bit impressed by that kiss." He grins, and there is something behind it, something he knows, and he's not telling me.

"We didn't know it would turn out to be what it was. We didn't realize it would last beyond the game." I never imagined the media circus it would cause, and I would never have guessed I'd finally get called up and learn how much time she spends here. It was a moment, an afternoon at the ballpark, but it feels like so much more.

"Easton spends a lot of time here too. I'm certain he's going to want to meet you. In fact, I called him last night and told him you were getting called up. He wanted to be here today, but I convinced him since this was official business, he'd have to stay home."

"Great," I mutter, making him toss his head back in laughter.

"It won't be easy. Easton is protective of his daughters. And those girls of his, they are all strong and full of independence. You're going to have your work cut out for you."

"I'd like to think she's worth it."

"You know this from an afternoon sitting next to her at a baseball game?"

"Yes."

"I like a man who knows what he wants." He stands from his chair and walks around his desk. "How about that tour?" he asks, slapping a hand on my shoulder and moving to walk out of his office.

I scramble to my feet to follow him. He rambles on about my stats, and I manage to keep up with the conversation, but in my mind, all I can think about is seeing her. He said she's here a lot, and the idea of running into her has my body on high alert. Is she as beautiful as I remember her?

"This is the gym," he says, pushing open the door. "This is where the required workouts will take place, and you are free to use the facility anytime you want."

"Thank you."

He nods, turns, walks out of the gym, and heads down the hall. "This is the locker room," he explains. My eyes scan the lockers, and that's when I see it. C. Taylor followed by the number twenty-two.

On their own accord, my feet carry me to my locker, and I run my hand across my name.

"It's a good feeling," Drew says from his spot next to me. "To see your name in the big leagues. I will never forget that day as long as I live."

"It's surreal," I admit.

"We're glad to have you as a part of the team." He claps his hand down on my shoulder. "Come on, let me introduce you to the trainers," he says. With one final look at my locker, I rush to catch up with him.

"We have a state-of-the-art training facility. When our players are injured in any way, we want to make sure they, you"—he grins—"receive the best care from our team of trainers and physicians to get you back on the field fully healed."

"Come on in." He pushes back on the door and allows me to step in ahead of him. "Ralph," Drew calls out. "I'd like for you to meet Cameron Taylor. He's a first baseman we just brought up. Cameron, this is Dr. Ralph Thomas, the team doctor."

"It's nice to meet you," I greet the doctor, offering him my hand.

"Welcome," Dr. Thomas replies. "Most of the training team is off today getting ready for our away game tomorrow. But we do have our newest member. Paisley!" he calls out.

My entire body is on alert. I can feel the way her hand felt in mine, and when I see her come around the corner, all I can think of is that she's even more beautiful than I remember her being. My eyes trail her as she walks toward her boss. She hasn't even seen me standing here.

"Paisley, I'd like to introduce you to—" Dr. Thomas starts, but the introduction isn't necessary.

"Cameron," she breathes.

"Paisley." I smile at her. Reaching out, I take her hand and bring it to my lips. "It's good to see you," I murmur.

"What's going on here?" Dr. Thomas asks.

"Ralph, it looks like you're the last one to put it together." Drew chuckles. "Cam here is the gentleman who Paisley was kissing on-screen a few weeks ago."

"Uncle Drew," Paisley hisses under her breath.

He ignores her. "Like I told Cameron, there are no rules against the two of you dating as long as it doesn't interfere with my ball club. You two keep it professional, and we won't have any issues."

"We're not dating. It was the kiss cam," Paisley says, exasperated.

"We could be," I chime in, keeping my eyes locked on her.

"I'm just saying." Drew holds his hands up in surrender. "And you're welcome. I told your dad to stay home today."

"My dad?"

"Yep." Drew winks at her. "Told him Cameron here was getting called up.

He wanted to be here to… meet him."

"Oh, God," she groans and covers her face with her hands.

The sound goes straight to my cock.

"Cameron, there's still some paperwork for us to fill out," Drew says, not bothering to be the least bit affected by Paisley's embarrassment.

"Paisley?" My voice is soft as I take a step toward her. I'm not letting her leave this time without a way to get ahold of her. Sure, we now both work for the Blaze, but that's not enough. I need… more. "Can we grab lunch or dinner, maybe?" I ask her.

"I-I don't think that's such a good idea."

"Come on. You have to eat."

"I have a lot to do here before we leave tomorrow."

I nod. "How about you give me your number, and I'll check in with you later? See if things have changed?"

"Cameron." She sighs. "We work together now."

"And you heard Drew. As long as it's not an issue for the club, it's not an issue for him."

"But it's an issue for me."

"Cameron?" Drew calls out. I can hear the amusement in his voice. He's enjoying watching me struggle.

"I'll get you to change your mind."

"Good luck with that," she sasses, and a small piece of the fun-loving girl I met that day at the game finally reappears.

"Game on, baby." I smirk and turn to follow Drew out of the room.

Chapter Five

PAISLEY

MY HEART IS RACING SO FAST I FEAR IT MIGHT POUND RIGHT OUT OF MY CHEST. I CAN'T believe that my uncle Drew, or hell, even my dad or my mom, didn't tell me Cameron was getting called up. Sure, I've avoided them, but after dinner at their place the other night, I thought we were all past the kiss cam incident.

Apparently not.

I knew this was a possibility. I mean, he plays for the Outlaws. And the main purpose of that team is to feed the Blaze. I get that. I know how it works, but I don't know. I guess I just thought I had more time. When John Hastings pulled his hamstring in the game over the weekend, I should have known that they would call someone else up. If I had done my research like I should have, I would have known that Cameron was a first baseman.

It's probably better that I didn't research him. I would have been worrying this entire time. Now, here I am, trying to settle into my new job and work past the hype that my last name and connections are the only reason I'm here. I also have to deal with working side by side with the sexiest man I've ever met, who just so happens to kiss like he was born to do so.

I'm screwed.

I ignore Dr. Thomas, who I think is also ignoring me, as I make my way to the small break room and grab a bottle of water from the fridge. I drain half the contents before replacing the lid. "Just breathe," I whisper to myself. "He's just a man." After a few more calming breaths, I get back to work, making sure that my training bag is packed up and ready for the road trip this week. We have two back-to-back games, one away and one at home, and then another stretch of home games. This is my dream job with a team that feels like home. No, this team is home to me. It's family, and I refuse to let some sexy, incredible-kissing stranger interfere with that.

Once I have everything we may need while away, I place the bag by the door with the rest of the training equipment to be loaded onto the bus tomorrow, then gather my purse and keys and hightail it out of the stadium. Normally, I would hang around and make sure nothing else needed to be done. That's been my norm since I started, but today, I'm too raw. I need to go home and dissect today's new revelations.

Just as I'm pulling into our condo, my phone rings. "Hey, Wil." I sigh into the phone.

"Rough day?" she asks.

"You could say that."

"Well, I was thinking I'd pick up Mexican for dinner. I'm exhausted too, and you're going to be gone the next few days. I thought we could just hang out and catch up before you leave tomorrow."

"That sounds good to me. I have a lot to tell you."

"Oh, now this I have to hear. Does it involve any of those hot-ass men you work with?"

"Yep." I don't bother elaborating.

"I'm on my way. You get packed so we have the entire night to gossip about whatever it is that has you in a mood."

"Extra queso and chips," I tell her. It's one of those nights.

"On it. Be home soon."

The call ends, and I can't help but smile. I already know what she's going to say. That he's good-looking and I should just roll with it. She's been pro-Cameron since the day we met him. It's not that I disagree with her, but my job is important to me. It's been my dream for so long, I don't want to do anything to jeopardize it. Besides, I have to at least make him work for it a little, right? I mean, I can't come off too eager or easy. I don't want to play games, but I also don't want to fall at his feet. That's not who I am.

Grabbing my things, I climb out of the car and head inside. I immediately kick off my shoes and plop down on the couch. I know I need to pack, but that won't take me long, and I just need a minute to reflect.

He looked good today. Damn good. He was dressed in slacks and had on a polo that showed off not only his muscles but also his tattoos. What I wouldn't give to trace them up close and personal. Not that I expected him to look anything less. I've seen the replay of our kiss many times. The way his calloused hands cradled my face and the way his muscles were tight underneath that plain T-shirt he wore.

I shake out of my thoughts. I can't go there with him. He's a player. I'm a trainer now, and it was a one-time, isolated event. Nothing more, nothing less. It's a good memory to have, but that's all that it will ever be. I'm a professional now. "Right." I laugh at myself. "There is nothing professional about the way that man makes you feel, Paisley Gray," I mutter.

I hear the front door open, and Willow calls out, "P! Guess who I ran into?" as she comes walking into the room.

"Me first," I say, standing from the couch to help her.

"Paisley," a deep voice greets me. I don't have to turn around to know who it is.

"Guess who also lives here?" Willow says. I can hear the smile in her voice.

I turn slowly, bracing myself at the sight of him standing in our small kitchen. "Cameron," I greet him.

"Looks like we get to have dinner together after all." He winks.

"I invited him," Willow blurts. "I bought way more than the two of us can eat, and I don't want to eat leftovers the entire time you're gone." By means of explanation, it's a good one, except for the fact that I needed to vent to her. About him.

"Thanks for picking this up, Wil," I say, ignoring Cameron's reference to how we're having dinner together even though I turned him down.

"Sure thing. I'm just going to run and change. Be right back." She shoots off down the hall to her room, and I want to yell for her to wait for me.

"How was the rest of your day?" Cameron asks.

"Uh, good. Good. Yours?"

"Overwhelming," he says with a chuckle. "I've waited what feels like a lifetime for this, and it's finally happening. It all seems pretty surreal."

"You're going to do great," I reassure him.

"Yeah?" he asks. "I'm glad you have faith in me. I have this feeling I'm going to get out there and choke."

"Come on now. A big, strong, tough guy like you? I'd have thought you'd have all the confidence in the world, ready to take the game by the horns and all that."

"No. I do, but it's still got me a little shook up. This is my chance, you know? I could just be filling in for Hastings, or I could stay, and I really, really want to stay."

"The team is great, and Coach Drummond is fair. Just do what you do best. Play ball. Don't let the hype or the fact that it's a different team get to you. Go out on the field, play your game, and it will all work out." Baseball talk I can handle, especially if it's the Blaze. It's a safe topic for us.

He steps up beside me, but I don't stop pulling food out of the bags. "Hey." He places his hand on my arm, which forces me to stop and look at him. "Just breathe, beautiful." He smiles at me.

"Look. The game was fun, but we work together now. It's important that we remain professional."

"The game was fun." He gives me a wicked smile. "And I agree with you. We should maintain professionalism while we're working."

"Good." I stand up a little straighter. "I'm glad we can agree on that."

"Paisley?" He tucks a stray strand of hair behind my ear.

"Yeah?"

"We're not working right now."

"N-No, we're not, but we are coworkers."

"Meh, not really. I'm a baseball player. You work as a part of the training team. We work for the same facility, but technically not together."

"Until you need me for something in regard to the game."

"I need you for something now."

"Oh, yeah?" I can't help but ask. "Do tell?" I turn to face him and move to cross my arms over my chest. Cameron, however, is faster and captures my wrists, bringing one, then the other to his lips for a kiss.

"I just need your time, Paisley. I just want to spend time with you. That's all." The conviction in his voice has me reaching out to grip his shirt.

"Friends," I blurt. It's the first thing that comes to mind, and I'm reeling for a way for us to remain professional. We've both worked our asses off to get where we are. Sure, I had some family connections, but I'm not the least bit naïve to think that if I were not qualified, my dad or even my uncle Drew wouldn't call me out on it. I've put in the time and the work to be where I am.

"That's a start," he concedes. However, when he leans in and presses his lips to my forehead, I want to take the words back. I want to tell him that I'll be whatever it is he needs me to be.

"Let's eat," Willow says, bouncing back into the room. She doesn't comment on our position. Instead, she finishes unpacking the food and setting out plates.

"So, Cameron, what a coincidence that you live in the same complex as we do," Willow says once we're all three seated in the living room with our plates full of food.

"I got lucky there was an opening. I thought it was fate, you know, with the facility being called Baseline Condominiums." He chuckles.

"My dad thought so too. When we graduated from college, he insisted on finding us the perfect condo to move into since we refused to move in with him and Mom and my two younger sisters."

"Hey, I would have had no issue with living at Casa de Monroe. Your mom's cooking skills are on point." Willow points her fork at me.

"Right. You say that, but we would never have any privacy, and it's not just because my two little sisters would be running around. My dad, now that he's retired, has way too much time on his hands. We would never have had a moment to ourselves."

Willow shrugs. "There are worse things."

"Stop!" I cringe.

"Wait? What am I missing here?" Cameron asks. His eyes flick from Willow to me and then back again.

"Oh, you know, just the fact that my best friend has a crush on my dad!"

"You've seen Easton in those pants, right?" Willow asks Cameron. The look on his face has me cracking up laughing.

"I've seen him play, but I'm sorry, Wil, that's just not my team."

"Oh, you're a Blaze player now," she reminds him.

"Oh, the Blaze is my team, but I'm more team Paisley than I am team Easton."

Willow tsks at him and points her fork in his direction. "That is no way to win over the parental units. Let me tell you, bud, Easton is fierce when it comes to the ladies in his life."

Cameron takes a pull from his bottle of water. "Good. I wouldn't want it any other way."

"He's not going to make it easy for you."

"Nothing in life worth having is easy."

"Like our girl here." Willow nods to where I'm sitting.

"Like our girl."

Something in his tone of voice, the conviction of him referring to me as his girl, sends tingles down my spine. "Cameron and I are just friends," I tell Willow.

"I don't kiss my friends like they're the air I breathe. I mean, we could try it if you want, but to be honest, I'm just not feeling you like that, sweet cheeks." She winks.

"You don't know what you're missing, Willow," Cameron tells her.

"Thanks for dinner, Willow," I say to change the subject.

"Always. So, tell me about your day. What was so rough about it?" she asks.

I subtly shake my head, but she just grins. "Cameron? Do you have any idea why our girl here had a bad day?"

"Hmm, maybe it's because she refused to have dinner with me?" He poses it as a question, but all three of us know he's being coy.

"Well, looks like luck is on your side." Willow grins.

"That it is. In fact, my day turned out so much better than I could have imagined. It turns out that I live right next door to two pretty kick-ass neighbors."

"Next door?" I ask him.

He nods. "Next door." He takes a bite of his rice and swallows it before speaking again. "Although, there is this woman, she's gorgeous and pretty much my dream girl, but she refuses to give me her number."

"Oh, well, lucky for you, she has a best friend that can help you with that."

"Willow!" I hiss.

"Hey, when you have a man like Cameron who wants your attention, you let him lavish you with it."

"We agreed to be friends," I remind both of them.

"Friends share numbers." Cameron grins.

"And meals," Willow adds.

"Maybe the two of you should exchange numbers."

"You know," Willow states, "that's not a bad idea. Toss me your phone," she tells Cameron.

I sit back and watch as he hands her his phone, rattles off the passcode, and then she types in what I'm sure is not only her phone number but mine as well.

I'm in over my head with the two of them ganging up on me. I'm just going to have to try harder to keep Cameron in the friend zone. That's where he needs to be.

Our jobs depend on it. At least that's what I keep telling myself. Self-preservation and all that.

Chapter Six

CAMERON

AS I BOARD THE BUS FOR THE AWAY GAME, I'M ON SENSORY OVERLOAD. I'M STILL TRYING to wrap my head around the fact that I got called up, and tomorrow night, I'll be wearing a Blaze uniform as I step out onto the field. That's surreal within itself. From the time I was a little boy, I dreamed of playing in the big leagues, and now, here I am.

Then there's Paisley. To say it was a shock to find out she and Willow are my new neighbors is an understatement. However, it's good to know that I have an ally in Willow. She not only gave me her number last night but she also gave me Paisley's. I'm sure that goes against some kind of girl code, which tells me that Paisley is more interested in me than she's letting on. I feel confident Willow wouldn't have given me her number if that were not the case.

Making my way down the aisle, I see Paisley sitting by the window with her eyes closed and her earbuds in. I have to bite down on my cheek to keep from smiling. Instead of making a scene, I drop into the seat next to her. I am the new guy, after all. I don't have a bond with the other players, so sitting with the trainer, the sexy-as-fuck trainer, is an obvious choice. At least that's what I'm telling myself.

I get settled and look across the aisle to see none other than Drew Milton watching me. I shrug as if to say *what do you do*, then close my eyes and rest my head back against the seat. I'm not thrilled he's going to get a front-row view of my time with Paisley, but it's only a two-hour drive, so it will be fine. It's not like I plan to seduce her right here on the bus.

When the bus begins to move, I feel her shift beside me. I open my eyes in time to see her rest her head against my shoulder. She's snuggled up underneath a Blaze blanket, and she looks peaceful. I want nothing more than to wrap her in my arms and hold her against my chest. A throat clearing pulls my attention.

I turn to see Coach Drummond watching me intently. "Sir?"

"I've got my eye on you, Taylor," he whispers.

"I wouldn't expect anything less." And I mean it. I'm glad he's looking out for her, but what he doesn't understand is that I'm the last person he needs to protect her from. I'm sure Drew has talked to him, and hell, from what I've heard about Easton Monroe, I wouldn't put it past him to have called to talk to the coach either. I just want the chance to get to know her. Maybe hold her in my arms while she sleeps. Is that too much to ask?

Paisley moves, causing her blanket to fall over into my lap. Underneath the cover, my hand seeks out hers as I lace our fingers together. With my head back against the headrest and her head on my shoulder, I let the lull of the tires against the pavement put me to sleep.

"SHIT." I HEAR A SOFT MUMBLE.

Slowly, I blink open my eyes to find Paisley staring at me wide-eyed. "Hey, beautiful," I whisper into the quiet of the bus.

"Hi," she says shyly. "I-I'm sorry. I didn't mean to sleep on you."

I give her hand that I'm still holding under the blanket a soft squeeze. "It's okay. We still have a good hour and a half to go," I say, looking at the time on my phone. "Go back to sleep."

"We can't just…" Her voice trails off.

"We can," I assure her. She chews on her bottom lip. Her unease is evident. "Hey." I turn to face her, keeping my voice soft. "No one is paying a bit of attention to us."

"They might."

"I don't care if they do."

"I'm the trainer for this team."

"And I'm a player on this team."

"Cam." She sighs.

"You said we're friends, right?" I'm desperate for this time, for this connection with her. "Friends take naps."

"Holding hands?" she whispers, her eyes wide.

"We do." I give her a slow smile that has her shaking her head and fighting one of her own.

"Come here, Paisley." I motion with my head for her to come closer. She does as I ask and rests her head against my shoulder. "There's my girl," I say, pressing a kiss on the top of her head. "Rest."

It takes her a few minutes, but eventually, her body relaxes into mine as she drifts back to sleep. I close my eyes and try like hell to do the same, but I can't. My mind won't shut off. There's so much happening all at once, I don't know what to give my attention to first. I know I need to be in the right headspace for the game tomorrow night, and I'm certain I'm there. Then there's Paisley. Sure, getting involved with a trainer isn't the smartest idea I've ever had, but in our defense, there was a connection before either of us knew who the other was. That's what I need to remember. She's more than just the sexy trainer. She's Paisley, a woman who loves the game as much as I do. She's the woman who charmed me one Sunday afternoon at a Blaze game.

She's the only woman who could ever make me think about her over the game. Unable to help myself, I press a kiss to her temple.

"What are people going to say about that?" she asks softly, her eyes still closed. She doesn't need to clarify that she's referring to this kiss.

"I don't care what they say, Paisley."

She tilts her head back to look at me. "You mean that, don't you?"

"With everything I am." I can't explain it. But when she looks at me with those big brown eyes, something happens to me. My chest feels tight yet lighter at the same time.

"I barely know you."

"Then get to know me."

"This has complicated written all over it."

"Only if we let it become complicated."

"I thought you wanted to be friends."

"I do want to be your friend. But, Paisley, it's more than that. I want to be your everything."

She sucks in a breath. "That's a bold statement, Taylor."

"I'm well aware."

"It's on the tip of my tongue to tell you not to play me, but I can see the look in your eyes. You're being real, aren't you?"

"Yes."

"It's so soon."

"When you know, you know."

She rolls those bright brown eyes. "Come on now." She grins.

"What? You don't believe me?"

"It's not that. I mean, I've heard stories of knowing when you know, but it's never been in association with me."

"We'll take our time and get to know each other. You can say we're friends if that makes you feel better, but we're more than friends. I'm not going to be seeing anyone else, and I'd prefer that you didn't either. I've never been much on sharing."

"You're saying you won't share me."

"That's exactly what I'm saying."

"What if I want to be shared?" she asks. She's trying to get a rise out of me, and it's working.

"Paisley," I growl, and she slaps her hand over my mouth. I kiss her palm, and her eyes glass over with heat. With want. For me. Slowly, she takes her hand from my mouth. "You're playing with fire," I warn her.

"I do work for the Blaze," she teases.

I don't think about where we are or who may see us. I don't think about the fact that our boss is sitting in the seat across from us and has a direct line to her dad. All I can think about is kissing her, so that's what I do. It takes very little effort for me to lean in just a fraction of an inch and press my lips to hers. It's chaste as far as kisses go, but it's her lips against mine, and that's the important part.

"You're beautiful," I blurt, resting my forehead against hers.

"You don't need to waste your flattery on me," she breathes.

"It's not flattery; it's facts. And nothing, no part of me would ever be wasted on you." I kiss the tip of her nose and pull away, settling back against my seat.

"This is crazy, Cameron," she says after a few minutes of silence.

"Tell me, Paisley. Do you think about that day? The game? The kiss? The connection?"

"All the time."

"Then this isn't crazy. I don't care what the world thinks. I don't care what your uncle Drew thinks, or hell, even your dad. All I care about is what we think, and all I can think about is you. We owe it to ourselves to see where this goes. We left it to fate, and beautiful, I believe fate has spoken."

"Can we talk about this later?"

"Sure, baby." I slide my hand underneath the cover and rest my hand on her thigh. "We *will* be talking about it, though."

"Okay," she agrees, resting her head back on my shoulder. Once she's settled and her breathing evens out, I close my eyes, and I'm finally able to fall asleep.

FLOPPING BACK ONTO THE BED, I STARE UP AT THE CEILING. IT'S BEEN A LONG DAY OF travel, practice, dinner with the team, and I just finished a long-ass hot shower. Now, I need some Paisley time so I can fall asleep and get rested for the game. Reaching for my phone, I dial her number.

"Hello?" she answers after the first ring.

"Hey."

"You sound exhausted."

"It's been a long day."

"How was dinner with the team?"

"Good. I'm the new guy, but everyone has been nice and friendly. I missed you, though," I tell her honestly.

"I was there."

"What?" I ask. She's got my attention. "What do you mean you were there? I didn't see you."

"I sat with Dr. Thomas and Uncle Drew."

"You should have told me. I would have joined you."

"That would defeat the point of a team dinner. You know, bonding and all that."

"You could have sat with me."

"It was better this way." She tries to appease me, but it's not working.

"Now I feel like I got ripped off. What did you have?"

"A grilled chicken salad." She laughs. "Is it really necessary for you to know what I eat?"

"I want to know everything about you."

"Does that go both ways?"

"Yes. I'm an open book to you." I'm not just saying it. I'll tell her anything she wants to know. I have nothing to hide.

"Tell me about your family," she prompts.

"Easy. I was raised by a single mom. My dad ran off when Mom told him that she was pregnant, so I've never met him. My grandparents helped my mom raise me."

"Do you ever wonder about him? Your dad?" I can hear the hesitancy in her voice. We're diving right into the grit of getting to know each other, but I'm okay with that.

"Sometimes, but not because I want to know him. He had his chance, and he blew it. It's more of me wondering if he has a family now, you know? As far as I'm concerned, my father is gone."

"So, if he were to come back into your life today, you'd push him away?"

"No. I wouldn't have to. He made his choice, and I'm doing fine without him. My mom busted her ass working two jobs to raise me. With the help of my grandparents, she made sure I had what I needed for baseball and that I was at every game and every practice. I had a warm bed to sleep in at night, and my belly was always full." I pause, collecting my thoughts. "And I knew I was loved. Sure, there were times growing up when I wished that I had a father like my friends, but that's not how life works, and as I got older, I saw the hard work and the sacrifices my mother made to give me the world."

"She sounds incredible," she replies softly.

"She is. She's going to love you," I tell her honestly.

"That's a pretty strong statement."

"Not when it's true. She's going to love that you keep me on my toes and make me work for it." I know she can't see me, but I can't contain my smile when I think about Mom meeting Paisley. "Growing up, she always told me my smile could charm any woman and most men." I laugh. "She'd tell me that it would take a strong woman to put up with me. That's how I know she's going to love you."

"So, she's going to like the fact that I don't give in to your every whim?"

"Exactly. Now, what about your family?"

"Is that how this is going to work? Because you answer, I have to as well?"

"Yes. We're getting to know each other. That's how this works. An even exchange of information."

"I'm sure you already know all about me. I mean, my father is Easton Monroe."

"Believe it or not, I didn't seek out the internet when I found out who you were. Any information I get, I want it to come from you, so spill, Monroe."

"Well, I'm the oldest of three girls. My dad, he adopted me when I was a little girl. I was four years old when he met my mom and me."

"I didn't know that," I say, keeping my voice soft. I have an all-new respect for Easton Monroe, and I was already giving him mad props for his skills on the field.

"Yeah. My mom fought it, but he just kept showing up. Anyway, they got married, and he adopted me. A few years later, my middle sister, Parker, was born, and a few years after that, the baby of the family, Peyton."

"Three girls. I bet your dad had his hands full." I laugh.

"Well, there are over seven years between Parker and me and three years between Parker and Peyton. So Dad still has his hands full." She chuckles. "I like to tell my little sisters that I paved the way for them. They both have to name their firstborn children after me," she teases.

"How bad does your dad hate me after the kiss cam went viral?"

"He was disappointed in me. Not because it was you, or even from the kiss cam. He's just… overprotective. He wanted to know who you were and how I knew you. Those kinds of things."

"I'm guessing when you told him we were strangers that went over like shit floating in a punch bowl."

"W-What?" She splutters with laughter. The sound wraps around me like a warm caress. "You did not just say that." She chuckles.

"You telling me I'm wrong?" I ask her.

"No," she says, the laughter still evident in her voice. "You're not wrong."

"I'm sorry you had to deal with that on your own. Next time, I'll be there."

"Next time? You plan on kissing me again, and it going viral on all the sports networks?"

"Kissing you again, most definitely. If they happen to capture it, then yeah."

"You're something else, Cameron Taylor," she says over a yawn.

"It's late. You should get some rest."

"Yeah, you have to be rested for your Blaze debut tomorrow."

"Have breakfast with me?"

"You're scheduled to have breakfast with the team."

"You're a part of the team."

"If I happen to see you, then I see you."

"Oh, baby, I'll make sure of it. Night, beautiful."

"Night, Cam." The call goes silent on the other end, and I know that she's hung up. Dragging my tired ass off my bed, I plug in my phone, then slip off the towel and pull on some boxer briefs before sliding under the covers. I wish she were here next to me, but having her voice be the last thing I hear before falling asleep is a good second. We'll get to her falling asleep and waking up in my arms. I'm a man who never backs down from something he wants, and I want Paisley Monroe.

Chapter Seven

PAISLEY

IT'S LATE, WELL AFTER MIDNIGHT, BUT WE PLAY AGAIN TOMORROW AT HOME. THE BUS IS buzzing with excitement as the players board still high off their win. The life of a professional athlete has a lot of extravagances, but there is a lot of hard work, dedication, and time on the road away from loved ones too. That's what the fans don't see. They don't see the hours of practice and travel. They don't see the injuries and the pain that the players push through. They also don't get to see the smiling faces as all of that hard work pays off and the team celebrates together.

I choose a seat near the front of the bus and curl up next to the window with my blanket. Closing my eyes, I listen to the sounds of the players and staff as they make their way on board. We have two buses, and I try not to think about whether or not Cameron will end up on mine. He texted me, asking me to wait for him so we could sit together, but instead of replying like an adult, I snuck onto the bus and chose a seat, and now I'm pretending to sleep.

"Yo, rookie, your girl is on the second bus." I hear one of the guys say. "Yeah, she's sitting alone." I hear him speak, but no reply. He must be on the phone. "You better hurry. I may just take your seat." I don't hear what the person, who I assume is Cameron, says on the other line, but the raucous laughter coming from the tattletale tells me that line didn't sit so well with him.

Footsteps carry on past me, and I snuggle further into my Blaze blanket, trying to block it all out. It's not that I don't want to sit with Cameron. It's the opposite. If I could spend all of my time with him, I would, but that'll only complicate both of our lives. So instead of waiting for him, I'm here taking the coward's way out, but I have a feeling with that phone call, the jig is up.

Someone drops into the seat next to mine. I lie as still as possible, still pretending to be asleep. Thankfully, I pulled the blanket up over my face to help with the act.

"Found her, huh?" a deep voice asks.

"Yeah, Miller gave me the heads-up," Cameron's deep voice replies.

Miller, that has to be Corey Miller, the outfielder. We don't have any other Millers on the team.

My mind is racing with how his teammates knew to look for me. Do they just assume since the kiss cam incident that we're dating? Is it their assumption that we're an item since we've sat together a few times? Did he tell them to let him know which bus I was on? A million questions filter through my mind right now, yet I can't voice any of them since I'm pretending to be asleep.

It feels as though hours have passed by the time the bus begins to move. In reality, it was maybe another five minutes, but my racing heart begs to differ. When his hand slides under the cover and laces with mine, I turn to face him.

"Hey, beautiful," he whispers, using his hand that's not holding mine to brush my hair out of my eyes. "You didn't reply."

"Yet you found me."

"Yeah, I found you."

"How?"

"I told a few of the guys to let me know which bus you were on."

"Why?"

"Because this is two hours that I get to spend with you."

"But your teammates may get the wrong idea."

"What idea is that, Paisley? That I'm into you? That fate put me in the stands and seated next to you that day, and we shared a kiss that rocked my world? That the thought of one of those fuckers getting this time with you had my gut twisted in a knot?"

I open my mouth to reply, but I've got nothing. I have no response to his speech. All I can do is stare at him as the truth of his words reflects back at me.

"I don't care who knows, Paisley. I already told Drew that I wanted to date you. As the GM, he's the one we should worry about, and he said he was okay with it."

"You told him that?"

"Well, I asked him for your number, and he wanted to know why." He shrugs. "I told him I wanted to ask you out and asked if it would be an issue. He said I had my hands full with you, but there were no rules against it as long as it didn't interfere with either of our jobs."

"Getting your teammates involved could interfere with your job."

"Not unless one of them tries to take you from me."

"I didn't realize I could be taken from you."

"I hope not." He flashes me a grin. "Come here." He releases my hand and slides his arm behind my shoulders, pulling me into him. "Sleep."

"You involved your teammates to find which bus I was on so we could sleep?"

"Yes. I knew I wouldn't get any rest, not knowing who was sitting next to you. This way, you're in my arms, and we can both get some rest."

"I could have slept just fine."

"No, you wouldn't have been able to. I would have been blowing up your phone. I'm a needy fucker when it comes to you, Paisley. You may as well get used to that."

"You barely know me, Cameron."

"We're fixing that, baby. Now, get some rest." He leans his head over on mine and exhales. In no time at all, his breathing evens out, and I know he's asleep.

A part of me wants to pull away just to prove that I can. To prove I'm an independent woman who can make my own choices, and he can't call the shots. Then another part of me wants to enjoy how he wants me close, and soak up his warmth, and catch a few hours of sleep. That part eventually wins out. He's so warm, and his chest might be ripped with muscles, but it's also oddly comfortable. That's my last thought before drifting off to sleep.

"MY PLACE OR YOURS?" CAMERON ASKS.

I stop in my tracks and turn to look at him. It's the early hours of the morning, just a few hours before sunrise, and we've finally arrived back at our condos. Cameron wanted me to leave my car at the stadium and drive me home. I argued and won, so he insisted on following me home. I didn't fight him because he lives right next door to me. There really was no point.

"What?"

"Your place or mine?"

"What are you talking about?"

"I need sleep, P. I have to play again tonight, and I sleep better when you're next to me."

"You don't know that."

"I know that I slept like shit last night and that I feel more rested after two hours on that fucking bus with you in my arms than I have in weeks. So, your place or mine?"

"Willow is home."

"We're just going to sleep, babe. Choose. We're both dead on our feet."

"Mine." I need to feel like I have some kind of leverage when it comes to him. I could fight him, but what would be the point? I'm exhausted, and if I know anything about Cameron, it's that he fights for what he wants. I can hear it in his voice, see it in his eyes. He's tired, and he's not going to sleep unless I'm with him. I'd be lying if I said it didn't send a thrill through me.

"All right." He places his hand on the small of my back with a nod and leads me to my door.

My hands tremble as I place my key in the lock and turn the knob. The condo is dark as we step inside. I wait for Cameron to follow me inside before locking up and leading him down the hall to my room. As quietly as I can, I close my bedroom door.

"Bathroom?" he asks.

"Yeah, through there." I point at the door.

"Thanks, babe." He kisses my temple and quietly disappears into the bathroom.

I give myself five seconds to freak out before jumping into gear and grabbing clothes to sleep in. I can't believe I'm doing this. This isn't me. I don't bring random men to my place, let alone with the intention of them spending the night. I'm not that girl. Sure, I've had hookups, but not in my space. Not in my home.

Before I can freak out any more, the bathroom door opens, and Cameron walks out wearing nothing but a pair of dark blue boxer briefs. I swallow hard as I take in his toned chest before averting my gaze back to his face. He gives me a lazy, sleepy grin before walking past me and placing his clothes on his bag. I rush to the bathroom and quickly change and brush my teeth before tying my hair up in a messy bun on top of my head.

Looking in the mirror at my sleep tank and shorts, I debate on removing my bra and decide I better keep it on. I'm a small C cup at best, but without the confines of my bra, it's obvious, and this tank is thin. Decision made, I switch off the light and open the door.

I move to the bed where Cameron is standing. "I wasn't sure which side you liked to sleep on." His voice is soft as his hands land on my shoulders.

"I sleep alone." My voice is soft but a stark reminder to both of us that this isn't me.

"Not anymore," he says, placing a kiss on my neck. "Isn't this uncomfortable to sleep in?" he asks, sliding his index finger under my bra strap.

I shrug. "It's fine."

"Hey." He turns me so that I'm facing him. The room is filtered with the glow of the full moon so I can make out his features. "It's just me, Paisley. I'm not here to seduce you. I just want to sleep with you in my arms so that I don't look like a monkey fucking a football out on the field tomorrow night." He chuckles softly. "Take it off. I want you comfortable."

All I can do is nod as I reach behind me and unhook my bra. It takes some maneuvering, but I get it off without removing my tank and toss it onto the chair in the corner of the room.

"Which side do you want?"

"Either."

"Okay. I'll take the one closest to the door."

"Why?"

He shrugs. "If someone would ever break in, they're going to have to get through me to get to you," he says as if it's no big deal. As if his words don't have a direct line to my heart. "Come on, let's get some rest."

"Should we set the alarm?" I know my body, and I'll wake up in plenty of time, but I don't know if he needs to be at the stadium before me.

"Nah, I don't have to be at the stadium until later in the afternoon. Let's just sleep." He reaches for the covers and pulls them back, motioning for me to climb onto the bed. I'm not sure why he asked which side I wanted when we're both using this one, but I don't say anything. I just climb under the covers and move to the opposite side.

"Come here, Paisley." His voice is husky. I hesitate for a second before moving back to the center of my queen-sized bed. Cameron pulls me into his arms, and I rest my head on his chest. His lips press against my head before he relaxes into the mattress with me in his arms.

It doesn't take long for his breathing to even out and drift off to sleep. Me, on the other hand, well, I can't seem to shut my mind off. I don't know what it is about this man that has me doing things I would have never done in the past.

Never would I let a man tell me he's staying with me or that I'm staying with him. Especially not one I barely know, but here I am, wrapped up in his arms as if I'm his and he's mine.

Chapter Eight

CAMERON

MY EYES AREN'T EVEN OPEN, AND I KNOW THAT I'M IN HER BED ALONE. I'D HOPED TO WAKE up with her in my arms, but I guess waking up in her bed is second best. Rolling over, I peel my eyes open to glance at the clock. It's just after nine in the morning. It's too damn early for either of us to be awake, which means Paisley is probably freaking out that I spent the night in her bed. Time to do damage control. Tossing the covers, I stand and stretch before going in search of her.

Slowly, I open her bedroom door and hear voices down the hall. I stop and listen to see what I'm dealing with in the light of day.

"How was your trip?"

"Good," Paisley answers.

"Did you get to see Cameron?"

"You could say that."

"Vague. Come on, Pais, spill."

"He sat with me on the way there."

"Nico," Willow comments.

"And on the way back."

"My man," Willow cheers, and I can imagine her giving me a fist bump if I were in the room with them.

"And he kindofspentthenight," Paisley rushes to say.

"Whoa, back up the cookie truck. Did you just say that he spent the night?" Willow screeches.

"Shh," Paisley shushes her. "Keep your voice down. You're going to wake him up."

That's my cue. I open the door and shut it, this time loud enough that they can hear me. I can hear their muffled voices as I grow closer to the kitchen. I find Willow sitting at the island while Paisley is sitting on the counter with a cup of coffee in her hands. I walk straight toward her, slide my hand behind her neck, and press my lips to her forehead. "Morning, beautiful," I greet her. My voice is still laced with sleep.

"Well, Cameron, fancy seeing you here."

"Morning, Willow," I say, turning to face her. I rest my back against the counter, settling between Paisley's legs. My hands rest on top of her bare thighs, and I need to watch myself. The last thing I need is my cock, that's already barely concealed, to get hard from the feel of her skin beneath my fingertips. At least not in front of her best friend.

"You two are up early." Willow grins.

"We are," I agree. Turning, I look at Paisley over my shoulder. "Why are we up this early?" I ask her.

"You can go back to bed," she tells me.

"Perfect." I turn my body to face her. Grabbing the coffee cup from her hands, I take a hefty sip before placing it on the counter. "Legs around my waist, babe," I tell her.

"W-What?" she sputters.

"Legs around my waist. We're going back to bed."

"I don't have to go with you," she argues.

"Yes. Yes, you do. See you in a few hours, Willow," I say, lifting Paisley from the counter. Instinct has her wrapping those sexy legs of hers around my waist as I carry her down the hall and to her room. Kicking open the door, I take her to the bed and release her. She flops, with a giggle falling from her lips.

"Scoot," I say, sliding in next to her.

"Are we really going back to sleep?" she asks, covering a yawn.

"We're really going back to sleep. I have a game tonight, remember?"

"Maybe you'd be more comfortable in your bed?"

"You want to go to my place?" I ask, knowing that's not what she means.

"No. I just thought you may sleep better in your own bed."

"I'll sleep better with you next to me. Decide, babe. My bed or yours? Either way, we're getting a couple more hours of sleep."

"Mine."

"Come here." I open my arms for her, and she comes willingly. "Get some rest," I say, kissing the top of her head and closing my eyes. It doesn't take long for sleep to claim me once again.

TWO HOURS LATER WHEN I WAKE, IT'S WITH HER IN MY ARMS. A SMILE TILTS MY LIPS when she stirs and peers up at me. "Did you get rested?"

"Yeah," she replies at the same time her belly growls.

"I need to feed you."

"No, that's fine. I'll just grab something."

"What kind of *friend* would I be if I left you hungry?" I make sure to emphasize the word friend when we both know we're more than that.

"Right. Friends," she says, moving away, but I capture her in my arms before she can get too far.

"You're more than that. I'm letting you tell me when you're ready to label this as something other than friends. Until then, we've agreed that neither of us are seeing other people."

"Did we agree to that?" she asks coyly.

"Damn right we did," I say, moving my hands to tickle her sides.

"Stop!" She laughs. "I'm going to pee my pants," she pants, squirming in my arms.

"Say it."

"N-No one else," she says, spluttering with laughter.

I release her, and she jumps off the bed, rushing to the bathroom. A few minutes later, she appears, leaning against the doorjamb. "That could have been bad, Cameron." She points at me.

"I'll take my chances. I need to go to my place and shower. Come over in twenty, and I'll feed you."

"Where are we going?"

"Nowhere. I'm going to cook for you."

"You cook?"

"Yes, I cook." I stand and adjust my cock. Her eyes follow the movement, and I don't bother to hide my smirk. "I'm a man of many talents, Paisley." I press my lips to her cheek. "I'm going to head to mine. If I don't see you in twenty, I'm coming to find you."

"Bossy," she sasses.

"Not bossy, baby. Confident. I know I want to cook for you." I shrug. "I'll see you in twenty," I say, pressing another kiss to her cheek. I have to force myself to step away from her and grab my bag. I don't bother getting dressed since my condo is right next door to theirs. Instead, I walk out of her place in my underwear and quickly slip inside mine. I drop my bag next to the door and make my way to the kitchen to see what I have that I can whip us up for breakfast. Luckily, I had groceries delivered the day I moved in. It looks like omelets and strawberries it is. They need to be eaten anyway before they go bad. With the menu planned, I head to my room to shower.

I'M SHOWERED AND IN CLEAN UNDERWEAR WHEN I START MAKING US A LATE BREAKFAST.

Hell, I guess it's lunch now. I crack some eggs into a bowl and whip them up before setting them to the side. I'm in the middle of chopping some fresh veggies when there's a knock on the door.

"Come in!" I call out.

"Oh."

I turn to find Paisley's eyes locked on my ass. "Give me ten, and this will be ready."

"Should you maybe, I don't know, put on some clothes?" she asks.

There's a flush on her cheeks, which is all the motivation I need to stay exactly the way that I am. "Nah, I need to feed you first."

"I can wait."

"Well, I'm starving. Have a seat." I motion toward the small kitchen table. I was lucky that this place came furnished when I moved in. It made the move a hell of a lot easier, especially since I lived in a house with five of my teammates from the Outlaws.

"Can I help?"

"Nah, I've got this. There's coffee in the pot and orange juice and milk in the fridge. Help yourself."

"Sure. What are you drinking?"

"Milk for me."

"Glasses?" she asks.

"Next to the fridge." I point at the cabinet and get back to work chopping vegetables.

"Is Willow coming?"

"No. She's already gone. She had to get to the office. Tonight is her late night."

"What does she do?"

"She's a social worker. Some of the things she sees, I don't know how she does it."

"She's making a difference in a lot of lives."

"She is," she agrees.

"What time do you have to be at the stadium today?"

"Two. You?"

"Same."

"Yeah, we need to be there to tape up the players, assist with stretches, assess injuries, those kinds of things."

"You love it, don't you?"

"I enjoy it. I'm still new, so I'm still getting into the swing of things, so to speak. It's not playing, but it's being a part of the game I love."

"Is that because of your dad? Your love of baseball?"

"Maybe." She laughs. "I can't really be sure. My first season of T-ball was the year he met my mom. Apparently, when I met his teammates, I claimed them as my uncles and roped them all into playing catch if they were around."

"Ah, Uncle Drew."

"Yeah." She smiles. "Uncle Drew. He and my dad are best friends, and he was victim to my request to play catch more times than I can count." She takes a sip of her orange juice. "Anyway, I don't know if that's why I loved the game that much, or if it was my dad and his friends and their willingness to play ball with me that made me fall in love with the game. All I know is that I've always loved it."

"I'd love to see pictures of little Paisley all decked out for a game."

"Oh, don't worry. My parents have plenty of embarrassing pictures of me. I think my mom kept all of my old uniforms from the time I started when I was four."

"Really? My mom did the same thing. She said I would appreciate seeing them when I made the big leagues. It was all just a pipe dream at that time."

"Look at you now."

I nod. "Look at me now."

"I remember when I first met my dad, I rambled on about wanting a pink glove. My mom looked everywhere, and she couldn't find one locally. She was a single mom, busting her ass to make ends meet. Anyway, Dad, he found me a pink glove. I loved that thing. I still have it. It's in a keepsake box in my closet."

"I'd love to see it."

"What?" she asks, surprised. "It's just an old tiny pink glove."

"Yeah, but it's important to you."

Before she can reply, her phone rings, I stay busy with making breakfast as she answers. "Hey, Dad," she greets. "The games were good. The Blaze pulled off back-to-back wins." She's quiet for a few minutes. "Oh, no, I've already eaten. I think I'm just going to get caught up on laundry before heading to the field." She listens again. "Great. I'll see you all later then." Another pause. "Love you too, Dad."

"Everything okay?"

"Yeah, that was my dad. He wanted to see if I wanted to grab lunch before heading to the field."

"Call him back and invite him over."

"What?" she shrieks. "Are you crazy?"

"I'm going to have to meet him eventually, Paisley."

"Whoa, let's back this up a little. We are not meeting the parents."

"Actually, my mom will be here for the game tonight. I was hoping to introduce you to her after the game."

"Cameron, I don't think that's a good idea."

"Why?" I can see her searching her mind for a good excuse, and there aren't any. I'm into her, really into her, and that's not going to change anytime soon. I want her to meet my mom. My mother is the most important person in my life, and that will only be rivaled by my wife and kids, and I think Paisley is a good contender for that title. Yeah, I know it's early, but I really like her. I want to see where this goes.

"We barely know each other."

"You keep saying that. That's what dating is for. I want her to meet you. I won't push you to introduce me to your family. I'll wait until you're ready, but, babe, I'm ready for you to meet my mom." I shrug.

"Why is it impossible to say no to you?" she asks as I place a plated omelet in front of her.

"Because I'm irresistible." I grin, placing a kiss on her forehead before plating my own omelet and taking a seat next to her at the small dining table.

"You're something, Cameron Taylor," she says, shaking her head, before digging into her breakfast.

The conversation is light as we eat, and once we're finished, Paisley insists on cleaning the kitchen, but I don't let her do it alone. Instead, we do it together. It's very domestic and not something I've experienced with a woman before. Until I met Paisley, there wasn't a woman I wanted to spend this much time and effort on. My gut tells me that she's different.

"Well, thanks for lunch, or brunch, or whatever we just had. It was great." She grabs her keys and her phone.

"Where are you going?"

"Back to my place."

"Let me get dressed, and I'll come with you."

"Don't you have some kind of pregame ritual or something that you need to do before the game?"

"No. The only thing I need to do is spend time with you. We can do that here or at your place."

"What if I had something to do today?"

"Well, I don't think that you do. You told your dad you were going to do laundry. So, if we need to go to yours so you can do that, we will. Otherwise, we can stay here and maybe watch a movie or something."

"You're not sick of me yet?" She raises her eyebrows. It's more than a question. It's a statement, one she thinks she's going to get a reaction to, but she's wrong.

"Never." My voice is steady, and my reply is quick.

"What kind of movie?" she questions, placing her phone and her keys back on the counter.

"You pick."

"You're letting me pick?" she asks in disbelief.

It takes me three steps to stand in front of her. "Yes, you get to pick. You see, my agenda here isn't the movie, Paisley. It's you. I just want to be close to you. I want to spend time with you and get to know you. I want you to see that when I tell you that I want you, it's not just your body I want. I want you in my life. I can't explain it, but you're different, and I want us to see where this goes."

"Wow."

I can't help it. I have to kiss her, so I press my lips to hers. It's just a quick peck, but I need to feel her lips against mine. "I'll set the alarm in case we fall asleep. Go pick out a movie while I grab my phone from the bedroom."

She nods and turns toward the living room. I've rendered her speechless, which I love. I meant what I said. I want us to see where this leads. Besides, I'm starting to think that Paisley Monroe is my good luck charm. I went to a Blaze game and met this amazing girl, shared a kiss to rival all kisses before her, and two weeks later, I'm finally called up to the majors. During last night's game, I was on fire, and here we are today. Life is better with Paisley. I just need for her to see that as well.

Chapter Nine

PAISLEY

CAMERON INSISTED WE RIDE TO THE STADIUM TOGETHER. HE SAID IT JUST MADE SENSE, considering we were traveling to the same place and then coming home to the same place. I didn't have a good argument or reason not to ride with him, so I gave in.

Luckily for me, once we got to the stadium, we both had jobs to do, so I've been able to avoid him. He's a lot to take on, and I'm trying to figure out his endgame. The only issue is that I can see the conviction in his eyes and hear it in his voice. This isn't a game to him.

It's overwhelming and confusing, but I'll be the first to admit it's also thrilling. I've never met a man like him before. One who seems to be more interested in me than my dad or my last name, or even the connections he can get from me. If that's his play, he's hiding it well.

After helping the senior trainers get the players that need it taped and stretched, I get busy preparing the drinks for the dugout. I'm the low man or woman on the totem pole, but making sure the players stay hydrated is an important part of a trainer's job, so I don't mind it. I'm in the dugout of the Tennessee Blaze. I'm in the heart of the sport and the team that I love. Life doesn't get much better than this.

"Can I get one of those?" I hear from behind me.

I let my smile free until the cup is full. Then I school my features when I turn to face Cameron. "Sure," I say, handing him the cup. I don't know why I'm trying to be so indifferent with him. I guess I'm still leery that he's out for something other than my attention. My heart tells me that's not the case, but I've been burned too many times to set the possibility free.

"You busy?" he asks.

"No. I just finished setting up." I point at the coolers behind me.

"Good. Wanna help me stretch?"

It's on the tip of my tongue to refuse, but it's my job to do so. "I can do that."

He moves to the field and lies down on the grass. Silently, we work through a series of stretches that I know he's already done. I saw him working with one of the other trainers earlier. I don't know him well enough as a player to know if the extra stretching is essential to his game or if it's just a way for him to be close to me. My guess is it's the latter.

"I got next," Travis Henderson, a second baseman, says, sitting in the grass next to Cameron.

Cameron gives him a hard look before turning his attention back to me. "So, Mom's going to stick around after the game. She's going to follow us home." I don't miss the way Travis's eyes widen when he hears Cameron say this.

"I can actually get a ride with my dad."

"No. We rode together. We leave together."

"Cameron, it's not a big deal. We're neighbors, and your mom is in town."

"She's staying with me tonight."

"See, all the more reason I should just have my dad take me home."

"I want you to meet her."

"Can we talk about this later?" I ask, lowering my voice.

He opens his mouth to argue, but I give him a pleading look, so he just nods. "Fine."

"You're all set," I say, moving to stand by Travis. I can feel his stare as I talk to Travis about any potential issues before we begin stretches. I pretend Cameron isn't standing vigil behind me and focus on doing my job.

"So good," Travis moans as I push a little harder on his leg.

I hear Cameron grumble behind me, but I ignore him and continue to focus on my player. "How's that?" I ask Travis.

"Great. Thanks for the workout, Paisley." He winks as he stands and jiggles his body to show that he's now loose. He winks at someone behind me, and I know it's Cameron before jogging off.

Slowly, I turn to find Cameron's eyes locked on mine. "He didn't need to be stretched."

"That's my job, Cameron."

"I know, but he was fucking with me."

"Then don't let him."

"Do you have any idea how it feels to have your girl stretching out your new teammates? To know what they're thinking as your hands are all over them? It's fucking torture, P."

"I'm not your girl, Cameron," I remind him. We both know I'm lying. The fact he slept in my bed last night pretty much debunks that theory.

"You are mine." His voice is steady. Solid. "I want to kiss you so fucking bad," he says, stepping even closer. Barely a few inches remain between his chest and mine.

"What's stopping you? It's not like us kissing hasn't been blasted all over the television networks and social media." It's a challenge, and we both know it.

"That's easy, baby," he says, his voice softening. "That kiss was theirs. It was for the kiss cam. Sure, it ended up being more than that, but that's how it started. We were giving them a show. The next time I kiss you like that, it will be just you and me. I want to be able to hold you close and run my hands over every inch of you. So I'm not going to kiss you today. Not here in front of the fans and the cameras. At least not the way I want to."

"Okay." I nod. There's not much I can say to that. Cameron Taylor has a way with words that makes me feel like I could melt into a puddle of goo at his feet.

"When I do kiss you like that, for the world to see, there will be no question between us that you're mine. We both know that you are, but you're struggling with it."

"What makes you think I'll ever be ready for that again?"

He smirks. "I can feel it here." He taps his hand over his chest, right over his heart. "It's deep, Paisley. Real fucking deep."

"All right, let's hit the field for the team warm-ups!" Coach Drummond announces. This is something that he's known for. He has the entire team on the field, and they go through a routine of stretches. It's meant to show teamwork and unity. Right now, the Blaze is the only team in the league that does it, and it started with Coach Drummond two years ago.

"You better go."

"Wait for me after the game." He reaches up as if he's going to touch me but thinks better of it and drops his hand.

"I'll wait."

His shoulders drop, and he exhales. "Thanks, beautiful. Wish me luck?"

"You don't need luck." He doesn't. From what I've seen, he's a great player.

"You're right. I have you." He winks and jogs off onto the field.

I watch him for far longer than I should before turning and going back to the drinks. I check my bag to ensure I have whatever I may need here in the dugout for the game and busy myself rearranging cups to keep from staring at Cameron out on the field.

It's going to be a long night.

"HELL YEAH!" COREY MILLER CHEERS. HE RUSHES TOWARD ME AND LIFTS ME IN THE AIR, spinning me around in circles before placing me back on my feet. "The Blaze is on fire!" he bellows as he makes his way to the locker room.

All I can do is shake my head and grin as I clean up the dugout. The rest of the training team will take care of the players. I'll help with whatever is needed as soon as this is cleaned up.

"What I wouldn't give to make you grin like that." I hear Cameron say from behind me.

"Good game, Taylor." I smile at him.

"Thank you. You still waiting for me?"

"Yes. I have to clean up here and then help out with anything the rest of the training staff may need, but my plan is to wait for you."

"Good." His eyes scan around us, and no one seems to be paying a bit of attention to us as they're wrapped up in their own celebration from the win. Moving in close, he crowds me, lowering his head and kissing the corner of my mouth. His lips are gone as soon as they press against mine, and he's walking away toward the locker rooms.

"Princess?" I hear, and I freeze.

I know that voice, and he's the only person on the planet who calls me princess. My dad. I know it's too much to ask that he didn't witness the kiss that Cameron just gave me. Knowing I have no choice but to face the music, I turn to look at him. "Hey, Dad."

He opens his arms for me, and I don't hesitate to walk into them and take the hug he's offering. "Your team did good, princess," he says, releasing me.

"Last I checked, they were your team too," I remind him.

He nods. "Blaze is in our blood," he says with a grin. "So, that was Cameron?"

I want to crawl under the bleachers. It's bad enough our kiss was all over the world, but for Dad to catch us, when the kiss was for us, and not for the world, it feels intimate, and I don't know how to handle that. I've always been a daddy's little girl, and I hate these awkward conversations. My little sisters owe me big time for breaking him in before they get to the dating-and-kissing-boys stage.

"That was Cameron."

"He's good."

"He is," I agree.

"You two together now?"

"We're—complicated," I tell him honestly.

"Is he good to you?"

I think back to last night. He held me all night long, and not once did he try anything. Not that I would have been opposed to it, but he gave me his word, and he kept it. Then this morning, he insisted on making me breakfast, and he just wanted to hang out with me. "He's good to me," I assure my father.

"No one will ever be good enough for you and your sisters. You know that, right?" He chuckles.

"Don't worry, Daddy, you set the bar high," I remind him, wrapping my arms around him again in a hug. "We know what true love looks like after watching you and Mom. We're not going to settle for anything less."

"Is that what this Cameron guy is to you? True love?" His brows furrow.

"We're talking? Dating? I guess you could say. It's still new and way too soon for declarations of love."

"He seems pretty intense. I watched him watching you throughout the game."

I blush, hearing that Dad witnessed Cameron and his intensity. "He's not pushing you, is he?"

"No." I'm quick to defend. "He's not. I promise you. I wouldn't put up with that. He's just… very sure of this. Of us. He wants to see where this goes."

"What do you want, P?"

"I want it all. I want my job with the team, I want Cameron to get a permanent spot on the Blaze, and I want him," I admit out loud for the first time ever. And to my dad, no less.

Dad nods. He looks a little sad, but I always knew this would be hard for him. I was his first little girl. As I said, my sisters owe me big time.

"I should get this cleaned up and get in there in case they need me."

"All right." He hugs me tight again. "Love you, princess."

"Love you too, Dad."

"I want to meet him. Officially."

"I'll see what I can do," I tell him—already making up excuses of why I could put the meeting off. Then I remember I'm meeting Cameron's mom tonight. This is moving really fast, but to my surprise, it feels right. My mom used to tell me how she fought my dad when they first started dating. She said he was so sure, so confident that she and I were what he wanted, but she resisted. Here they are, years of marriage and three kids later, and they're still madly in love. I know it's possible. I guess I never considered it would happen to me. I'm not saying that I'm in love with Cameron, but I'm definitely in like. A whole lot of like.

Chapter Ten

CAMERON

IT TAKES EXTREME EFFORT NOT TO GLARE AT MILLER WHEN I ENTER THE LOCKER ROOM. HE didn't do anything wrong except put his hands on her. It was respectful, and that's the only reason I'm not throwing hands with my new teammate.

Many of the guys already know I've got my sights set on Paisley. It wasn't hard to put two and two together when I asked them where she was and which bus she was on during our away game this week.

That's the effect that she has on me. She's all I think about. Hell, even when I'm on the field, she's on my mind, and that never happens to me. Usually, when I'm on the field, it's just me and the game, but from the day I met her, she's been there, always on my mind.

"Good job, rookie," Henderson, our second baseman, tells me.

"Thanks." I bump my fist with his as I make my way to my locker to grab some clothes to shower. Checking my phone, I see a missed message from my mom.

Mom: Great game, Cam!

Me: Thanks, Ma. Showering. Will be out soon.

I hesitate to tell her that Paisley is joining us and decide I don't want to catch her off guard.

Me: I have someone I want you to meet.

Mom: Someone, as in a woman? Have you been holding out on me? Oh, is this the kiss cam girl?

I chuckle at her question. For years, she's been telling me she's not getting any younger and wants grandkids. I've always assured her that if I ever met a woman who I thought may be able to make that happen, she'd be the first to know.

Me: Yeah, Mom, it's the kiss cam girl, and you're the first to know.

Mom: A win, a hug from my son, and I get to meet the one. This night just keeps getting better.

Me: Don't scare her away.

Mom: Best behavior. Now hurry up!

Me: Yes, ma'am.

I toss my phone back into my locker and head to the showers. By the time I'm finished, the locker room has cleared out a good bit.

"Yo, Taylor. Drinks at The Pub?" Henderson calls out.

"Nah, my mom's in town. Taking her to dinner."

He nods. "All right. Catch you later."

I finish getting dressed, and pack up my bag and go in search of Paisley. I assume she's going to be hanging around outside the locker room for me. We didn't really discuss where she was going to wait for me, just that she would wait.

Pushing open the locker room door, I'm just in time to hear Henderson asking Paisley if she wants to head to The Pub for a drink.

"No, thanks." She declines with a smile that I know has him puffing out his chest. She has that effect on you. Trust me. I know firsthand.

"You got plans?" he asks her.

"She does," I answer for her.

"Dinner with Mom?" Henderson whistles. "So, it's like that."

"Yeah, it's like that." I nod, walking toward Paisley and sliding my arm around her waist.

"All right." Henderson holds up his hands in surrender. "You two will have to join us next time." With that, he turns and walks away, catching up with a few of our teammates who are already halfway down the hall.

"Was that necessary?" she asks.

"Yes. Yes, it was." I press my lips to her forehead. "You ready for this?"

"Do I have a choice?"

I stop walking and pull her into me so we're chest to chest. "Yes. You always have a choice. I know I can come on strong, but I don't want you to be miserable. If you're really not ready for this, then I'll take Mom to dinner and come home to you."

"No. It's okay. I'm sorry. I'm being prickly. I'm just… nervous."

"You have nothing to be nervous about. She's going to love you."

"You don't know that."

"I do, actually." I smile reassuringly.

"Care to enlighten me?" she asks, tilting her head back to look up at me.

"Because I've never introduced her to anyone before. She knows that this is important to me, that you are important to me by that fact alone. She also knows because I told her."

"I don't know what to say to that."

"You tell me if you want to do this or not. I won't force you. I don't want you to be miserable, but, babe, I promise that's not how this will go. If anything, my mom is going to come on too strong. She's excited to meet you, but she promised me she would be on her best behavior."

"You made her promise?"

"Of course, I did. I just got you. I can't have her scaring you away."

"You really want to do this?" she asks softly.

I move my hands to rest against her cheeks. "I really want to do this. With you. I want you to meet my mom."

"Okay."

"You're sure?" I ask, hardly able to believe my luck. It may be a small concession, but it tells me she's finally seeing the bigger picture. The one where we are together. Not just for a date or a night of fun. For a hell of a lot more than that.

She nods. "Yes. I'm sure. But just know that if this is where this is headed, you're going to have to meet my dad."

"You tell me when and where, and I'll be there."

"Just like that?"

"Just like that. You feel this too, right? It's not just me who feels this intense, crazy connection between us?"

"I feel it too," she confesses. "It's crazy and scary and so fast."

"It's me and you, P. That's what matters. As long as we're both on the same page, that's all that matters."

"What page are you on? You know, just in case."

"The one with a happily ever after," I say, pressing my lips to hers briefly. "We need to get going before Mom sends out a search party."

Her eyes widen at my confession. I watch as a slow smile graces her lips. "Right. Okay. Well, I apologize in advance for making either of us look like fools tonight."

"Not possible, babe. Just be you."

With her hand in mine, we make our way down the hall and out of the stadium. I know my mom is going to be waiting just outside the door with security. We talked about where to meet earlier. I'm kicking myself in the ass for not clarifying where to meet Paisley, but my girl waited outside the locker room for me. Coming off a win with the Blaze, I smile, thinking this night just keeps getting better and better.

"SO, PAISLEY," MOM SAYS, AND I GIVE HER A LOOK ACROSS THE TABLE, WARNING HER TO be nice, "you work for the Blaze?"

"Yes. I'm one of their athletic trainers."

"I take it you love the game too?" Mom asks.

"I do. My dad actually played for the Blaze when I was growing up. They're our home team for sure."

"Oh, anyone I know?"

"Easton Monroe."

My mom pretends to ignore me as a smile lights up her face. "Cameron had a poster of your dad on his bedroom wall growing up. He never missed a game."

"Mom," I groan.

"What? It's sweet."

Paisley turns to look at me, and I expect her to be smiling too, ready to give me shit, but her face is stone serious. "You were a fan of my dad?"

"Yeah, I think all boys my age who liked baseball were Easton Monroe fans. Especially those of us who played first base."

"You were a fan of my dad's, but you didn't know who I was?"

Fuck. I see where she's going with this. "No. I mean, I knew he had three daughters, but I promise you the day we met, I had no idea who you were. At least not until the media told me."

"It's true," Mom chimes in. I know she's only trying to help, but I'm not sure anything she could add would help me in this situation.

My head spins, trying to come up with the words to make her believe me. I didn't have any idea who she was that day, and I'm glad. I wouldn't change the way we met for anything.

"That day, Cameron called me as soon as he left the field. He liked to go to as many Blaze games as he could, and I was supposed to go with him that day.

I got caught up at the hospital. I'm a nurse," she adds. "Anyway, we were short-staffed, so I canceled, and I knew it wouldn't matter anyway. You get my boy to a baseball field, and he checks out. He's been that way since he was little. I made it home during the fourth inning but started it over on my DVR. I record all of his games."

"Mom," I say in warning, but it's no use. She's determined to say whatever it is she feels like saying, and my objection isn't going to stop her. I'm surrounded by stubborn women.

She ignores me, keeping her eyes on Paisley. "He called me as soon as he left the game. I was expecting to hear about the win and all the other comments about line drives and foul balls. That's what we usually talk about after a game, whether he was playing or not, so that's what I expected. However, that's not what I got."

My eyes are now glued to Paisley. I watch as she swallows hard, her full attention on my mother. "What did you get?" she asks, her voice gravelly.

"All I heard about was this woman. She was into baseball. Not just into it, but she understood it. She cheered at the right times, yelled at the players and umps at the right times, and she was beautiful."

I exhale, sitting back in my seat. My mother has sealed my fate. There is no playing it cool, not that I've really been trying, but she basically just gave me away.

"All he could talk about was you. You have no idea how hard it was for me to ask questions. It was even more difficult for me not to point out that this was a first for him. At least when it came to me. You see, Cameron has always told me that when he found someone worth me meeting, I would be the first to know. He didn't tell me I was going to meet you that day after the game, but it was clear that you made an impression on him. Imagine my delight when I turned on the news and saw the two of you kissing on the kiss cam."

If Mom's grin grows any wider, her face is going to crack. "Okay," I say, but my mother continues to ignore me, keeping her eyes on Paisley.

"I knew when I heard the excitement in his voice that you had made an impression on him. When I saw the kiss, I could tell it wasn't one-sided. Then tonight, my son tells me that he has someone he wants me to meet. I didn't have to ask him if it was you. Sure, I might have given him a hard time, but I knew, in here"—she places her hand over her chest, right over her heart—"that you were the someone I was going to meet tonight. So, while my son might have been a fan of your father's growing up, I can assure you he didn't know about you. It's impossible for anyone to fake that kind of excitement." Mom takes a sip of water and places her glass back on the table. "If you'll excuse me, I need the ladies' room." She slides her chair back and leaves us to discuss the bomb she just dropped.

Turning in my chair, I reach out and take Paisley's hands in mine. "I fell hard for you that day. You were unlike any woman I'd ever met. You were cool as hell to hang out with, and you loved the game that has meant so much to me in my life. You more than loved it. You understood it. You weren't there to land a player. You were there for your love of the sport."

"It has nothing to do with my dad?"

"No. It had everything to do with the beautiful, outgoing, baseball-loving woman who was sitting next to me. It was your smile and that kiss... life-changing," I say, leaning in and kissing the corner of her mouth.

"Life-changing? That's a tall claim, Taylor."

"I stand behind it."

"I've never in my life met anyone like you before."

"Is that a good thing?" I ask with a grin.

"I'll let you know."

"You do that," I say, leaning in and this time kissing her full pouty lips.

"Come on now, there are no cameras," Mom teases as she takes her seat across from us. "Now, Paisley, tell me how you plan to keep my son in line," she says, giving my girl her full attention once again.

Paisley laughs, and for the rest of the night, I can barely get a word in edgewise while my mom, the most important person in my life, bonds with the woman I'm falling hard and fast for.

Chapter Eleven

PAISLEY

"PAISLEY, IT WAS A PLEASURE MEETING YOU," GRACE, CAMERON'S MOM, SAYS AS WE make our way out of the restaurant.

"You too," I tell her. "Thanks for all of the stories on this one." I point to where Cameron stands beside me.

"Oh, honey, I have so many more. We should exchange numbers." Grace laughs.

"All right, you two." Cameron steps up and wraps his mom in a hug. "Thanks for coming tonight."

"Nowhere else I'd rather be."

"You want to follow us home?" he asks her. She raises her eyebrows in a silent question. I'm guessing it was the "us" that is raising her suspicions. "Paisley lives in the same complex as I do."

"Wow. That's… well, fate is the only thing I can think of to describe it."

"See." Cameron leans his shoulder into mine. "Come on, ladies, let's go home." With one arm around my shoulders and one around his mother's, he leads us to the parking lot.

"She's nice," I say, once we're in his truck and on the way home.

"Told you so." He reaches over and laces his fingers with mine. His hand is warm and calloused.

The rest of the drive is quiet. The radio plays softly in the background, and it appears that Cameron and I are both okay with just being together. There's no need for chatter to fill the silence. It's comfortable and just another thing to add to the list of things I like about him. He puts me at ease, even when he's being his bossy self.

We pull into the parking lot, and he shuts off his truck but makes no move to get out. "Stay with me tonight."

"You need this time with your mom before she drives home tomorrow."

"She just lives an hour away. I can see her anytime."

"Really, with the Blaze schedule?" I challenge.

"Fine. I know I can't, and I want to spend time with her, but I want to spend time with you too."

"You've been with me for over twenty-four hours. You need this time with her."

"Can you come back later and sleep in my bed with me?" He sounds like a little boy asking, and it makes me smile.

"I don't think that's a good idea, Cameron. Spend time with your mom. Take her to breakfast before you have to be at the field tomorrow, and we can catch up tomorrow night."

"I don't like this plan."

"I think some time away will do us both some good. It will give us time to think about this." I point between the two of us.

"I don't need to think about you any more than I already do."

"I mean, what this means. What we are. You've made some big claims, and you know maybe once you get some time away and a little perspective, you may change your mind."

"I'm not changing my mind." He turns to face me. "Every minute that I spend with you, I fall harder. You heard my mom tonight, right?"

"I did, but this is all so new, and you've had a lot of change in your life. You got called up to the big leagues. That's huge, Cameron, and you can't lose focus. Not now."

"I won't. The only thing that could make me lose focus on that field is losing you."

"You don't really have me to lose." We both know that's a lie.

"Don't I?" He leans in close and presses his lips to mine. "We can't keep doing this, Paisley. Can you just admit that we're dating? We can't be just friends. It's not possible for me. I'm willing to slow down and let you catch up, but I just need you to admit that we're dating. That neither of us is seeing anyone else. We're a couple. You're my girlfriend, my steady girl, whatever you want to call it. However you want to say it, I just need that."

"You really want to label this?"

"Yes." There is no hesitation in his answer.

"What if it hurts your chances of staying with the Blaze?"

He slides his hand behind my neck and pulls me close, pressing his forehead to mine. "That's a risk I'm willing to take. I've never met anyone like you. I've never met anyone who could make me think of something besides the game. That's worth everything."

How do I say no to that?

It's simple. I don't.

I don't want to. I can't resist him. I have a list a mile long of reasons we should just be friends, but none of them seem to matter. He's in this. I trust that. I can see the conviction in his eyes and hear it in his voice. I'm who he wants, and to be honest, I'm tired of fighting him on this when he's who I want as well.

"Okay."

"Okay?"

I nod. "Yeah. But I want to slow us down just a little. That means you sleep at your place tonight."

"Say it."

"Say what?" I'm being coy, and we both know it.

"Paisley," he warns.

"I'm your girlfriend." Saying the words makes me feel like I'm back in high school, but the way his eyes light up under the glow of the streetlamp makes that childish feeling worth it.

"Fuck yes, you are," he says, as his lips crash with mine. He rests his palms against my cheeks as he kisses me breathless.

I don't know how long we kiss, but when I remember that his mom is waiting for him to let her into his condo, it's like a bucket of cold water is tossed over my head. "Cam, your mom," I say against his lips.

"More kissing. Less talking."

"Cameron." I laugh, pushing at his chest, effectively breaking our kiss. "Your mom is waiting on you."

"Oh, shit," he mutters.

"Yeah. Oh, shit."

"This is real, right, Paisley?" he asks softly. "I'm not going to wake up tomorrow and realize this was all just a dream?"

"It's real. But you need to go."

"Come on. I'll walk you to your door." He climbs out of the truck, and that's when I see his mom climb out of her SUV that's parked beside us. My face heats with embarrassment. Not the best first impression of his girlfriend.

Knowing I need to face this head-on and I have no other choice, I reach for the handle and climb out of the truck. I take my time walking to the front and meeting them on the sidewalk. As soon as I'm within arm's reach, Cameron slides his arm around my waist.

"Mom, I have someone for you to meet," he says. His voice is chipper and filled with wonder.

"You feeling okay, son?" Grace asks him.

He laughs. "I'm perfect. Mom, this is my girlfriend, Paisley Monroe."

"Well, that's a new development. A welcome one." Grace steps forward and wraps her arms around both of us in a motherly embrace. When she pulls away, she's smiling wide, and it may just be the lighting, but I'm pretty sure she has tears in her eyes.

"Where's your bag?" Cameron asks.

"Oh, I just have this small one." She points at a small suitcase at her feet.

"I'll take that." Cameron reaches for the bag and begins to wheel it toward his condo.

"You make him happy," Grace says, keeping her voice low and just between us.

"He makes me happy." It's the first time I've admitted that. It's the truth. I don't know him all that well, but from what I do know, Cameron is one of the good guys. I know that people can change, but I'm pretty sure with Cameron Taylor, what you see is what you get.

"I may get grandbabies after all." Grace laughs as she moves ahead of me to step inside Cameron's condo.

I stand still, processing her words. We're not there yet—not even close—but I guess at least I have his mother's approval. I know how important she is to him, so to know she approves of us is a relief.

"Mom, I'm going to walk Paisley home," Cameron says, standing at the open doorway of his condo.

"I'm right here." I point behind me where my front door is a mere foot away.

"I'm walking you," he says, leaving no room for argument.

"Good night." I wave to Grace.

"Good night, sweetheart. I'll see you again soon." She sounds just as assured as her son as she waves and closes the door behind her.

"You sure I can't convince you to stay?" Cameron asks as we stroll hand in hand the steps it takes to get to my front door.

"I'm sure. You need this time with her."

"I need this time with you too," he says, pulling me into his chest.

"Well, you see now that we're official, that means you get to see me whenever you want. So, this one night with your mom, that's just a blip on the radar."

"Us being official means I need to be with you every spare second I can."

"Are you going to be one of those boyfriends?" I tease.

"I'm your boyfriend," he says, kissing me softly.

"And you're Grace's son. She drove here to see you, to spend time with you, and that's what you need to do."

"Hard-ass," he mutters, but I can hear the humor in his voice.

"Go. Enjoy your time with your mom."

"Fine." He brings his lips to mine for a soft kiss. "Good night, beautiful."

"Night, Cam," I say, stepping out of his hold. He stands behind me while I unlock the door and slip inside.

"I didn't think you would ever get home," Willow says, scaring the hell out of me. I whip around to find her sitting on the couch.

"I didn't expect you to still be up."

"Well, we have a lot to talk about. Namely, Cameron sleeping over last night, and you spending the day with him before going to work."

"Wil," I say, plopping down on the couch next to her. "I don't know what I've gotten myself into."

"What? Did he hurt you?" My best friend is on immediate alert.

"No. Nothing like that," I assure her. "He's just intense and so sure of himself. Of us."

"Oh, so there's an us?" she asks, tucking her legs underneath her as she turns to face me.

"As of tonight, there is an us," I say, barely able to contain my smile.

"Paisley has a boyfriend," she sings.

"Stop." I laugh. "He wanted to put a label on it, and honestly, he's hard to resist."

"So, last night?"

"He said I was staying with him or he was staying with me. He was adamant about it, and well, I chose here."

She nods. "And today?"

"He insisted on making me breakfast, and afterward, he wanted to hang out. So we just watched a movie at his place, and then we went to work. Oh, and he insisted we ride together too."

"It's great you two are together, but I don't want you to lose yourself in him either. You have choices. Cameron's bossy self is just going to have to deal."

"I know. It's not like that, though. He's confident in what he wants, and he wants what he wants, but tonight when he thought he was pressing too hard, he backed off."

"Pressing too hard?"

"We had dinner with his mom. She was in town for his game."

"Wow. He wanted you to meet his mother?"

"Yep," I say, popping the *p* and tilting my head back to stare at the ceiling. "Fast, huh?"

"I mean, not really. There are no set parameters for a relationship. As long as you're both on board with the pace, I say go with it."

"You know this means he's going to have to officially meet my dad, right?"

"Ah, and how do you think Daddy dearest is going to take the fact that his princess is in a relationship?"

"You know the answer to that question." I raise my head to look at her. "He ended up being cool with the kiss. My dad, I mean. So, maybe there's hope that he'll be cool with Cameron too."

"I don't know. Remember prom?" She laughs.

"Don't remind me."

"I thought Nick was going to shit his pants when your dad asked him his intentions with his daughter. And then when he asked him if he not only carried protection but how old it was and if he knew how to put it on. I swear, I'm surprised I didn't piss my pants."

"Can we not go down memory lane?" I beg.

"Easton Monroe is not only a badass on the baseball field. He's lethal when it comes to the women in his life."

"That." I point at her. "That is why I have never brought a guy home. Not after senior prom."

"You never really had a boyfriend in college, P. Sure, you dated, and there was that what six-month stint with Henry, but you never labeled him as your boyfriend. No matter how hard he tried."

"Yeah, well, Henry wanted to get to my dad, which is why he never did. He was going to school to be a sports agent." I can't help but roll my eyes as I think about Henry, the asshole that he was. He was pissed when I called off our little "fling" I guess you could call it. I intercepted a text message of him telling his friend that as soon as he and I quote "met the rents," he was in there, and his career would be launched. Needless to say, he never got to meet my parents, and I kicked his using ass to the curb.

I wish I could say that Henry was the only guy who tried to use me to get closer to my dad, the league, or my uncles, but I'd be lying. Maybe that's why I've been letting my guard down so much with Cameron. He's already playing in the majors. Sure, his spot isn't a definite as he fills in for Hastings, but he's here. He doesn't need me to help him.

It's refreshing.

"Tonight, Cameron's mom told me he had a poster of my dad on his wall when he was little. I started to freak out. I thought that I hid it well, but his mom pretty much nailed my mood and immediately put my mind at ease. I really think Cameron is with me for me. Not for my dad, my name, or any potential connections."

"Has he asked to meet him? Your dad?"

"No. But he has said that he knows it's going to happen, and he's ready for anything Dad happens to toss his way."

Willow tosses her head back in laughter. "He doesn't know Easton Monroe like he thinks that he does."

"Right?" I smile. "Thanks for listening. I should let you get to bed. I know you have to be up early tomorrow."

"Meh, I've gone on less sleep."

"That we have," I agree.

"What's your schedule tomorrow?"

"Another home game, and another the day after that."

"Damn, girl, I'm exhausted just hearing about your schedule."

"Yeah, it's great, right?" I smile at her.

"Only you would say that." She stands from the couch and offers me her hand, pulling me to my feet. "Where's your man tonight?" she asks as we shut off the lights and head to our rooms.

"His mom is staying with him. He tried to get me to stay, but I shut him down."

"Good. Keep him on his toes."

"That's going to be a hell of a lot harder than it sounds."

"You've got this, P."

"Thanks, Wil." I give her a hug and then head to my room. I plug my phone in to charge and notice a message.

Cameron: I miss you already.

Me: It's been fifteen minutes. Max.

Cameron: That's too long.

Me: Are you the clingy boyfriend type? Maybe I should rethink this?

Cameron: Paisley.

Me: Cameron.

Cameron: Don't mess with me.

Me: Good night, Cameron.

Cameron: Good night, beautiful.

My smile is wide as I change and settle into bed. He's definitely going to keep me on my toes. It's thrilling. I never really know where I stand with guys who ask me out. But I know with Cameron, which is comforting, allowing me to let my guard down. I'm excited to see where this goes.

Chapter Twelve

CAMERON

WE'RE ON THE ROAD FOR A THREE-DAY STRETCH IN PENNSYLVANIA, AND WE'RE TWO FOR two. We're definitely kicking ass and taking names. But that's all I'm going to say about that because I don't want to jinx us.

The bus pulls up to our hotel, and all I want to do is order room service, curl up with Paisley, and get some sleep. I'm exhausted. This schedule is grueling. Not that I'm complaining. This is everything I've ever dreamed of. It's still hard for me to believe that this is my life—playing for the Tennessee Blaze, and my game is tight if I do say so myself.

Then there's Paisley. She's an unexpected surprise in my life, one that I cherish, and I couldn't imagine her not being a part of this dream I'm living. We've been going strong now for a couple of weeks. I finally got her to agree to put a label on us. I'm not an idiot. I know a good thing when I see it, and Paisley Monroe, she's as good as it gets in my book. Of course, I'm locking this down.

Us.

Her.

Me.

She's what I've been missing.

I grew up with a single mom who always talked about me growing up and falling in love. I didn't quite understand it since she's still single herself. That didn't stop her from telling me that love is one of the greatest joys in life and that I should embrace it when I find it. It wasn't until I was older that I asked her how she could be so "pro-love" when her heart was clearly still broken. I will never in my life forget what she told me. "*I lost the love of my life, but that doesn't mean I don't still love him. Love is different for all of us, Cameron, but I would rather have loved and lost than to never have loved at all.*"

"Yo! Taylor, you coming?" Henderson calls out as we're walking into the hotel.

"Nah. I'm calling room service," I call back.

"Where's your girl?" Miller asks.

"She's coming."

"My man." Henderson throws his fists in the air and rocks his hips. I can't help but laugh at his stupid ass. He looks ridiculous.

"I don't know, Taylor. If these are your friends and the company you keep, I may need to rethink this whole boyfriend thing." I hear her voice from beside me.

Tossing my arm over her shoulders, I pull her close. "Not a chance, baby. You're stuck with me." I lead us to the elevators, and she doesn't hesitate to lean into me as we ride to her floor.

"Good game," she tells me as she scans for her room and pushes open the door.

"Thanks, babe."

"Are you as tired as I am?" she asks. "Wait, don't answer that. You're playing out on that field when all I'm doing is watching. Of course, you're exhausted."

"I'm tired. The schedule is grueling."

"Yeah. I mean, I knew what it was like from Dad playing all those years, but we didn't really live it with him. We did travel with him when we could, but not every time, so this is definitely an adjustment."

"Everything going okay with your position?" I ask.

"Oh, yeah, that's fine. I love my job. It's just adjusting to the schedule. And

I came in toward the end of the season. I can only imagine what next season will be like."

"I can't say, and I'm not sure if I'll be here next season." I voice the words that have been playing in the back of my mind. My game is on point, but rumors of Hastings getting better and coming back to the field are swirling, and that could mean that I go back to the Outlaws.

It would suck since playing for the majors has always been my dream. What would suck even worse than that? Not seeing Paisley every day like I do now. I'm addicted. She's my calm and my driving force. I don't know how I would handle being away from her. I keep telling myself that this is too fast, but my heart just can't seem to accept that memo.

"What are you talking about?"

"Rumors are going around that Hastings is better and may be coming back."

"He's not," she assures me. "I worked with him yesterday. He's still in a lot of pain, and he's not there yet."

I nod. "You're not breaking some kind of rule by telling me that, right?" I ask her.

"No. It's team knowledge. There were other players in the room when he and I were discussing his prognosis along with Dr. Thomas."

"There are what? Six weeks left in the season?" I try to calculate the date in my head, but when you work this schedule, it all starts to run together.

"Yes. And I don't know that he's going to be ready by then. Have you heard anything from the front office?"

"No." That's something else that has me thinking that this is only temporary. My only saving grace is that I'll go back to the Outlaws, which means I stay close in Tennessee. Sure it's about two hours from here, but at least Paisley and I will be in the same state.

"Hey." She rubs her thumb over what I'm assuming is the frown line on my forehead. "We'll cross that bridge if we ever get to it," she says softly. "Right now, we're here together, and you're playing the hell out of the game. Enjoy it."

"You know what I want to enjoy?" I ask, wrapping my arms around her waist.

"Room service?" She smiles up at me.

"You." My lips find hers, and just like the first time, and every time since then, it's like a jolt of lightning. She gasps when I nip at her bottom lip, and I take the opportunity to stroke her tongue with mine.

I will never get enough of this woman. Never.

Every touch feels as though it's the first time I'm touching her. My mom used to tell me that finding love was just as important as doing what you love. I never understood what she meant until I met Paisley. I remember asking my mom how I would know. She used to tell me that you just know, and I thought she had lost her mind. I was sure my dad, who is better described as a sperm donor since he bailed on her when he found out she was pregnant, had her brainwashed or something. He doesn't deserve her love, and as I got older and understood fully, I told her so. She said the heart wants what the heart wants. I still don't understand how her heart could still want him.

My mom is one of the greatest people I know, and I wish she could find love and happiness again. Especially if this feeling that I have with Paisley is what she was telling me about my entire life. She needs this. Everyone needs to feel this… content.

"I need to feed you," I say against her lips. What I don't say is that unless she plans on being my meal, we need to slow the hell down.

"I want it all." She laughs, falling back onto the bed.

"You shower first. I'll order us some food."

"Or, we could eat and then shower. Together."

"Woman," I growl. "You're testing my patience."

"Good." Her smile lights up her face.

"I'm taking my time with you."

"We have all night." She smirks.

"You know what I mean. This is real to me."

"It's real to me too, Cameron. You think I offer myself to just anyone?"

"No." I hold her stare. "But I want to do this right."

"I've been sleeping in your arms for weeks. You refuse to sleep without me, yet you won't have sex with me."

"I want you, Paisley. Don't ever question that. Fuck, baby, it's hard for me to resist you, but I refuse to be like the assholes of your past who used you."

"How is having sex with me when I'm offering myself to you, using me?"

"I don't know how to explain myself here. I'm an athlete, not a poet." I sit on the bed, offer her my hand, and pull her up so she's sitting next to me. I place her hand over my hard-as-steel cock that's beneath my sweats. "This is what you do to me. Just thinking about making love to you does this to me."

"I don't understand."

"I want it to be special—our first time. I've never cared about that before, but with you, everything is different. I'm here for the series, not just the game. I don't want it to be a quick fuck after a game. You're worth more than that, P."

She exhales loudly. "When you put it like that," she says, leaning her head on my shoulder.

"I want you, Paisley. I'm with you for more than just a good time. I want all of you. I want our lives intertwined so we can't differentiate what's mine and what's yours."

"That's a big claim for a couple who has only been dating for a few weeks."

"When you know, you know."

"So philosophical, Taylor," she teases.

"I have my moments." I kiss her softly. "I'm going to order us some food, and we'll go from there." Her eyes light up like she may be getting her way, but I'm sorry to tell her that I'm not budging on this one.

My cock is just as disappointed as she is, but it's important we wait. What I feel for her is strong and more real than anything I've ever felt.

"I CAN'T EAT ANOTHER BITE," PAISLEY GROANS, PUSHING HER PLATE AWAY.

"Your plate is still half full," I tease. "You said you wanted it all."

"Next time, just ignore me when I say that." She laughs.

"How about a bath?"

"That actually sounds perfect right now."

I stand from my cleared plate and kiss the top of her head. "I'll get it started." I leave her to do what she needs to do as I make my way into the bathroom. Her suite has a separate shower and a Jacuzzi tub. I wish I had some candles or bubbles or something to make this a little more romantic, but it is what it is. I could probably call down to the front desk, but I don't want people in our business. What I do with my girl behind closed doors is between us. No way do I want the paparazzi getting ahold of anything private between us. They got our first kiss, and the vultures are still playing those clips. They'd have a field day with me requesting bubble bath and candles for my girl in her hotel suite while on the road.

No thanks.

When the tub is about half full, I stand from the edge to let Paisley know it's ready for her, except I freeze when I look up to find her standing naked in the doorway of the bathroom. "Paisley." I breathe her name.

"Is it ready?" she asks softly.

I swallow hard. My eyes rake over her naked body, and fuck me, she's gorgeous. "Y-Yes," I say, my eyes coming back to hers.

She takes a hesitant step toward me. Then another and another, until she's in front of me. All I would have to do is lift my hand, and I could feel the weight of her breasts in my palm. Or bend my head and capture one of her hard, pretty pink nipples in my mouth. I could slide my hand between her legs and see if she's wet for me.

"Thank you, Cam." She places her palms against my chest and stands on her tiptoes to kiss me. It's a chaste kiss as far as kisses go, but my lips burn from the contact.

She drags her hands across my chest as she walks past me. She grips my bicep as she steps into the tub. All too soon, she's releasing her hold to sink down into the steaming hot water. My eyes follow her as her breasts bob just above the water, the tub still not yet full. My cock aches to be inside her. I shift my position, and with my hand in my sweats, I adjust to a less painful position.

"You okay there, slugger?" she asks coyly.

"You're torturing me, Paisley."

"Who me?" She cups water in her hands and lets it fall over her tits.

"Yes. You," I growl.

"A bath was your idea," she reminds me.

"I'm aware of the error in my ways."

"You know. You could climb in here with me. This tub is big enough for both of us."

"Are you trying to test my restraint?"

"Yes." She smiles sweetly. "Please, Cam, will you get in with me?"

I have no willpower—none when it comes to her. I stare down at the most beautiful woman I've ever laid eyes on. The woman who is quickly becoming everything to me. She's begging me to soak in the tub with her. My muscles ache, almost as bad as my cock. Can I do this? Can I soak with her and not make love to her? My cock twitches at the thought of holding her naked body against mine, and my decision is made. I'm a disciplined man. I have to be for my job. I can do this. I can hold her naked body against mine and control my cock. Decision made, I begin to undress.

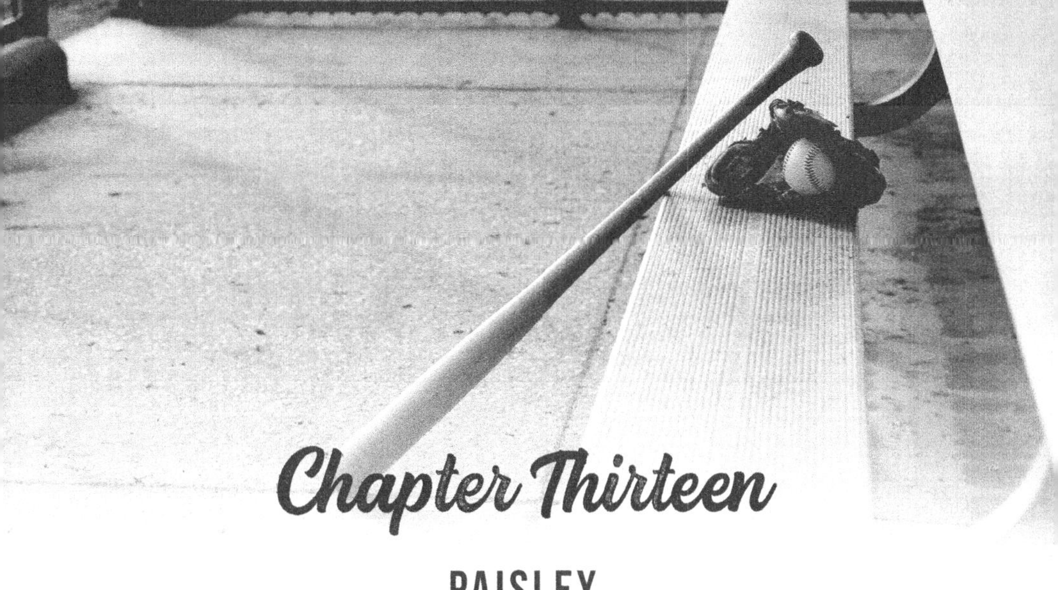

Chapter Thirteen

PAISLEY

A SEDUCTRESS I AM NOT. HOWEVER, WITH CAMERON, I'M DIFFERENT. THE WAY HE LOOKS at me, and the confidence he has in us, it's liberating. I've been sleeping in his arms for weeks, and he's been the perfect gentleman. That's great, he's a good man, and he's proven this to me.

I have needs, though, and only Cameron can handle those needs for me. I've been waiting for him to make a move, and nada. I don't know why, but tonight I hit my boiling point and decided to be the one to make a move. So far, my efforts are fruitless, but it's nice to see how I affect him. His breathing is labored, and his cock, let's just say he sees me.

When he reaches for the neck of his T-shirt and pulls it over his head, tossing it to the floor, a thrill races through me. Finally, I got him to cave. I don't take my eyes off him as he slides his sweats down his thighs, kicking them to the side.

"You're almost there," I say, nodding to his boxer briefs. I lick my lips in anticipation of him stripping out of them. I've seen him just like this every night for weeks. I know what he's hiding beneath the thin layer of cotton, but that's not the same as seeing it with my own eyes. Speaking of eyes, mine are lasered in on his crotch.

"Paisley." His voice is gruff.

"Cameron," I mock, my eyes never leaving his package.

"Eyes up here, beautiful."

With great reluctance, I pull my gaze to his eyes. They're full of fire and want. All for me. "You're teasing me."

A laugh bubbles from his lips. "No, baby. You're the only one doing any kind of teasing."

I run my hands up my thighs over my belly and cup my breasts in the palms of my hands. "Me?" I ask coyly.

"Fuck," he rumbles.

"Cam?"

"Yeah?" he asks. His voice is thick with need.

"Please join me." I watch as his shoulders relax and his face softens. He nods, and that's when it happens. His hands slide under either side of the waistband of his boxer briefs, and he tugs them down his thighs, letting them fall to the floor. His cock juts out, resting against his belly. Long and thick, bigger than anyone from my past. Even though my experience is limited, I know sex with Cameron is going to be life-changing.

"Move up," he says huskily. I do as he asks and lean forward. He steps into the tub and takes a seat behind me. "Come here, baby," he whispers. He grips my hips and pulls me against him.

His hard cock presses against me, and it takes extreme effort not to squirm or shift my position, putting him where I need him. Instead, I rest my head back against his chest and close my eyes.

"I've never seen anything more beautiful," his deep voice whispers in my ear. His hands move to my breasts, and softly, he palms them as if he's testing their weight. "Your skin is so soft," he muses.

I keep my eyes closed. I can't watch him touching me. I'm a pile of embers close to igniting the way that it is. I would embarrass myself if I watched him touching me. Instead, I just feel. Feel the rough pad of his thumb as he traces over my nipple and the way his breath is hot against my neck.

His hands roam over my belly and venture between my thighs. "Are you wet for me, Paisley?" he pants. The sound of his voice tells me he isn't unaffected. "Can I touch you here?"

"Please." My reply is breathy and a little desperate, but I don't care. All I care about is his hands on me.

Anywhere.

Everywhere.

"Jesus, baby." He curses under his breath as he slides his fingers through my folds. "You test a man's patience," he says, nipping at my ear. "I want you so fucking bad, but I promised myself we were going to wait, and I stand behind that."

I grip his arm, holding his hand where it is. "Don't stop."

"Is this what you want?" He dips one finger inside. I lift my hips in reply, and he chuckles softly. "I've got you," he assures me.

Sliding my arms under his, I grip his biceps holding on as he adds yet another digit, bringing me to a level of bliss I've never known. How is it this man is better with his hands than my previous bed partners? Again, there hasn't even been a handful, but there is a stark difference in Cameron and the men who aren't worth mentioning of my past.

"Is this breaking your rules?" I ask him.

"Nah. This is me taking care of you. You know that's all I want, right, Paisley? I just want to be with you. To take care of you."

"I'm a handful."

"Oh, baby, I know." He kisses just under my ear. "You're my handful."

Before I met Cameron, I never knew what it meant to melt under the words of a man or swoon. I imagined I knew what it felt like, but nothing could have prepared me for this man and the effect he has on my heart, my body, and my mind. It's not just the way he makes me feel. It's the fact that I crave the feeling. I crave his sweet words and his kisses. I crave the touch of his arms wrapped tight around me at night. I'm in deep, and even though that scares the hell out of me, I'm pushing forward. For the first time in my life, I'm not letting the fear of the unknown dictate my future. Instead, I'm letting my heart guide me.

He curls his fingers just a little, pulling me out of my thoughts as a moan spills from my lips. "There," I praise him.

"I've got you, baby. Just feel." The water splashes as he rocks his hand between my thighs, and all I can do is hold on as he takes me higher and higher until I feel as though I'm falling off the cliff of ecstasy.

My chest is rapidly rising and falling, my breasts moving in and out of the water from the rapid rate of my breathing. My body feels like Jell-O as I lie in his arms. Cameron's hands are everywhere they'll reach. The soft caress of his calloused hands is soothing.

When I feel as though I can function, I move to the side so I can see him. His eyes are heated yet soft as he stares back at me. "You're flushed," he says, running his index finger over my chest. "Beautiful," he murmurs.

I move to reach for him, his cock specifically, but he stops me. "No. This was for you."

"I can't just leave you like this," I tell him.

He smiles softly. "I can take care of myself."

"I want to."

"I know, baby. But I only have so much willpower."

"Good." I reach for him again, but again, he stops me.

"Paisley, I want you more than I want my next breath. I want to know what it's like to slide my cock deep inside you. I crave that, but I don't want it to be here. To be now. I have plans for us. Long-term plans, babe. Not just here and now. I want us to go the distance, and… I think we need to wait a little longer."

"This is important to you?"

"Yes. You're important to me." He kisses my forehead.

"Okay," I agree, even though my body is screaming to push him. I know that if I pushed, I could get him to give in to me. But that's not what I want. For some reason, us waiting is important to him, and who am I to take that from him? From us?

"Thank you." His lips connect with mine, and his tongue sweeps past my lips, dueling with mine. "I have to stop," he says a few minutes later. "The water's getting cold anyway. I need to take a quick shower."

"Why—" I cut off when it hits me. He's going to "take care" of himself. "Never mind. You sure you don't want some help with that?" I ask, wiggling against him.

"Shameless." He laughs. "Hop up, baby."

I do as he says and carefully step out onto the tile floor. Why is it that hotels never have bath mats? I guess they like the fact that their guests risk their lives stepping out on the slick-ass tile floors. Grabbing a towel, I toss it onto the floor and then reach for another to wrap around my body.

"I'll be quick," Cameron says, standing.

I turn to look at him and watch as the water trails down his body.

Let me just tell you. Cameron in baseball pants is a sight to behold. Truthfully, every woman, hell, every man should witness the gloriousness that is my boyfriend in his uniform. However, Cameron in nothing but what the good Lord gave him? Yeah, that's got me all kinds of worked up, and I know I need to shut it down, or I'm going to attack him while he's in the shower, or maybe while he sleeps.

"You're staring." He smirks.

"Have you seen you?"

He tosses his head back in laughter. "Go change. I'll be right out."

"I'm struggling with what's about to go down. I can't just go out there and go about my business when you're in here, doing… that."

"You don't have a choice."

"Oh, but I do," I say, dropping to my knees.

"Paisley." It's meant to be a warning, but it's more of a plea.

"Let me do this for you. I promise I won't push us for more. You took care of me, and I should get the opportunity to do the same for you. I promise we'll clean up and go to sleep." I peer up at him under my lashes and see the slight nod he gives me. He braces his hands on either side of the small wall in the bathroom as I take him into my mouth for the first time.

Closing my eyes, I just feel. I've never really been a fan of giving oral sex, but this time, all I want to do is feel him on my tongue. Taste him. It's new for me, but that's just how things are with Cameron. Over and over again, I take him with my mouth, using my hands, my lips, my tongue to drive him crazy.

"Pais…" he pants. I hear his fist hit the wall, and with how he's unraveling, I'm desperate to take him deeper and see him spiral. I grip him a little tighter, and he moans from deep in his throat. "I'm close." He drops his hand and taps my shoulder. "Baby," he grunts.

I don't stop. I can't stop. I need to taste him. I want everything he's willing to give me. If this is all I get for now, then I want it all. I want the full experience.

"Shit. I can't. You have to stop," he warns again.

I don't stop.

I go harder.

I go faster.

I go deeper.

"Fuck!" he roars as his release coats my tongue and the back of my throat. I don't stop until he slides out of my mouth. I barely have time to think when he glides his hands under my arms and lifts me. Instinctively, I wrap my legs around his waist and my arms around his neck. "You're incredible." He kisses me so soft and sweet, not the least bit worried about tasting himself on my lips.

"Thank you for tonight."

"Oh, Paisley," he says softly. "Baby, you never have to thank me for giving you what you want. What you need. Just hang with me a little longer. I want it to be right between us."

"Okay. I respect your choice, but maybe we can pencil a few more nights like tonight into our schedule?"

He chuckles softly. "We can do that." He kisses my forehead. "Shower tonight or in the morning?"

"In the morning."

He nods and starts to move. He carries me to the bed and places me gently onto the mattress. I scramble to get under the covers to ward off the chill of the air-conditioning. Cameron stares down at me with an odd expression on his face before turning off the lights and climbing into bed.

We reach for each other under the covers, and he wraps me in his warm embrace. My head rests on his chest, and I can't remember a time I've ever been more comfortable. It's just us, skin to skin. If I was asked my most comfortable night six months ago, I would have said any night before this one, but tonight once again changed that. I'm just about asleep when his lips press to the top of my head. "I'm gone for you, Paisley."

I don't speak because I know he thinks I'm asleep. I want to tell him that he's not alone. I want to tell him I'm falling in love with him, but that's crazy. It's too soon. It's just the emotions of the night, after what we shared. Instead, I close my eyes and drift off to sleep, knowing that I'll wake safely in his arms.

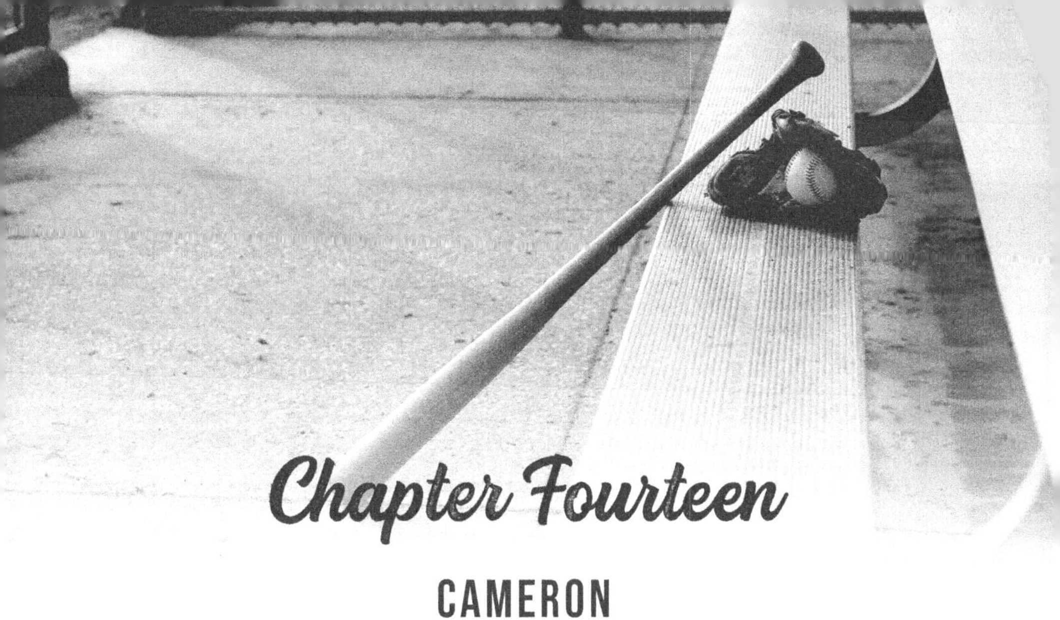

Chapter Fourteen

CAMERON

THE LOCKER ROOM IS CHAOTIC AS WE CELEBRATE ANOTHER WIN. TODAY IS OUR LAST HOME game before leaving for the road tomorrow morning. We have another three-game stretch, this time in Cincinnati. The travel is exhausting, grueling, but at least I have Paisley with me. The other guys on the team aren't that lucky. Sure, we're new, but having her with me, calms me.

We've been dating for a little over a month, and things are going great. She's my addiction, and she knows it. That's fine, though. I wouldn't have it any other way. I can't sleep if she's not with me. Luckily, she travels with the team, and I leave my shared room at night to sleep with her in her single. My game is on fire, and I know it has a lot to do with her. Baseball players are superstitious, and Paisley is not only my person. She's my good luck charm.

Yeah, my person. It happened fast, but I wouldn't change what we have for anything. I can't ever remember a time in my life when I've felt more… relaxed. That's the best way I can describe it. I'm living my dream, but with her by my side, it's better than just my dream. It's everything I never knew I wanted. She's everything I never knew I wanted or needed in my life. Now that I have her, I don't ever plan to let her go.

I know, those are strong words, but the heart wants what the heart wants, and mine, well, it wants Paisley. I haven't told her yet. I know that I'm a little further along in our relationship than she is, and that's okay. I'll wait for her to catch up. In the meantime, I'll love the hell out of her without telling her because there isn't a doubt in my mind that I'm in love with her. Not one. Speaking of Paisley, my phone vibrates, and her name pops up.

Paisley: Hey. My parents came to the game. They want to grab dinner.

Me: Okay. I'm going to grab a quick shower, and I'll be right out.

Paisley: Just like that?

Me: Just like what?

I know what she's asking. If I had my choice to meet her parents, would it be sprung on me after a game? Probably not. However, this is my life. Baseball is my career, and hers as well, and we have to take these moments when we can get them. Besides, she met my mom weeks ago. And we've all had dinner a couple of times when Mom comes to the home games. It's time for me to meet her family. In fact, I want to meet them. I want to get to know the people who made this amazing woman who she is.

Paisley: No hesitation.

Me: They're your family.

Paisley: This is a BIG deal, Cameron.

Me: I know.

Paisley: I've never introduced them to anyone. Not unless you count senior prom.

Paisley: It was a disaster.

Me: I've got this. I'm getting in the shower now. We don't want to keep them waiting.

Paisley: Okay...

Me: It's going to be fine. I promise. I'll be out in a few.

Tossing my phone back into my locker, I head to the showers. The guys are all making plans for drinks while I'm planning on meeting my girl's family, who just so happens to be my childhood idol. Talk about a mind fuck. I rush through my shower while declining drinks with the team again.

"You too good to hang out with us?" Corey Miller asks.

"Nah, having dinner with my girl's family." I leave it at that. They all know that Paisley is mine. I've had to give a few hard stares, but after my night of searching for her on the bus, they all know.

"No shit. You're having dinner with Easton Monroe?" Henderson asks as we head out of the locker room.

"I'm having dinner with my girlfriend's parents and her younger sisters." And her dad, who just so happens to be one of the greatest first basemen of all time. Who played for our fucking team, no less.

"Dude, it's Easton fucking Monroe. How are you so chill?" Henderson asks.

I shrug. "He's not Easton Monroe to me tonight. He's Paisley's dad tonight. I'm not going to meet the greatest first baseman of all time. I'm going to meet my girlfriend's dad."

"Still, meeting the rents is a big deal," Miller chimes in.

"It is," I agree.

"You don't seem the least bit fazed," Miller challenges.

"I'm not. I know what she means to me, and I know what they mean to her. That's all that matters tonight. I'm meeting people who care about her like I do. We have that in common. The rest will come."

"Oh, shit," Henderson mutters. He's looking over my shoulder.

Slowly, I turn to see Paisley, her dad, a woman who I assume is her mom, and her two younger sisters. All five of them are looking right at me. "I'll catch you guys later," I say to the teammates whose questioning got me into this mess.

I plaster a smile on my face and slowly make my way toward them. I'm going through the conversation we just had, making sure I didn't say something stupid. I'm positive I didn't, but hell, you never know.

I reach Paisley, who is watching me with a watery smile. "Hey, you." I slide my arm around her waist and press my lips to her temple. "Hi, I'm Cameron." I wave at her family with my free hand.

"Hi, I'm Parker." The oldest of the two sisters waves.

"I'm Peyton," the younger one chimes in.

"Hi, Cameron. I'm Larissa, Paisley's mom. It's nice to meet you."

"You too," I say, accepting her hand for a shake.

I turn my attention to Easton. "Cameron Taylor." I offer him my hand. He takes it, and his shake is firm.

"Easton, Paisley's dad."

"Good game," Paisley says, pulling my attention back to her.

"Thanks, babe." I kiss her temple again because when she's this close, I can't not. It's physically not possible, not to mention I'm not going to pretend to be someone I'm not. What I'm not is a man who can resist this woman. I'll keep it clean, but no way can I go all night and not shower her with affection. That's just not who I am with her.

"So, we should go," Larissa says.

"I want to ride with Paisley," Peyton, who, if I remember correctly, is twelve, says.

"You're riding with us. So is your sister," Easton tells her. The tone of his voice leaves zero room for argument.

"Actually, Dad," Paisley speaks up, "Cameron and I will meet you there. We rode together." Her shoulders are squared, and her head is held high, but I can feel the slight tremble as it makes its way through her body. I know she's not afraid of him, but the fear of disappointing him is real. I didn't grow up with a dad, but I feel the same way when it comes to my mom. So I know how she's feeling.

Easton stares at his daughter, and I wish more than anything I could read his expression. They're in a standoff, and there isn't a damn thing I can do to break the tension. "Fine. We'll meet you there."

"My next day off, we'll spend some time together," Paisley promises Peyton.

"Okay," Peyton agrees. She doesn't seem thrilled that she has to wait, and I get it. I crave time with Paisley too. I make a mental note on our next day off, whenever that may be, to plan something that her sisters can be a part of. Her sisters and me. Because let's be honest, I feel like Peyton when I don't get my time with her.

"We'll meet you at the restaurant," Paisley tells her family. Then she looks up at me. "Ready?"

"I'm with you," I tell her.

"See you guys." She waves at her family.

My arm that's around her waist eases to rest on the small of her back as I lead her out of the stadium and to my truck. "You okay?" I say once we're inside.

"Yes. I just… I've never introduced them to anyone."

"You said senior prom."

"Oh, God, Cam. It was a disaster," she moans.

My cock is instantly hard at the sound. Did I mention we've not slept together yet? Yeah, there's that. It's not that I don't want to. Hell, I know she wants to, but this all happened too fast between us, so I've slowed that part down. Sure, I want to share that intimacy with her, but we'll get there. I'm content to hold her in my arms each night as I fall asleep and wake up to her smile every morning. I just want to be near her.

"Come on, I'm sure it wasn't that bad," I say, as I discreetly adjust my cock.

"Oh, it was that bad." She goes on to tell me about how her dad acted with her prom date. "I've never brought another guy home. Either he was using me to get to Dad, or I just wasn't feeling him."

"So you're telling me I'm the only one to make the cut?" I glance over at her and flash her a grin.

"Yes!" she exclaims. "Now you see the issue. This is nerve-racking."

I reach over and place my hand on her thigh. "Babe, it's fine. I'm all yours. They're going to see that, and if they don't, I'll tell them, and they'll see it in time. It's going to be fine."

"You say that."

"Are you afraid of your dad?" I haven't gotten that vibe from her, but she's really nervous.

"No. I'm not afraid of him, but I hate disappointing him."

"By having a boyfriend?"

"I'm Daddy's little girl. Well, we all are, but I was the first, and he chose me, you know?" she asks. "He didn't have to step up and be my dad. He didn't have to love me the way he loves my little sisters, but he does. He adopted me, gave me his last name, and—" She pauses, and I can hear the emotion in her voice. "He's an amazing man, and he's given me so much. I just don't want to disappoint him."

"You think being with me will disappoint him?" I force the question past my lips.

"No." She's quick to defend. "It's not you. It's just I know my dad. He's always said no one will be good enough for his girls, and well, I guess I just worry he's going to be rude to you, and you don't deserve that."

"I can handle it." I can handle anything as long as she's mine.

"You shouldn't have to handle it. That's what stresses me out. I won't let him be that way. Not with you. You're different, Cam. You're with me for me, and you're so good to me. If my dad can't see that, then I-I don't know what…"

I guide my truck into the parking lot of the restaurant and park before removing the keys from the ignition and turning to look at her. "Hey." I reach over the console and cradle her cheek. "I don't want you fighting with your family for me. I'm a man. A man who is crazy about you. I can take what they dish out. Okay?"

"I-I don't want you to decide this isn't worth the hassle."

Fuck me. "Baby, that's never going to happen. I'm in this. Me and you. I fought too damn hard to get you to be with me. Do you really think I'm going to let your dad run me off?"

"I really like what we have, Cameron."

"Me too, baby. Me too." Leaning over, I kiss her softly. "Now, let's go inside and have dinner with your family. I don't want you to stress or worry about anything. I can handle it. I promise you that. As long as I know at the end of the day you're mine, none of this will get to me."

"Cam, I—" She starts but then stops. "Thank you," she says instead of what was on the tip of her tongue.

"Anything for you. You ready?" I ask.

"As I'll ever be."

I nod. "Stay put. I'll get your door."

"You don't have to do that. I've told you this."

"And I've told you that I like doing things for you. Give me this, please?"

"Fine," she grumbles, but I can see the slight tilt of her lips as she tries to hide her smile.

Climbing out of the truck, I see her family waiting in front of the restaurant for us. I can feel their stares as I make my way to the passenger side to open Paisley's door. I offer her my hand, and she takes it, this time her smile lighting up her entire face. "You're beautiful," I tell her as we walk hand in hand toward the front entrance of the restaurant.

"Are you trying to charm me, Cameron Taylor? I think it's my dad you want to use all that Taylor charm on."

"Nope. All my charm is yours," I say, making her throw her head back in laughter.

"What did we miss?" Parker asks.

"Nothing. Cam's just being Cam." Paisley smiles up at me, and my heart misses a beat. I'll do whatever it takes to see that smile on her face every single day.

"Ready?" Larissa asks us.

"Yes," Paisley says. Her body is relaxed as she leans into me, and her voice is steady. Hell yes, my girl is ready. She's got me in her corner, and I'll always be here for her to lean on.

Chapter Fifteen

PAISLEY

CAMERON PULLS OUT MY CHAIR AND WAITS FOR ME TO SIT BEFORE TAKING THE ONE BESIDE me as his own. He immediately places his hand on my leg under the table, and the contact is soothing.

"Paisley, guess what?" Peyton asks.

"What?" I give her my full attention. Well, as much as I can. There's always a part of me focused on Cameron, even when he's not this close and touching me.

"I'm signing up for drama club."

"Really? That's awesome. What made you decide to do that?" I ask my youngest sister.

"Well, Mom's always saying how dramatic I am, so I thought I might as well try it and see how it goes."

"Are you giving up softball?" I ask her.

"No." Her answer is hard and firm. "This is just something to keep me occupied until softball season starts."

"Will it overlap?" I clarify.

"I don't know. I guess I better make sure. I'm not giving up softball," she says adamantly.

"I'm sure it will work out, lady," Dad tells her.

Our server appears, and we place our orders. As soon as he steps away from the table, Dad turns his attention to Cameron. "So, Cameron, tell us about you," he says, sitting back in his chair. He's at the head of the table with Mom at his side. I'm on the other side with Cameron next to me. Peyton is next to Mom, and Parker is directly across from Dad. At least I'm between Dad and Cameron.

"I went to college at the University of Tennessee. My degree is in sports management. I started playing for the Outlaws right after college, and I've been there until just recently."

Dad nods. "You finished your degree?"

"Yes, sir. I promised my mom I'd have a fallback. It's a good plan. This career isn't guaranteed."

"It's always good to have options." Mom smiles at him.

"What about your family?" Dad asks.

"It was just my mom and me growing up. My mom's parents helped with me a lot. Mom worked full-time and went to college to become a registered nurse after I was born."

"She's so sweet," I add. "You and Grace would get along great," I tell my mom.

"You've met her?" Dad asks.

"I have. A few times, actually." I hold his gaze as he processes what I just said.

"This is serious then?" Dad asks. This time, it's Cameron he's looking at instead of me.

He tightens his grip on my leg under the table while holding my dad's stare. "Yes." Just one word. No explanation. Then again, none is needed.

"It's a little soon to be serious, don't you think?" Dad asks.

"Easton!" Mom scolds him.

"Baby, I'm just speaking the truth. They've known each other a handful of weeks, and it's serious. She's too young for that."

"Easton Monroe. Have years of marriage and three girls made you lose your memory? Do you not remember our dating history?"

"That's different."

"Explain that." Mom crosses her arms over her chest and gives him a look that tells us she's not playing. It's her mom look, the serious one.

"She's our little girl. She's only twenty-two. She's too young to be serious."

"I'm not even going to dignify that with a response." Mom rolls her eyes. "Paisley is an adult. She's a college graduate, has a career, pays her own bills, and has the freedom to date whomever she wants."

The server delivers our food, and we all dig in. The table is quiet, and my heart sinks. I was so hoping this would go better. Cameron's mom was so good to me, and that was weeks ago when we first met. I love my dad, but sometimes he's just too over-the-top.

"Hey," Cameron murmurs in my ear. I turn to look at him, and he's still leaning in close, ignoring anyone and everyone but me. "You all right?" he asks softly.

"No."

"You want to get out of here?"

"That's just going to make it worse," I whisper.

"I don't care, Paisley. What I care about is you. If you're over this, we'll leave."

"That's going to give him more ammunition," I tell him.

He drops his fork and lifts his hand to cradle my face. I hear Mom sigh and Dad grunt, but I ignore them. "You are my priority," Cameron says. This time, his voice is strong and no longer a whisper. "Say the word, baby. I've got you always," he says, leaning in to press his lips to my forehead.

"Mr. Taylor, can you remove your hands from my daughter?" Dad seethes.

"No, sir," Cameron answers, never taking his eyes from mine. "She's upset."

"Princess?" Dad asks. This time his voice is soft and a reminder of the man who raised me. Not this stubborn brute who is trying to scare off my boyfriend.

"Dad?" I reply, turning to face him.

"What's wrong?"

"Really? Are you going to sit there and ask me that? You're being an ass, Dad."

"Paisley," he warns.

I look across the table. "Thanks for dinner, Mom. Parker, Peyton, I'll call you both soon." With that, I push back from the table and stand. Cameron eases back his chair and does the same, placing his hand on the small of my back.

"Sit down, young lady," Dad says, his voice stern.

"I'm a grown woman, and you no longer get to dictate my life. Cameron is a good man. The best I've known next to you. He's good to me. He puts me first. I don't know what more you could ask for? Call me when you decide to be reasonable." With that, I turn and walk away.

When I feel Cameron's hand drop from my back, I stop and turn to look for him. He's still standing at the table, his eyes locked on my father. His arms hang at his sides, but I can tell he's upset. Not sure what's going to happen, and not wanting to cause any more of a scene, I rush back to him, lacing my fingers with his.

"Cam?"

"Your daughter is the most incredible woman I've ever met. She's kind, loving, and her smile lights up my world. I happen to agree with you. I'm not good enough for her, but you're missing something." Cameron pulls his gaze from my dad and turns to look at me. His eyes soften before he looks back at my dad. "I'll fight every damn day to be the man who she deserves. I know what hard work looks like. I know what it's like to have a dream and work your ass off to make that dream happen." He presses his lips to my temple. "Ready, baby?" he asks softly.

All I can do is nod. I'm too overwhelmed with emotion. With my hand locked tight in his, Cameron leads us out of the restaurant. We don't stop until he's at the passenger door of his truck. He opens the door for me and waits until I'm buckled in before closing the door and making his way to the driver's side. He climbs behind the wheel and grips it tightly.

"I'm sorry, Paisley. I'm so fucking sorry. I should have kept my cool in there, but I couldn't stand that he was giving you a hard time because of me."

"Cameron." My voice cracks, which has his head turning to look at me. Panic dances in his eyes.

"I'm so sorry." He leans over the console and slides his hand behind my neck, resting his forehead against mine.

"You have nothing to be sorry for," I say through my tears. "You told me you would have my back, and you did. You didn't let the fact that you were sitting at dinner with Easton Monroe sway you. You were really there for me. Not my father."

"Of course I was there for you." He pulls back and stares deep into my eyes. "I'm in love with you, Paisley. I meant every word I said to him. I know I don't deserve you, but I'll do my best to be a better man every day. A better man for you."

"You're perfect for me."

"No one will ever love you the way that I do," he says softly.

"I love you too." I do. I love him. I know our relationship has been a whirlwind, but I feel it in my soul that Cameron is my other half.

"Let's get you home." He kisses me softly before pulling away. I watch him as he puts on his seat belt and starts the truck. I keep my eyes on him all the way home. He glances over a few times, giving me a sexy smile, which only makes my heart feel like it's going to burst open with love for this man.

When we pull into the parking spot in front of our building he turns off the truck. "Your place or mine?" he asks.

"Yours."

"Do you need anything from yours?"

"No. I just need you." Five words we both feel deeper than the surface of their meaning. I resisted him at first, and he fought for me. He fought for us. He's proven that there is no ulterior motive. Just me. He just wants me.

"You know how to bring a man to his knees, you know that?" he asks.

"You look fine to me."

He places his hand over his heart. "Right here, baby. This is where your words hit me. Deep, Paisley."

"You were wrong, back at the restaurant. You're good enough for me. You're the first man I've ever dated who was really with me for me. Well, besides poor Nick. He never really had a fighting chance."

"He did, but he wasn't willing to take it."

"We were eighteen," I remind him.

"I'll give him that." Cameron smiles.

"We were kids."

He shrugs. "I would have fought for you."

"You don't know that."

"Neither do you," he counters.

My phone rings, and I pull it out of my purse. *Dad* flashes on the screen. I turn the phone to show Cameron.

"Answer it," he urges.

"I'm not ready to talk to him."

"Maybe not, but he loves you."

"Why are you defending him?"

He shrugs. "I'm trying to put myself in his shoes. He has three beautiful daughters, and he's famous. He has to be worried about men taking advantage of you, even without his fame. Maybe cut him some slack."

"After the way he treated you?"

"I got to defend myself. I also got the girl." He winks. "Come on, let's go inside, and you can call him back." He climbs out of the truck, and I do the same.

"I was going to get your door."

"I know how to open doors, Cameron," I remind him.

"I know you do. It's not about you not being able to. It's about me spoiling you and showing you in small ways, like opening your door, how much you mean to me."

"Silver tongue," I mutter, making him laugh.

"Come on, beautiful." He places his hand on the small of my back and leads me to his door. He unlocks it and pushes it open, allowing me to walk in first.

As soon as we step inside, my phone rings again. "It's him again," I tell Cameron.

"Answer it, baby. You'll both feel better once you do. I'm going to go change." He kisses me quickly before walking down the hall to his room.

Plopping down on the couch, I swipe at the screen and accept what is now a video call. "Hey."

"Princess." My dad's voice cracks.

"Dad."

"I owe you an apology."

"You owe Cameron an apology."

"He chose you."

"Of course he did. He loves me," I say without thinking.

Dad sucks in a breath. "I had to make sure. I know that dating has been hard for you. Your mother and I talked," he confesses. "I know he's playing for the Blaze, and he has his own career, but I had to be sure. I needed to push him to see how he felt about you."

"I understand what you're saying, but you need to learn to trust me. I can make my own choices. I've made it this far and done all right for myself."

"It's not that I don't trust you, princess. I do. I just… I love you so damn much. You made me a dad for the first time, and I know you're an adult, but dammit, I'm having a hard time with that."

Cameron comes to sit next to me and kisses my cheek. "Cameron," Dad says.

"Mr. Monroe."

"My daughter tells me you're good to her."

"I love her."

Dad nods. "I owe you an apology. Part of me was being an ass earlier, and part of me was testing you. I know Paisley has had too many guys in her life using her. Whether that's to get to me or to the league or to her uncles, hell, I don't know, but my daughter is my priority."

"She's mine too."

Dad nods. "I'm having a hard time with that. For too long I was the man in her life. It's not sunshine and roses knowing you're being replaced."

"Daddy, I'm not replacing you," I say, tears welling in my eyes.

"I know you're not, princess. But your old man is still having a hard time."

"I love you," I tell him.

"I love you too, Paisley Gray. More than you will ever know. Always speak from your heart, baby girl." He shuffles, and Mom's face appears on the screen.

"We love you, sweetheart," Mom tells me. "You two enjoy the rest of your night. We'll do dinner at our house when the two of you get back to town."

"Thanks, Mom."

"Night," my parents say at the same time.

"Night," Cameron and I reply, and the call ends.

"Feel better?" he asks.

"I do. I guess I never really looked at this from his perspective."

"Always two sides to every story."

"We made some big claims tonight, Taylor." I smile at him.

"We did?"

I push at his chest, laughing. "Oh, you forgot already? Maybe that means I should head to my place tonight."

"I'm coming with you."

"You sure about that?"

"Yes. Do you know what else I'm sure about?"

"What's that?"

"That I love you."

My smile remains as I press my palms to his cheeks. "I love you too." I give him a loud, smacking kiss that makes us both laugh.

"You ready for bed? We need to get up early so we can pack and head to the stadium."

"Yes. It's been a long day."

"That it has." He stands and picks me up, tossing me over his shoulder in a fireman's hold, and carries me to his room. He drops me on the bed, causing me to laugh harder. With a wink, he disappears into the bathroom while I grab one of his T-shirts to sleep in and quickly change.

Tonight started out as a shit show, but when Cameron stood up for me and then told me he loved me, my night turned around. And Dad calling, I know that was hard for him, and I love him for stepping up and calling me, calling us to apologize.

It's as if hearing Cameron stand up for me solidified our relationship. It's almost as if I'm finally able to love him freely without worry. He's with me for me. I knew this, at least I hoped, but after tonight, I'm sure of it. Cameron Taylor loves me, and I love him. Excitement bubbles up inside me for what the future may hold for us.

Chapter Sixteen

CAMERON

FINALLY, A DAY OFF. I WANT NOTHING MORE THAN TO JUST STAY IN BED WITH PAISLEY ALL damn day, but I have a surprise for her. Time off during the season is rare, and we have to make the best of it. Besides, if I get my way, my girl and I will be back at my place for an early dinner and lots of cuddle time.

Checking the time on my phone, I realize we're going to be late. "Paisley!" I call down the hall to where she's getting ready in my room, the room that I think of as ours. "We gotta go, babe."

"This would be easier if you would tell me where we're going."

"I can't do that. That would ruin the surprise."

"Fine," she grumbles, leaving my room, before leaning over the back of the couch to kiss me. "I'm ready."

"Great." Standing from the couch, I offer her my hand and lead her out the door. When I head toward her place, she pulls on my hand.

"What are we doing?"

"You'll see," I say as I continue to her door. I knock once, and the door flies open. Willow greets us, smiling.

"Hey. Ready?" she asks.

"Wil?" Paisley asks. "What's going on?"

Willow points her finger at me. "Your man here told me I wasn't allowed to tell you." She shrugs, and bounces off to my truck.

"Cam, what's going on?"

"I told you. I have a surprise for you."

"I thought that was code for you and me spending the day together."

"We are spending the day together."

"Alone," she says under her breath.

"That's later. Trust me. No way am I not getting some alone time with you on our day off. But first, I have a surprise for you." She opens her mouth to speak but quickly closes it. "Speechless?" I ask her.

"Kind of, yeah. I can't figure out what you're up to."

"You'll see." I lead her to the passenger side of my truck and open the door for her.

"When can we tell her?" Willow asks when I slide in behind the wheel.

I glance in the rearview mirror at her. "Not until we get there."

"Please, let me tell her," Willow begs.

"No." I busted my ass to arrange today. It's been a challenge, and at times, I even felt like I was cheating on her. I was dodging phone calls so I could take them when she was in the shower or away from the locker room, which is a whole other mess. It's a lot of work to plan a surprise, especially when you spend so much time with the person you're trying to surprise.

"Fine," she grumbles, sitting back and crossing her arms over her chest. I can't help but chuckle at her.

"The suspense is killing me," Paisley says from her seat beside me.

"Give us about fifteen more minutes or so, and we'll be there."

"Wait," Willow announces. I glance at her in the mirror, and she's digging through her purse. She smiles as she lifts an eye mask. "We should make her wear this."

I glance over at Paisley and think about her reaction when she sees what I've organized for today. "Babe? You up for being blindfolded?"

Her eyes heat, and she bites down on her lip.

"None of that," Willow says as she leans forward and sticks her head between the seats to talk to Paisley. "We're not talking kinky here, P. It's just for the surprise," she quips.

"Fine," Paisley agrees. "I'm already this far in. What's a little blindfold to top off the experience." My cock twitches at her willingness to be blindfolded. I'm not into that particular brand of kink, but I can definitely see the benefits of blindfolding her and kissing every inch of her skin.

"That's the spirit," Willow tells her.

Willow and Paisley make small talk about work and friends they know from college. I'm content to just drive and listen to them. It's nice to know we have the entire day to do whatever we want. We don't have to rush to the stadium or the bus or airport for an away game. The season is almost over, and I don't know what that means for me. I do know that Hastings is out for the rest of the season, so I know I'm here until then. After that? Well, I'm not so sure. It's up in the air right now.

"Okay, P, we're getting close," Willow says. She hands Paisley the blindfold and helps her put it on. "How many fingers am I holding up?" Willow asks. She leans forward and holds up three fingers in front of Paisley.

"Uh, Wil, I'm blindfolded." Paisley laughs. The sound fills the cab of my truck and has a smile of my own tilting my lips. I love seeing her happy.

"Hey, I was just checking," Willow says, sitting back in her seat.

Pulling my truck into the lot, I see a Range Rover, and I know it's her family. I park next to them and grab my keys from the ignition. "We're here. Stay put. I'm going to come and get you," I tell her.

"Okay." She smiles and wipes her hands on her thighs.

Climbing out of the truck, I shut the door and wave to her dad, who meets me at the sidewalk. "She knows?" he asks.

"No. I was able to keep it a surprise. Willow even went as far as blindfolding her. I was thinking you all could go on inside and have everyone together when we surprise her."

"This is your show, Taylor." He claps me on my shoulder and walks off to tell everyone the plan.

Willow climbs out of the back seat and gives me a thumbs-up before jogging to the rest of our group and walking inside with them. "You ready, baby?" I ask after opening her door.

"I'm ready. I'm nervous," she admits, wiping her palms on her thighs again.

I grab her hands and press a kiss to each palm. "I promise this is a good surprise. And you were the one who agreed to the blindfold."

"Yeah, well, I may have been thinking about something else," she mutters.

I bend my lips to her ear. "Make sure you slip it into your purse."

"Cameron!" she scolds me. "Who can hear you?"

"It's just us, babe. Willow went inside."

"Phew. Okay. Can we do this? The suspense is killing me."

"Come on, beautiful." I grab her hips and lift her from the truck, placing her feet on the ground. After shutting the door, I slide my arm around her waist. "I'll guide you. Just follow my voice. I promise I won't let you fall."

"I trust you, Cam," she says softly.

My chest swells with so much love for her, something that happens more frequently than not when I'm with this woman. I hope she's excited about today. "Watch your step," I tell her as I guide her up onto the sidewalk. "We're almost to the door." I dictate our steps. "I'm going to pull open the door," I tell her. I reach for the door, and with my arm still around her, guide her into the building. Everyone is standing front and center and ready for the big reveal.

"Ready, babe?"

"Yes." She laughs. "Show me already."

Carefully, I remove her blindfold. She blinks to adjust to the light and gasps when she sees her family and my mom standing in front of her. She turns to look at me with tears in her eyes. "What is this, Cameron?"

"Well, I know we've been running like crazy, and you miss your family. You told Peyton your next day off, you would call her and plan something, and that got me thinking about planning something so we could all spend time together. Get to know each other better."

The words are barely out of my mouth before she launches herself at me, hugging me tightly. "I love you. I can't believe you did this."

"I love you too," I whisper in her ear, before releasing my hold on her.

"You—" She points at her sisters. "You both said Mom and Dad wouldn't let you miss school today."

"Hey, we stretched the truth for the greater good," Parker says, coming forward and hugging her big sister.

"It was so hard not to tell you," Peyton says, stepping forward for her hug.

"Move over. Momma needs a hug," Larissa says, pushing into the fold of her daughters and wrapping Paisley in a hug.

"Move it or lose it, queen," Easton tells his wife. He steps forward and hugs both Larissa and Paisley at the same time. They step back, and my mom steps forward.

"Paisley, it's nice to see you again," Mom says.

"Grace!" Paisley hugs her snugly, and something in my chest tightens and releases. The two most important people in my life are embracing with smiles on their faces, and I can't tell you how happy that makes me that the two of them get along so well.

A week after they met, Paisley asked for Mom's phone number. I guess they had talked about some show over dinner and she wanted to tell Mom something about it. They've been texting back and forth ever since. In fact, my mom messages me less. When I called her out on it when planning for today, she said my girlfriend does a great job of letting her know how I am. I wasn't mad or even offended. I was happy they were getting along so well.

"Cameron," Paisley calls out.

"Beautiful," I reply, stepping next to her.

"What's the plan?"

"Well, this entire place is ours until about three, which is when the doors will open to the public."

"This entire place is ours?" she asks as her eyes scan the fun center.

"Yep."

"Yes!" Peyton cheers. "Paisley, I'm thinking you should keep this one," she calls out.

"Yeah." Paisley smiles up at me. "I think you're right, Peyton."

"Lady, I just got used to the idea of the guy. Let's not go marrying your sister off just yet," Easton tells his youngest daughter.

"Lady?" my mom asks.

"Oh." Paisley smiles. "My dad is a little over-the-top. When he met my mom, I was four, and he started calling me princess. When they got married, he started calling Mom queen. So, naturally, as my little sisters were born, he had to find names for them. Parker, my middle sister, is duchess, and Peyton, the youngest, is lady."

"I love that." Mom smiles over at Larissa. "You have a beautiful family."

"Thank you. I'm Larissa, by the way." Larissa holds out her hand for Mom to shake.

"Grace."

"And this is my husband, Easton, and well, you know the girls now." Larissa laughs.

"It's nice to meet all of you," Mom tells them.

"I'm Willow." Willow steps up to Mom, offering her hand as well. "Paisley's best friend and roommate."

I'm waiting for her to comment how she's not been much of a roommate these past few months. We spend most nights we're in town at my condo instead of hers. We have more privacy there. Don't get me wrong, Willow is great, but sleeping skin to skin with my girl is something we started, and it's easier if we're in the condo alone.

"Paisley, let's go race go-karts!" Peyton grabs each of her sisters by the hand

and begins to move toward the go-karts.

"Wait for us," Larissa calls out. She links arms with my mom and Willow, and follows after the girls.

"This is a good thing you did, Cameron," Easton says, his eyes on the women walking away.

"She was missing her family. I thought the laid-back environment would be good to introduce you and Mrs. Monroe to my mom."

"Easton and Larissa. You've earned that right."

I nod. I want to toss my fist in the air and pound on my chest that I finally got her father's approval, but instead, I go for cool. I wait several seconds before speaking. "So, who do you think is going to win?" I nod toward the go-kart track.

"My girls are all competitive. And Willow, that girl loves to win." He laughs.

"My mom was both Mom and Dad growing up. She's not a newbie to the go-kart scene."

"I guess we better get over there and cheer them on."

Together, we make our way to the track and do exactly that. We cheer for the girls, which has Peyton coming out as the victor. Easton and I join them on the second ride. And that's how the day goes. We hop from go-karts to arcade games, to Skee-Ball, to miniature golf, and back to go-karts. It's a fun day. I feel like a kid again, and everyone seems to be getting along well and enjoying the day.

We have a late lunch, which consists of junk food from the concession. Pizza, nachos, and soft pretzels all around.

"We should get going," Larissa says, looking at her watch. "It's about to open to the public," she tells our group.

I open my mouth to reply when a pair of arms wrap around my waist. Arms I don't recognize. Looking down, I see Peyton hugging me. "Thank you, Cameron. Today was the best day." She smiles up at me.

"You're welcome," I tell her, hugging her back. I catch Paisley's eyes, and she's smiling at us.

"Thanks, Cameron," Parker says as she too steps up for a hug. "It's been forever since we got to do something like this with Paisley."

I hug her back as well, because what else do I do? The hugs don't stop there. Larissa, Mom, and Willow all take their turns. "Thanks for today," Easton says once Willow steps out of my hold. Paisley sneaks between us and wraps her arms around my waist, resting her head on my chest. A sign of our solidarity, I'm sure, but her dad and I are in a good place now. He knows what she means to me, and as her father, I respect his need to know for sure.

"I'm just glad it worked out, and everyone was able to make it. And no one let the cat out of the bag." We all turn to look at Willow.

"Hey." She holds her hands up, laughing. "If she was home more, I might have let it slip, but we made it." She smirks. That's a subtle dig that Paisley spends more time at my place than theirs. I knew it was coming. I'm just glad she was inconspicuous with her wording.

After another round of goodbyes and a promise that all of us will get together at the Monroes' for dinner soon, we head our separate ways.

"I'm not even going to ask if you're coming to our place," Willow says when I pull in front of our building. "Not after what lover boy did for you today."

"The day's not over," I tell Willow.

"Stop." She holds up her hand. "I don't need to know about your plans for the rest of the day. Paisley, what time do you work tomorrow?"

"We're on a three-day home stretch."

"Lunch tomorrow?"

"Definitely."

Willow looks at me. "No objection?"

"I get her until tomorrow at eleven. No sooner, and we'll call us even."

Willow tosses her head back in laughter. "I want details, P," she says as she reaches for the handle and climbs out of my truck.

Chapter Seventeen

PAISLEY

CAMERON UNLOCKS THE DOOR TO HIS PLACE AND PUSHES THE DOOR OPEN FOR ME TO WALK in ahead of him. I walk inside and kick off my shoes. Thankfully, he told me to dress casually and comfortably today. I still can't believe he organized for both of our families to get together. On our day off. *His* day off.

As soon as the door closes, I turn to face him. "I don't know what you have planned for the rest of the day, but I'm going to need you to strip down."

"What?" He laughs.

"You heard me. Strip."

"If I'm stripping, it's only fair that you do as well."

I hold my hand out for him, and he places his in mine. Turning, I lead us to his bedroom. A room that feels more like ours than just his alone. Pushing open the door, I gasp at what I see. The bed and the floor are littered with red rose petals. There are candles all around the room, and the blackout curtains are pulled tight, blocking out the light of day.

"That's a fire hazard," I blurt.

He chuckles as he wraps his arms around my waist from behind. "They're battery operated." I turn my head, and he kisses me just below my ear. Our hands are entwined, and the feeling of being home washes over me. It has nothing to do with the location and everything to do with the man who holds me as if I'm precious to him.

I am precious to him.

The feeling is mutual.

"How did you pull this off?" I ask him.

"Willow. She had her sister come over and set this all up for us. It couldn't be just anyone. I needed someone who wasn't going to run to the tabloids and exploit either of us, and everyone I trust without question was going to be with us today."

I turn to face him. He's dressed in jeans today. They fit him just as well, if not better than his baseball pants. It's a treat to see him in jeans. He's wearing a plain white T-shirt that molds to his muscles and leaves his tattoos on display. He has on a black baseball hat, and he's wearing a smile for me.

The floral scent in the room is a reminder of what he did for me. For us. I don't need him to tell me to know that this is our moment. The one we've both been waiting for but denying ourselves. Well, more Cameron than me. He has Thor's strength when it comes to not giving in to me. Believe me. I've tried. However, today that's all about to change.

I'm wearing cutoff shorts and a tank top, something I won't be able to do in a few weeks when the weather starts to turn cool. My hands find their way to the button of my shorts. I don't take my eyes off him as I shimmy my shorts down my legs. They pool at my feet, and I kick them to the side—next is my tank. I reach for the hem and lift until it's over my head and somewhere on the floor. I'm left standing in front of him in a sheer black bra and panties.

"You're beautiful," he says, swallowing hard.

"You're overdressed," I counter.

He pulls his hat from his head and tosses it to the floor. The corner of his mouth lifts in a grin as he reaches behind him, grips his plain white T-shirt, and pulls it over his head, letting it fall to the floor. "Better?"

"Keep going, Taylor." I point at his jeans.

He kicks off his shoes and makes quick work of stripping himself out of his jeans. "How about now?"

"We're getting there."

"Yeah?" he asks, stepping toward me. He wraps his arms around me, pulling me into his chest. "I think you're the one who's now overdressed." With deft fingers, he unhooks my bra and assists me with sliding the straps over my shoulders and down my arms, adding to the pile of clothes beginning to gather on his bedroom floor. "Now we're even," he murmurs, and he bends his head and sucks a nipple into his mouth.

Closing my eyes, I fight back the moan that threatens to spill free. "Is that how this is going to go? Tit for tat?"

"Is that how you want this to go?"

"I asked you first." Suddenly, I'm nervous. I've wanted this moment with him for a long damn time, and now that it's here, the nerves move in.

"What I want is to cherish you. I want a night when I know I can take my time to give you the attention you deserve. I want a lazy morning of lying in bed and making love to you."

"Is that night tonight?"

"Depends." His eyes lock on mine. "If you allow me the honor to make love to you, then yes, tonight is that night."

"Finally," I say dramatically, making us both laugh.

"Sassy," he says, kissing my lips before trailing kisses down my neck.

"You love me sassy."

"I love you any way I can get you, Paisley." He drops to his knees and spends some time kissing my belly. Settling his hands on my hips, he looks up at me. "I love you."

I bury my hands in his hair. "I love you too."

Sliding his hands in the waistband of my panties, he works them over my hips, my thighs, and down my legs. Bracing my hands on his shoulders, I lift one foot, then the other to step out of them.

"I don't know where to start," he murmurs, kissing just below my belly button.

"We can just get down to business."

"Oh, you think you're ready?"

"Try me," I challenge.

He smiles. "On the bed, beautiful." The predatory gleam in his eyes causes a shiver of anticipation to race down my spine. Doing as he asks, I sit on the bed and move back until I can lay my head on the pillow.

I don't take my eyes off him as he strips out of his boxer briefs and reaches into the nightstand. I watch him as he takes out a box of condoms and opens it for the first time. He pulls out a strip and tosses it on the bed next to me. When he walks toward the end of the bed, I speak up. "Where are you going?"

"I'm taking care of you," he replies as he climbs onto the bed from the bottom. He settles on his knees before picking up my left leg. He massages my foot before working his way up. When he kisses the side of my foot and trails his lips along my leg, I know I'm in for an experience of a lifetime. He wasn't just spouting random bullshit. He truly intends to take his time.

"Cam."

"Yeah, baby?" He stops his caress of my right foot and gives me his full attention.

"I need you."

His eyes soften. "You have all of me."

He's not getting it. Then again, maybe he is. This man is stubborn as hell, and I know that no amount of begging or pleading will hurry this process. He's got his heart set on seduction, which is a waste of his efforts because I'm a sure thing, but that's not what this is about. It's the experience. He wants our first time to be memorable. My badass baseball player is a giant softy and a romantic. At least where I'm concerned. Knowing this is his show, and I'm just a spectator, I rest back on the pillow and enjoy the feel of his hands and his lips against my skin.

He moves to stretch out, lying flat on his stomach. Lifting up on my elbows, I watch as he lifts my legs and places them over his shoulders. The look in his eyes is one I've never seen before. It's love, and desire, and something predatory "You okay?" he asks.

"I'm perfect. You okay?" I toss the question back at him.

"This is the best day of my life," he says as he dips his head and sucks my clit into his mouth.

"Cam," I moan as I drop back against the pillow.

"Let me hear you, baby. There's nobody here but us. No thin hotel walls, no nosy fans, no paparazzi. It's just us, Paisley."

I don't bother to reply to him. We both know he's not waiting on an answer when he begins to torture me with his mouth and his tongue. It's the best kind of torture I've ever experienced. I've had very limited experience with oral sex. But I don't want to think about the past. Not when I have Cam taking my body to levels of pleasure I've never experienced.

I grip the sheets, but it's not enough. I move to bury my hands in his hair, and he moans, which sends a pulse throughout my entire body. My back arches off the bed, and my hands hold him still. I need him to stop. I need him to give me more. I don't understand this mixed feeling coursing through me. I'm a mess of want, need, and something else I can't name.

When he slides his fingers in deep and works them in tandem with his tongue, the last of my control starts to slip. "Cam—" I start but can't finish. Not that I know what I was going to say anyway. He's officially stolen my ability to think, let alone speak.

He doesn't stop his relentless pursuit of my pleasure. His mouth and hands are everywhere. At least that's how it feels. I feel a burn deep in my core, and my legs clamp around his head. He moans again, and that's all it takes. The vibration shoots me off like a rocket as my orgasm tears through me. The intensity of the flames of desire racing through my veins is unlike anything I've ever felt before in my entire life.

Cam holds his position, not removing his mouth and hands from me until my body drops to the mattress. I'm sated and exhausted, but I've never felt more alive, more cherished. I guess that was his plan all along.

He presses his lips to both of my inner thighs before he carefully places my legs back onto the bed. Then he's there, hovering over me. His dark eyes are filled with so much love, I could cry. "You okay?" His brow crinkles with concern.

"I've never been better," I assure him. It takes extreme effort, but I manage to lift my arms and wrap them around his neck.

He stares at me for several deep breaths before lowering his mouth to mine and kissing me. I can taste myself on his tongue, and if any other man from my past would have tried to kiss me, I'd have pushed them away. I do the opposite with Cameron. I pull him closer. This time it's me who pushes my tongue past his lips.

I want more of him.

I want more of us.

My kiss is feverish and borderline desperate. I can't get close enough to him. I need to be closer. I need to feel his skin on mine. I need him inside me. "I need you," I murmur against his lips.

"I'm right here."

"I need all of you. I need you inside me."

"I promise you this night will not end without me making love to you. But first—" He reaches over to the nightstand. I follow his movements, and that's when I see a single red rose. I suppose it's left over from all the petals. He grabs it and moves next to me on the bed.

He holds the rose by the stem, and I can see that the thorns have been removed. When he uses the petals to trace over my pebbled nipples, I arch my back as goose bumps break out against my skin.

"What are you doing to me?" I'm breathless and sated and more turned on than I have ever been in my entire life.

"Cherishing you."

The look in his eyes is one I recognize. I've seen it on him a hundred times. Determination. This time, it's not on the baseball field, and he's not facing an opposing team. No, this time it's in his bed, and his opponent isn't an opponent at all. It's me, his girlfriend, and I know without a shadow of a doubt, we're not close to being done.

Chapter Eighteen

CAMERON

I NEVER WANT THIS NIGHT TO END. I WANT HER HERE IN MY BED FOREVER. I KNOW THAT'S not possible, but tonight, I'm going to pretend that it is. Rose in hand, I trace the petals over her pretty pink nipples. She sucks in a breath, and I lean down, taking one of the pebbled buds into my mouth to hide my smile. I've waited a long damn time to drive her wild, and I can't help the satisfaction of my success.

It's been so hard not to take her. Sleeping naked next to her night after night is thrilling, and I'm constantly hard. I've jacked off more times since we've been dating than I have in my entire life combined. I knew waiting would be worth it, though. Selfishly, I wanted to be able to take my time with her. I also wanted to wait so she knows that I'm with her for her, and not because she's fucking me.

Another part of me, a deeper part, wanted to make sure I had the time to take care of her. To show her how we can be together. That same part of me hoped that when we finally had a night like tonight, I would ruin her for all other men. Lord knows she's already ruined me. Even before tonight, there was no chance I would ever look at another woman the way I look at Paisley.

Trailing kisses between her breasts, I work my way to the other nipple, lavishing it with attention as I stroke the petals of the rose over her thighs. "Cam."

I don't reply. She's not expecting me to. Instead, I trace every curve of her body with the rose. From one breast to the other, down her stomach. I lift the bud just before I reach her pussy, and she groans, making me smile. I continue down one leg, then the other, all the way up to her thighs. I don't stop until the petals of the rose have touched every inch of her, well, all except for where she really wants me.

Softly, I let the rose trace over her pussy. She arches her back off the bed as a moan from somewhere deep inside her spills from her lips. Her legs fall open and give me the space I need to run the petals of the rose over her most intimate parts.

I spotted the rose, and the idea just came to me. I thought that it would be sensual and turn her on. I didn't stop to think about what it would do to me. My cock feels like a steel spike resting against her leg. I've never wanted a woman like I want Paisley. I know that I never will. She's changed something in me—something I can't name but can only acknowledge.

Unable to resist, I move between her legs and lazily kiss her there. I'm taking my time, teasing and torturing us both.

"Please," she pleads. That one word calls to me. Moving up her body, I fuse my lips to hers. I kiss her like she's the air that I breathe. Like if I don't kiss her this very second, I might not make it. The truth is, I might not. I need her.

"Cam?"

"Yeah, baby?" I say, barely lifting my mouth for her to answer, before devouring her once more.

Her hands find their way back to my hair, and she tugs so I'll lift my gaze to hers. There are tears in her eyes, and my heart drops, thinking I hurt her in some way. That this seduction to show her what she means to me has somehow backfired. I open my mouth to apologize, but she beats me to it.

"I'm so in love with you," she whispers. Tears shimmer in her eyes.

Do you know what it feels like to have your heart melt inside your chest? Yeah, me either, at least not until now. Her words send a warm flow of satisfied content and love… so much fucking love throughout my body. I know that my words aren't doing the feeling justice.

Dropping the rose to the bed, I accept defeat. It's time. My elbows rest on either side of her head as I push her hair out of her eyes, careful of my weight so I don't crush her. "What's after love?" I ask.

"What?" She looks up at me as if I've lost my damn mind.

Maybe I have.

"What's after love? That word, *love*, it's not enough, Paisley. It doesn't do justice to what I feel for you. I love you with every fiber of my soul. What word do I need? Help me out here," I tell her.

"Oh, Cameron." She sighs as a tear slides out the corner of her eye.

"I love you too," I tell her. "My heart, my soul, my body, my mind, they're all yours, Paisley." I press my lips to hers. I take my time, relishing the feel of her mouth on mine. Over and over and over again, I kiss her—slow, languid strokes of my tongue with hers. Without words, I'm trying to show her how I feel, how no one will ever take her place in my life. She is my number one. Nothing will ever change that.

When she pulls away and cradles my face in her hands, her brown eyes bore into mine. "Make love to me."

"I want nothing more," I reply honestly. Reaching for the strip of condoms, I tear one off and move to settle on my knees. A quick glance at my girl and I see that she's watching my every move. My cock twitches knowing what's about to happen. We're about to slide into home. Shaking out of my thoughts, I tear open the small pack and sheathe my cock.

Settling with my elbows once again on either side of her head, I hold her gaze. "You're it for me. This is my last first time," I tell her.

She swallows hard. "That's… a big claim."

"The biggest," I confirm.

"You make my heart feel like it could explode. It's racing so fast, just from six words."

"They were a good six words." My mouth tilts in a smile.

"So modest," she teases.

"Are you ready to start the rest of our lives together?" I push the hair out of her eyes.

"More than anything."

With that, I push inside her for the first time. Closing my eyes, I take a slow breath to memorize the moment. One I will never in my life forget. It's more than the fact that her pussy is tight, hot, and wet, and all for me. It's the knowledge that this is my forever. *She* is my forever. This is what I have to look forward to as the years pass us by, and that knowledge alone is enough to bring a man to his knees.

"You with me?" she asks, her hands once again finding their way to my cheeks.

I open my eyes to see her smiling up at me. "I'm perfect. You're perfect." I drop a quick kiss to her lips before sliding my arms underneath her and rolling us over so she's on top.

"Oh," she moans, rocking her hips.

I had to move so she could be in control because I was too close to losing mine. I know that even when we're fucking, we're making love, because that's what this is. Love. But tonight, I'm barely hanging on by a thread. My control is at its limit, and feeling her… I need her to take control. I want this to be everything she's imagined it would be these past several weeks since I've denied us pleasure. It's already the best night of my life. I want to ensure that it's hers as well.

Bending forward, she places her palms flat against my chest. Her hair is hanging over her shoulders, and her eyes are locked on mine. "I don't know what to do here, Cam. You have to help me."

"You've never been on top?" I ask, and she shakes her head.

My cock twitches inside her, causing her to moan. She's three years younger than me, but I forget that her experience is not as broad as mine. She's kept herself sheltered from the opposite sex and intimacy because she could never tell the true reasons they were with her. That mixed with the fact that she's been trying to get me to cave and make love to her for weeks now. She's never let her lack of experience guide her, hence her ploys to get me to make love to her sooner.

"What feels good?"

"You," she breathes.

I smile up at her. "There's nothing you could do that I'm not going to love." I place my hands on her hips and gently lift her before pulling her back down on my cock.

"Oh." She tilts her head back, so I repeat the motion a few more times. I change it up, trying to help her find what works for her, because, let's be honest, my cock is buried deep inside her. It's all good for me. Hands gripping her hips, I rock her back and forth, and she sighs.

"Take over, baby. Just do what feels good to you. Fast or slow, it doesn't matter."

She peers down at me, and a slow, sexy smile lifts her lips. I keep my eyes locked on hers as she swirls her hips, then rocks back and forth before lifting off my cock and lowering back down slowly. She repeats this process over and over again until she's gained a rhythm. My hands slide over her thighs before they find their way to her pussy. She moans a low throaty sound when I press my thumb to her clit.

She clenches around me, and I know she's close, which is good because I've been fighting my orgasm since the moment I slid inside her. "I'm… close," she pants.

"What do you need?"

She grabs my hands and moves them to her hips. I start bouncing her on my cock, quick and fast. She moves her hands to grip her tits as they bounce. "I need you there," I tell her. The sight of her holding her tits is more than I can take. Add the fact that she's bouncing on my cock, and the moans that are coming from her, and I'm ready to lose it.

"C-C-am," she whimpers.

The sound goes straight to my cock. "Paisley," I grind out. "Now." It's a command. One I'm not sure she can carry out, but I need her to. I can't come before she does.

"Cam!" she screams and grips me like a vise as she stills above me.

I can't hold on a second longer. I groan as my release crashes through me. I spill everything I have inside her. She collapses against my chest, and I wrap my arms around her. I hold her tightly as a million different emotions make their way through me. The biggest of all is love. The love that I have for this incredible woman has changed me. I'm no longer me without her.

"I think you killed me," she mumbles, making me laugh.

I run my hands up and down her back. "You're still very much alive," I assure her. "I can feel your heart beating against mine."

She lifts her head to look at me. "When can we do that again?"

Laughter bubbles up in my chest. "I need some recovery time." Although if she keeps looking at me like that, probably not much.

"How about we shower and get something to eat, and then maybe we can do that again?"

"Shower, sustenance, and sex with the love of my life? I'm in." I smack her ass, and she giggles as she slowly moves off me.

It was important that our first time together be special, and I can say without a shadow of a doubt this is a day I will never in my life ever forget. I hope that when we are old and gray, sitting on our front porch watching our grandkids play in the yard, I can easily recall this day. The day I made love to her for the first time.

Chapter Nineteen

PAISLEY

TONIGHT'S OUR THIRD HOME GAME STRETCH, AND WE'RE OFF TOMORROW FOR A RARE DAY. When Willow found that out, she demanded that we have a girls' night. Not that it mattered. I miss my best friend, so I readily agreed. Cameron, on the other hand, whined, but he gets it. Besides, he needs to hang out with his team. We've had drinks a handful of times after away games, but we always leave after one and head to my room. He needs to bond with them more than just on the field. There still isn't any word on his future with the Blaze. I've stopped myself a dozen times from just picking up the phone or heading up to Uncle Drew's office to ask him what's going on. I'm trying to stay out of it. Well, as much as I can, being his girlfriend and all that.

It shouldn't be a hardship since the guys are coming off another win. They've been kicking ass this season, and I couldn't be prouder of them. All of them. Not just my man.

"You're all set," I tell Marty Harris, one of our power hitters. He took a ball to the shoulder during the game, and we worked it a little and added some ice. "Check back in tomorrow when we get to the field."

"I'll be fine," he assures me.

"Probably. However, I want Dr. Thomas to take a look just to be sure." I'd have him look now, but he had to rush out as today is his anniversary. Once the game ended and there were no threatening injuries, he bolted. Not that any of us blame him. This schedule is grueling and can strain the best of relationships. I witnessed that growing up. My parents are the most in love two people can be, and they even struggled at times. I'm fortunate that Cameron and I get to travel together with the same team. I don't even want to think about what it will be like if that's no longer possible.

I quickly clean up the area and sanitize the table he was on before grabbing my things and heading to wait outside the locker room exit for Cameron. When I push open the door, I hear a squeal, and then my best friend is there, hugging the life out of me.

"Wil, I can't breathe," I sputter with laughter.

"I've missed you," she says, releasing me. "I can't tell you how excited I am for tonight."

"How was the game?" I ask.

"I got my fill of baseball asses, so it was good."

"Please tell me that you behaved while you were around my little sisters," I beg.

"Cross my heart." She takes her hand and makes an X motion across her chest. "Besides, Parker is fifteen. She understands the greatness of baseball ass. My guess is even Peyton at twelve understands."

"You're probably right," I agree. "However, I don't want my bestie to be the one corrupting them."

"Oh, you want that privilege all to yourself then? I mean, come on, P. Your dad played, your honorary uncles played, and you're dating Cameron. They're surrounded by baseball ass. They're bound to discover the wonder that it is."

"What am I going to do with you?"

"Hey, you know I'm right, missy. You are dating one of those baseball asses."

"Who are you calling an ass?" Cameron asks as he wraps his arms around me from behind and presses a kiss on my cheek.

"Just discussing the glory of baseball pants and the asses that fill them," Willow replies, not missing a beat.

"Do I want to know?" Cameron whispers in my ear.

"Probably not," I tell him with a laugh.

"You change your mind about tonight?" he asks.

"Nope," Willow answers for me. "Back off, Taylor. You get her all the time. It's girls' night," she says, reaching for my hand, but he has me locked tight in his arms. I'm not going anywhere until he's ready for me to.

"Where are you going?"

"Nope," Willow says again. "We are not telling you so that you and your boys can crash girls' night."

"What if I have them wear their uniforms?"

Willow taps her chin, pretending to consider his offer. "No dice," she finally tells him.

"Well, shit, Willow, I was sure that would sway you."

"Do not underestimate the power of girls' night, Taylor." She points at him.

His deep throaty chuckle surrounds me. "I think we can make a run for it," he tells me.

I turn in his hold, looping my arms around his neck. "You need to hang out with your team, and I've been neglecting my best friend."

"Fine." He relents and presses his lips to mine. "Are we meeting back at my place or yours?"

"Yours is fine."

"What time?"

"I'll text you."

"Let it be noted, I'm not a fan of girls' night," he mumbles.

"You'll get used to it," Willow chimes in. "Especially in the off-season."

"We have to keep her, right?" he asks with a wicked grin.

"Hey!" Willow swats at his shoulder.

"Go. Have fun with the guys."

"Yo! Taylor? You coming tonight?" Henderson calls out as he walks past.

"Yeah, I'm coming," Cameron says, kissing me one more time.

"You can bring your girl and her friend," Henderson says. I look over to see him standing next to Willow.

"Go." I push at Cameron's chest. "Have fun. I'll text you when we're on our way home."

"I won't drink in case you need a ride."

"No way, Taylor. We never get you to hang out with us. You're drinking. Our game isn't until tomorrow night. You have time to sleep it off."

"Fine. One beer," Cameron concedes.

"Have fun." I wave at him.

"Love you, P."

"Love you too," I call out.

"Fuck, man, you're in deep, aren't you?" I hear Henderson ask him.

Cameron stops walking and looks over his shoulder. "Not deep enough." He winks and turns back around, walking off with his teammate.

"Wow," Willow comments as we watch the two of them walk off.

"Yeah," I agree. I'm certain her wow has something to do with Henderson and the jeans he's wearing, and well, mine has everything to do with Cameron.

"Right. Let's go home and change. The girls at work were telling me about this great little bar not far from here. They claim it's super low-key. I thought that was best, considering you're famous now and all that."

"What do you mean 'I'm famous'?" I ask in disbelief.

"You and your man are all over the social networks and sports channels. Baseball's golden girl falls for an up-and-comer. And they love the fact that he plays the same position that your dad played."

"Just ignore all that crap," I tell her.

"Oh, I do, but others not so much. I thought keeping it chill, sharing a few drinks, and catching up was the best avenue to take."

"We can just grab some takeout and a bottle of wine and stay in."

"No. We can't do that because I miss you. I've been working my ass off, as have you, and we need a night out—both of us. Besides, I don't know when I'll be able to convince Cameron to let me have you for another night," she teases as she bumps her shoulder into mine.

"Stop. He doesn't control me."

"I know. I was kidding. But really, I know the two of you are attached at the hip, and your schedule is crazy, and if they keep winning, it's not going to get any better as you go into the playoffs or whatever they're called. So we are going out." She links her arm through mine, and we make our way out of the stadium.

"Where did you park?" I ask.

"Oh, your parents picked me up."

"They did?"

"Yeah. Your mom called, not wanting me to come here alone, and since I knew we were going out after, I thanked them politely and said yes."

"All right, well, climb in. Girls' night is about to commence." We head back to our condo and change for the night and have a glass of wine while we do it. We take a lot longer to get ready than necessary, but we both needed this—just time to hang out and catch up. I love Cameron, but I miss my best friend. Tonight is a good idea.

"HOW HAVE WE NEVER BEEN HERE BEFORE?" I ASK WILLOW AS THE UBER PULLS UP TO THE curb and drops us off. I look up, reading the sign that says The Pub in neon lights. It's located on a back street, that despite living here my entire life, I've never been on. Talk about a sheltered life.

"I guess they're really strict on paparazzi and things like that."

"Really? That's odd. I mean, it is close to the stadium, so I guess that makes sense." She pulls open the door, and we're greeted with raucous laughter. I turn my head to see what the ruckus is about, and my mouth drops open.

Willow links her arm through mine. "Okay, so I might have known that this is where the players come after their games. I also know that you're in love with him and that he worships you, and being apart tonight was not something either of you wanted."

"I wanted to spend some time with you. And how did you know this is where they come, and I didn't?" I question.

"And we did hang out. We got ready together, had a few glasses of wine, and now we're going to hang out with your man and his teammates while we catch up. And as far as this place goes, the guys refer to it as VIP most of the time. At least that's what the rumor is. One of the girls at work asked if we ever hung out at the VIP. I told her no, that I thought it was a myth. I've never seen a VIP club. She then proceeded to tell me about The Pub. She's a baseball groupie if you didn't catch that." Willow laughs.

I turn and pull her into my arms for a hug. "I love you. You didn't have to do this. I want to spend time with you too."

"I know. We will. Besides, hanging out with you and Cam isn't the worst way to spend the evening. Especially not when there is so much eye candy to go around."

"Well, let's go to the bar and get a drink. We'll see how long it takes him to notice that we're here."

"Are you kidding? He has Spidey-senses where you're concerned," she says, just as his arms wrap around me from behind.

"It's not my birthday, but fuck if I'm not glad to see you," he says, kissing my neck. I can smell the beer on his breath, which makes me smile. He needed this time to bond with his teammates. I know he doesn't usually drink during the season and hardly ever in the off-season. He's laser focused when it comes to his body and his career.

"You can thank Willow." I point at my best friend.

"Thank you." The sincerity in his voice is humbling. "What do you want to drink?"

"Actually, you should go back to your friends. Willow and I are going to sit at the bar and have a drink and catch up."

"You can catch up with us." He points over his shoulder as more laughter fills the small pub. "We can go up to the VIP area. We only stay down here until the crowd picks up. At least that's what the guys told me."

"You need to bond with your new team."

"We don't know how much longer they're going to be my team," he says softly.

"Regardless. It makes for better chemistry on the field. Go. I'll come see you in a little bit."

"Fine." He grins as his lips press to mine. "Love you. Thanks again, Willow," he says before sauntering back to the table. All the guys turn and wave to us and motion us over. Cameron shakes his head and takes his seat, and they all go back to whatever it is they're cracking up about over there.

"I need to get me one of those," Willow says with a sigh.

"What? A baseball player?" I laugh.

"No. A Cameron. Not yours, of course, but a man who looks at me the way he looks at you."

I look over at the table, and Cameron turns to glance over his shoulder at the same time. He smiles and turns back to his teammates. "He's pretty great," I agree.

We both order a beer and catch up for about twenty minutes before Henderson appears next to us. "Monroe, you're killing the vibe," he says, taking the stool next to me. "Your boy keeps looking over his shoulder to find you. Fucker hasn't listened to a word we've been saying since you walked in."

"I'm sorry?"

He grins. "Come on. Enough avoiding. Come join us."

I look over at Willow, and she nods her agreement. "Okay," I say, sliding off my stool, as does Willow. Henderson moves to stand between us and throws an arm over each of our shoulders.

"This is going to be fun," he jests.

"Well, boys, I'm heading out," he says as we approach the table. The conversation stops, and all eyes turn to us.

Cameron's eyes find mine, and he smirks. He knows damn good and well he's the only one I'm going home with.

"Nothing?" Henderson asks him. You can hear the disappointment in his tone.

"She's mine," Cameron says. The tone is so casual it's as if any other option is ludicrous. Which it is.

"What about you?" Miller looks at Willow. "You wifed up like Monroe here?"

Willow smiles. "Nope."

"You snooze you lose, Miller," Henderson says as he drops into a chair and pulls Willow into his lap. She tries to move, but his hold on her prevents it.

"Paisley." That's all it takes. He just has to say my name to command my full attention. He scoots his chair back from the table and pats his lap. I waste no time going to him and taking my spot. His arms wrap around my waist, and he places a kiss on my bare shoulder.

"This place is quiet," I say about an hour later. Two older gentlemen sit at the bar, keeping to themselves, but other than that, it's just us.

"Yeah," Miller chimes in. "The owner tosses groupies out on their ass. He has a VIP room in case we don't want to be around anyone, but for the most part, people leave us alone here."

"What, you all don't like groupies?" Willow asks in disbelief.

"Have to be in the mood," Miller answers.

Willow turns to look over her shoulder at Henderson since she's still sitting on his lap. "What about you?"

"I've dabbled."

"You do know that's not who I am, right?" she asks.

"Yeah, I got that when I saw you with Monroe."

Willow and I make eye contact. I can see in her eyes that she's excited to have his attention, but as her best friend, I also see the worry there too. Willow, like me, isn't a fling kind of girl. Sure, she talks shit about the guys in their pants, and she can flirt with the best of them, but at the end of the day, she needs the connection. We both do. That explains why she's flirty tonight, but not her usual over-the-top self. She's making sure not to give him the wrong impression.

I watch as Henderson whispers something in her ear, and her shoulders visibly relax. "Is she good with him?" I turn to ask Cameron, keeping my voice low so only he can hear me.

"I don't know him well, but from what I do know, yeah, she's good."

I don't know him well either. He's only been with the Blaze for two years. Well, after my dad retired. I know him on the field, but not off.

"How long do we have to stay?" Cameron whispers in my ear.

I turn to face him. "You not having fun?"

"Sure." He shrugs. "I'd be having more fun if we were at home cuddled in bed."

"It's not even midnight."

"Fine. We leave at midnight."

"Thank you."

"You know I can't say no to you."

"That's not true. You denied me for weeks."

His eyes heat and then soften. "You know that's different. It was well worth the wait."

"Yes, it was."

"Are they always like this?" I hear Miller ask when Cameron's lips press against mine.

"Yep," Willow replies, and the table erupts with laughter.

Chapter Twenty

CAMERON

I JUST FINISHED A WORKOUT AND SPED THROUGH MY SHOWER. I DON'T HAVE TO BE BACK for tonight's game until four, which means I get the rest of the day with Paisley. Pushing my feet into my tennis shoes, I grab my bag and stand just as Coach Drummond steps in my line of sight.

"Cameron." He nods.

"Coach."

"Front office needs to see you."

My stomach drops. "Coach?"

"The GM," he clarifies.

Fuck. I nod and head upstairs. I may as well get this over with. I'm not worried about my game, but I am dating another Blaze employee publicly. Sure, he told me it was fine, but there may be fine print. I fucking hate fine print. Not to mention there is still Hastings and his injury. Originally, he was out for a few weeks at best. Those weeks multiplied, and then it turned into the entire season. Things change. Healthcare isn't an exact science. The human body is a marvel. So I have no fucking clue what to expect as I step off the elevator and greet his secretary, whose name I can't remember. I make a mental note to ask Paisley. That is even if I need to take the time to learn it.

"I'm here to see Mr. Milton." I refrain from using his first name. That could just be another nail in my proverbial coffin.

"Of course, Mr. Taylor. You can go on in." She smiles and points at the door to Drew's office.

Hiking my bag up on my shoulder, I make my way to his office, stopping at the door and knocking on the frame. Drew looks up and nods. "Cameron, good to see you. Come on in."

Doing as I'm told, I stride into his office like my insides aren't shaking. He points at one of the black leather chairs across from his desk, and I sit.

"Thanks for seeing me. I know you have some free time today, well, time away from the club." He laughs. "I know what it's like during the season. Every hour you don't have to be here is like a get-out-of-jail-free card. Don't get me wrong," he adds, "I loved the game. I still do, but a little downtime is nice as well."

"Agreed." I nod. I'm not sure what this meeting is about, and my guard is up. I'm not being an ass, but I'm not overly talkative either.

"Anyway." Drew sits back in his chair. "I'm sure you're wondering why you're here."

"Yes, sir."

He nods. "Hastings."

That sinking feeling in my stomach falls just a little further. "Hastings," I repeat.

"He's retiring." My mouth drops open in shock. "He's not healing like he expected to, and he's tired. He's been in the league for fifteen years and has decided it's time to call it quits."

I open my mouth to speak, but the words won't come. Hope wells in my chest. If I get a contract, if I get to stay, that means I get to stay close to Paisley. I don't have to leave her.

"I'd like to offer you a three-year contract. We're looking at twenty-two million for three years."

I nod. That's a fuckton of money. Money that Paisley and I can use to start our lives together. We can buy a house and have all our family over to our place.

"Cameron?" Drew says, pulling me out of my thoughts. "What are you thinking, son?" he asks.

"Paisley," I blurt.

"What about her?" He raises his eyebrows.

"I get to stay with her."

He throws his head back in laughter. "Taylor, I just told you that I was going to pay you twenty-two million dollars over the next three years to play for the Blaze, and your first thought was your girlfriend?"

I nod. "Yeah." I can feel the smile that's threatening to crack my face wide open.

He shakes his head, still laughing. "Here's a copy of the contract. Have your agent look it over, your attorney, and get back to me by the end of the week."

"Thank you," I say, taking the envelope from him.

"You good with your agent?" he asks.

"He's not really done much for me, except the phone call I got to come and replace Hastings."

"You have a contract with him?" he asks.

"Yes."

"Is there an out clause?"

"Yes. I made sure of it. I had an independent attorney take a look. I didn't want to make a wrong choice and be stuck in a situation I couldn't make it out of."

He reaches into his desk drawer and pulls out a business card. "Call this guy. Tell him I sent you."

"Thank you. Is there something wrong with my agent?"

Drew sits back in his chair, crossing his arms over his chest. "I called him. Offered you three years for fifteen million. He accepted without bothering to try to negotiate or even calling you from the look on your face when you walked in here today."

"Motherfucker," I mumble under my breath. "Why are you doing this? You obviously raised the offer, and now this...." I hold up the business card.

"Paisley isn't my niece by blood, but she's my niece. Consider this a favor to her, and before you ask me why the favor is for you more than her, your reaction earlier tells me that I made the right choice. I've been in this seat for several years now. Eight, to be exact. You are the first player I've ever offered a contract to whose first reaction is that he doesn't have to leave his girlfriend."

"I love her."

"I can see that. I hear you're good to her too." He smirks.

"No other way to be." I shrug.

"Welcome to the team, Cameron." He stands and offers me his hand.

I take it and give it a firm shake. "Thank you, sir."

"Drew. You're a part of the Blaze family now, and well, Paisley is family, so—" This time, it's his turn to shrug.

"I have some phone calls to make," I tell him.

"Right. Call the new agent, and if you have questions, Paisley has my number."

"Right. The agent. I'll do that too," I promise. Standing from the chair with the envelope and business card in hand, I make my way back to the elevator. I'm in a daze on the ride, so when the doors slide open, I jolt and step off. I make my way to my truck in the players' lot and pull my phone out of my pocket. Two people are on my short list of favorites. Mom and Paisley. My finger hovers between the two, debating on who to call first. Finally, I decide and hit Mom's name. She's sacrificed so much to get me where I am today. She needs to hear about this first before it gets out. Hopefully, by the time our call ends, I'll be home, and I can tell my girl in person.

The phone rings through the truck's Bluetooth as I pull out of the lot. "Well, this is a nice surprise," Mom answers.

"Hey, Mom."

"You ready for your game tonight?" she asks.

"I'm leaving the stadium now. We had an early morning workout. I'm headed back home to take Paisley out for breakfast. We're going to celebrate."

She gasps. "Cameron Joseph Taylor, did you propose and not tell me?"

I can't help but laugh. "No. I promise when I ask her to marry me, I'll tell you first."

"Deal. So what are you celebrating?"

"I just left the GM's office. I got a contract."

"What!" she shrieks. "Cameron, that's amazing," she says, her voice cracking. "I'm so proud of you."

"Thanks, Mom." I go on to tell her what Drew said about my agent and how he raised my contract price without negotiations.

"That's unheard of," Mom comments.

"Yeah. The Blaze is a good team. A family. Drew is a solid guy."

"And you're dating his niece."

"I'd like to think that's not the only reason, but yeah. I'm sure dating his niece helped."

"You're only going to be an hour from me."

"Perfect-case scenario," I agree.

"Call me after you talk to the new agent, and let me know how it goes."

"I will. Hey, I just got home. I'm going to jump off here so I can go tell Paisley."

"She doesn't know?"

"Nah. I called you first."

I hear her sniffle. "I love you, Cameron. I'm so proud of you," she tells me again.

"Love you too, Mom. Talk soon," I assure her, before ending the call. I turn off the truck and grab my bag. I left Paisley sleeping peacefully in my bed when I went to the stadium, but I'm sure she's up by now. I rush to my place and unlock the door. I find my girl standing in the kitchen in nothing but one of my Blaze T-shirts.

"Hey, babe." She smiles as she brings the cup of coffee to her lips.

I drop my bag by the door, and my feet carry me to her. I lift her onto the counter and take the coffee cup from her hands, setting it to the side. Then I slide my hand behind her neck and kiss the fuck out of her. The kiss is bruising, but my girl doesn't seem to mind. She wraps her legs around my waist, and her hands grip my shirt. Needing air, I pull back, resting my forehead against hers.

"What's gotten into you?" she murmurs.

"I got called into the GM's office today."

She pushes back at my chest so she can look me in the eyes. "Cameron?" There's hope in her voice, so much like my mom's. I'm surrounded by strong, beautiful women.

"Hastings is retiring. They offered me a three-year contract."

"Oh my God!" She does a little shimmy on the counter and wraps her arms around my neck, pulling me into a hug. "I'm so damn proud of you." She gives me a loud lip-smacking kiss as she giggles. "We have to celebrate."

"I was thinking I could take you to breakfast."

She grins at me. "Yeah. We could do breakfast," she says, not really committing to the idea. "Or—" She tugs me close and whispers in my ear, "You could take me to your room, and I could show you how proud of you I am."

My hands slide under her thighs, and I lift her into my arms, carrying her to our room. She doesn't live here officially, but she's been here pretty much since I moved in. This feels like our place, not mine. Stepping into the bedroom, I see the sheets are still rumpled from where we slept last night, which is fine by me. We're just going to mess them up again. I press my lips to hers, kissing her with all the love I have in my heart for this amazing woman. I don't break the kiss as I set her on the bed.

"We're celebrating you," she reminds me, breaking the kiss.

"Trust me, beautiful. This is a celebration for me," I assure her.

She nods. "I can make it better." She pushes on my chest, and when I step back, she stands. When she turns to face me, she places her hands on my hips and turns me so my back is facing the bed.

All I can do is stare as she drops to her knees and works my athletic shorts and boxer briefs down my legs. She peers up at me under her lashes. "Step out," she instructs.

I do so awkwardly, my shoes in the way. She giggles as she lifts one foot, then the other, removing my shoes so I can step out of my clothes. "You can go ahead and lose the shirt too," she demands.

"Yes, ma'am," I say with a smile. My girl wants me naked? Who am I to tell her no? Reaching behind my neck, I pull off the T-shirt and toss it at her. Her laughter fills the room.

"Funny man." She smiles. "Sit." I do as she asks, and she moves in close. "Now, just feel," she instructs, before taking my cock in her mouth.

I hiss out a breath at the feel of her mouth sliding over me. Hot, wet, and so fucking sexy. I fight the need to close my eyes and just get lost in the pleasure of her mouth on me, but the need to watch her wins out. I can't take my eyes off her as her head bobs and her hands work me in tandem. She slows and peers up at me.

I move to place my hand against her cheek, my cock still deep in her mouth. "I love you."

Her eyes shimmer from my confession, and she takes me deep. "Fuck." That must be the response she was looking for as she works me harder, faster. All too soon, I'm tapping her on the shoulder. "Close," I manage to say through the pleasure building inside me. She doesn't pull away. Not that I expected her to. Instead, she takes everything I have to give as I spill down the back of her throat.

She stands and wipes her mouth with the back of her hand. She then climbs into the bed behind me. "Cam." My name is a whisper on her lips. I'm spent, but I turn to face her. "Cuddle with me?"

Is there anything better in life than being offered a multimillion-dollar deal with a professional baseball team and cuddling with your girl? I think not.

Chapter Twenty-One

PAISLEY

TODAY IS A DAY OFF BEFORE A THREE-DAY HOME GAME STRETCH. MOM CALLED LAST NIGHT and insisted Cameron and I go to dinner at their place tonight. Cameron readily agreed, like the amazing guy he is. The last time we had dinner with my family, it was a disaster—until we got home, and my dad called to apologize. I don't know how tonight will be, but I hope it's the complete opposite of our last dinner. The day at the fun center turned out great, so I hope tonight will too.

"Why don't you call your mom and see what she's doing for lunch? We can drive up and see her," I suggest to Cameron.

His eyes light up as he reaches over to the nightstand to call his mom. It's a little after nine in the morning, and we're still in bed. We take full advantage of these days off.

The phone rings through the speaker twice before Grace picks up. "Hello."

"Hey, Mom. What are you doing for lunch today?" he asks her.

"I'm not sure yet. I'm off today. Why, what's up?"

"Well, today is an off day, and Paisley and I thought we would drive up and have lunch with you."

"Really?" she asks, pleasantly surprised if her tone is any indication.

Cameron's eyes find mine, and he winks. "How's noon?"

"It's perfect. Just come here. I'll make us lunch."

"You don't have to do that—" Cameron starts, but she cuts him off.

"I want to," she insists.

"All right, well, I guess we will see you in a few hours."

"Love you, Cam," she says, ending the call before he can even reply.

"I think she's excited." I chuckle.

"Yeah, I think so too. Great idea, baby." He leans over and kisses me.

"Both of our families in one day."

"We'll have more time in the off-season," he assures me.

"And more us time." I move closer to lay my head on his chest.

We're both quiet as he runs his fingers through my hair. We still have plenty of time before we have to start getting ready to go have lunch with Grace, and right now, we're both just content to lie here in each other's arms. "I've been thinking," he says, his voice soft.

"Yeah? About what?" I ask, not moving from my spot against his chest. The way his fingers are running through my hair is relaxing. He could probably put me back to sleep from his touch.

"What if you moved in here? With me? Or we could buy a place together."

I lift my head to look at him and find his eyes already on me. "You want to move in together?"

"We practically live together anyway."

"What about Willow?"

"When is your lease up?" he asks.

"Not until next summer. We moved in right after graduation."

"Was it a financial thing or just a best friend thing?" he asks.

"Best friend. She can support herself financially without my help."

"One of you were bound to move out eventually," he says cautiously.

"Yeah, but… is this too soon?"

"You tell me," he counters. "There is no timeline, Paisley. It's what we want. What we feel is right. If you're not ready, I understand. No pressure. I just like you here. It feels like our place more than my place anyway."

"Because you're a bossy ass and insisted we sleep in the same bed."

"You can't fault a man for wanting to be close to the woman he loves."

"You didn't love me then," I challenge.

"How do you know?" he fires back.

"I—" I've got nothing. I guess I don't know, but surely, he didn't. That's not possible, right?

"I think I've loved you since that very first moment in the stands. Even before the kiss. You were unlike anyone I'd ever met."

"And here we are."

"Here we are."

"Can we table this until the season is over?" I ask. "Let's get through the season, and we can take care of it then."

"That doesn't sound like a no."

"It's not a no," I confirm.

"GRACE, LUNCH WAS GREAT. THANK YOU." I'M NOT JUST BLOWING SMOKE UP HER ASS because she's my boyfriend's mom. She made us spaghetti and meatballs with garlic bread and salad, and I cleaned my plate.

"You're welcome. This was such a nice surprise. Thank you for spending your day off with me."

"How's work?" Cameron asks once we are sitting in the living room relaxing.

"Oh, you know, long shifts, bossy doctors, same old." She laughs.

"You know I signed that contract, right? With my new agent?" Cameron asks her.

"Yes. You told me. I'm so proud of you."

"You should quit your job and move closer to us."

"What?" She freezes as she stares at her son. She places her hand over her heart, and tears well in her eyes. "I love you, son, so very much, but it's not your responsibility to care for me."

"Why? You worked two jobs to give me what I needed growing up. I want to pay you back for that."

"Cameron, you are my son. That was my job. To take care of you and give you the world. And as far as paying me back, you've done that tenfold. Look at the man you are today. You have an incredible career in a sport you've loved since you were a toddler. You have an amazing woman in your life, and I couldn't be prouder of you."

"I want to do this."

"I want you to focus on you, Cameron. Build your life." Her eyes flash to me quickly before they are back on her son. "Build your family. Your future."

"I can do that and support you."

"I know you can, but I don't need you to. I'm happy here. I love my house and the memories I have of you growing up here. I may complain about my job, but I love it. I don't dread going to work every day like so many people I know. I'm good, Cameron."

"At least consider letting me buy you a place closer to us," he says. Grace's eyes flash to me again, and she grins. She didn't miss the way he said, "us," either. I wonder if it made her heart pitter-patter in her chest like it did mine.

"We can get you a job there." Cameron looks at me, but I'm not sure for what.

"It's an hour's drive."

"What happens when we have kids?" he asks her.

"We will cross that bridge when we come to it," she tells him gently.

"Mom. Please, let me do this for you."

"No. I love you for it. I love your heart, son. This is your time. Nothing makes me happier than to see you happy and thriving. Successful." She smiles, tears in her eyes. "When you become a father, you'll understand," she tells him.

"Stubborn woman," Cameron mutters, making Grace and me laugh.

The doorbell rings, and Grace stands to answer it.

"Hey." I reach over and place my hand on his thigh. "You all right?"

"She's stubborn."

"Maybe." I shrug. "I can't say. I've never been in her shoes, but she's entitled to her own life. You can't change that."

"Cameron." Grace's voice is hesitant as she steps back into the room, only she's not alone.

"Mom," Cameron replies. I don't have to look at him to know his gaze is more than likely locked on the man standing beside his mom with his hand on the small of her back.

"I'd like you to meet Gerald." She looks at the man beside her, and her shoulders visibly relax when he smiles at her. "He's…." She looks at Cameron and back at Gerald.

"I'm her boyfriend," Gerald answers. He steps forward and holds out his hand for Cameron. "It's nice to meet you. Grace talks about you all the time."

I have to elbow him to get him to reach out and take Gerald's hand. Gerald moves his eyes to me. "You must be Paisley. Nice to meet you," Gerald says, offering me his hand as well.

I accept it. "You too," I tell him, and Cameron growls from beside me.

"I didn't know you would have company," Gerald tells Grace. "I was hoping we could go see that movie you've been wanting to see."

"Oh." She blushes.

"The four of us could go," Gerald offers.

"Thank you," I tell him. "But we have dinner plans and about an hour's drive home."

"Next time." He smiles at me.

"Grace, do you mind if I grab a glass of water?" Gerald asks.

"Help yourself," she tells him. He gives her arm a gentle squeeze, and something passes between them. I'd bet my next paycheck he's not the least bit thirsty. He's giving us time, especially Cameron and Grace, to discuss his presence and declaration of being her boyfriend.

"When did we start keeping secrets?" Cameron asks.

"It was so new," she tells him with a heavy sigh. "I didn't want to bring it up if it was going nowhere."

"And now?" he asks her.

"He's a good man, Cameron. He's good to me, and I enjoy spending time with him."

"We should go." Cameron stands, and I see the hurt written all over his mom's face.

"Grace, can you give us a few minutes?"

"Sure." She turns and walks out of the room.

I move to climb onto Cameron's lap, and he wraps his arms around me, holding me tight. Like he always does. "I'm happy for her," I tell him.

He grunts.

"She's been alone a long time."

"She had me."

"That's different, and you know it. What would you do if you didn't have me to hold, to kiss whenever you wanted? What if I wasn't there to snuggle with at night or to make love to you?"

"That would be me living in hell."

I smile. "She's an adult. She can make her own choices. I, for one, am happy for her."

He sighs. "It's more that she didn't tell me. Why is she hiding him from me?"

"I don't think it was malicious. You told me she's never really dated. This is all new for her. However, I do think he's a good man."

"You just met him."

"I know, but I also saw the way his hand rested on the small of her back as he led her into the room. I saw that look he gave her as she introduced him, and I saw his eyes when he told us he was her boyfriend. He's in love with her."

"You don't know that."

"I do."

"It's not possible from a look, Paisley."

"Oh, but it is."

"Explain."

I place my hand against his cheek. "Easy. He looks at her the way you look at me."

His shoulders deflate, and he wraps his arms just a little tighter as he holds me. "I love you."

"I know you do. He loves her too."

We sit here for several long minutes. "Come on. I know your mom well enough to understand she's in the kitchen freaking out right now. Besides, we should get going and let them get to their movie, and we have dinner with my parents tonight." Climbing off his lap, I offer him my hand and pull him to his feet. Hand in hand, we make our way toward the kitchen.

I stop just outside the door when I hear Gerald's deep voice. "It's going to be fine, babe," he says reassuringly. "I didn't know they were here. We kind of sprung this on him."

"He's never seen me with a man."

"Well, he's going to have to get used to seeing me."

"Gerald."

"You mean too much to me. He's a grown man, Grace."

"He's my son."

"And I respect that. But you are my number one priority. I hate to see this tearing you up. I can't handle that."

"He's just in shock, I think."

I turn to look at Cameron, and the anger that was once there is gone. I cough, which is completetely obvious and over the-top, but I want to alert them we are on our way. I count to five and lead us into the kitchen. Gerald has his arms wrapped tight around Grace as her head rests on his chest. I wrap my arms around Cameron and put us in the same position, staring up at him. He nods. He gets it.

"Sorry about that," Cameron speaks up. "I wasn't expecting you." His eyes are locked on Gerald.

"It's all good," Gerald replies easily.

Cameron releases me and steps forward. He offers Gerald his hand, and the two shake. Grace smiles, her eyes watering with tears as she pulls away from Gerald and hugs her son. "Love you," Cameron mumbles.

"Love you too." She holds him a little longer before stepping away.

Cameron immediately returns to my side, wrapping me up close. Gerald does the same with Grace. "We're going to head out. Let the two of you get to that movie," Cameron tells them.

"We should plan something," Gerald voices. "Grace tells me your schedule is tight, but maybe once the season is over?"

It's not lost on any of us that if we make the playoffs, the season could run several more weeks. Gerald just told us without telling us that he plans on sticking around.

"Yeah. Our days off are slim, but we should do that." He looks down at me, and I see the question in his eyes. I nod. "You should come with Mom. To a game. I can, uh, make sure there are two tickets waiting."

Gerald nods. "You tell us when and we'll be there."

Cameron nods. "Right. Okay, well, we're heading out. Love you," he tells his mom with a wave. We make our way out to his truck.

I wait until we're on the road before turning to look at him. "You did good back there."

"Thanks." He laughs lightly, shaking his head.

"You know, it's like you and my dad reversed roles," I say, biting down on my cheek to keep from laughing.

"I owe your dad an apology."

This time, I do laugh. "No, you don't. You didn't do anything wrong but love me and put me first."

"You'll always be first."

His words send warmth to the center of my chest. I'm not sure who was looking out for me to bring Cameron into my life, but I'm grateful. He's one of the good ones, and he's all mine.

Chapter Twenty-Two

CAMERON

"ARE WE GOING HOME FIRST?" I ASK PAISLEY AS WE DRIVE BACK INTO TOWN.

"Yes."

"What time do we have to be at your parents'?"

"Dinner starts at six."

It's fifteen minutes until five. We stopped for ice cream on the way home and stayed longer than we should have. It was her idea, but I needed it. We sat on a bench at a nearby park and ate our ice cream like we didn't have a care in the world. We got a few looks, and I'm pretty sure some cell phones were pointed our way, but the park wasn't very busy, and those who were there left us alone.

"You sure you don't want to just head over there now?" I ask.

"I'm sure." She rolls her head to the left to smile over at me. That smile, I dream about it. It's one I can wake up to every day for the rest of my life.

When we pull in front of my condo, she jumps out of the truck and rushes to stand on the sidewalk before turning and waiting for me. "You good?" I ask.

"I'm perfect." She laces her fingers through mine and pulls me to the door. Shoving the key into the lock, I push it open for her, and she walks in. I follow her, and as soon as the door is shut, I turn, and she's there pressing her hands against my chest and pushing me against it.

She rises on her toes and places her mouth a breath from mine. "I want you." She falls back and unbuttons her jeans, sliding them down her hips.

Not one to ever disappoint her, I do the same, kicking my jeans and boxer briefs to the side, not giving a fuck where they land. Next is my shirt, and I'm standing before her naked. I reach for my cock and stroke it lazily as I watch her pull her shirt off as well. I lick my lips, gripping my cock a little tighter as she reaches behind her and unsnaps her bra. She's quick to remove it from her body, letting it fall to the floor.

She reaches out and places her hand over mine, and together, we stroke my cock. I slide my free hand behind her neck and kiss her feverishly. I will never get enough of her. Never.

"Cam."

"Yeah, baby?" I ask against her lips.

"I need you."

"Condom. My wallet," I tell her.

"Were you a Boy Scout?" she asks, bending to grab my wallet out of my jeans. She finds it easily, dropping my wallet after. She tears the pack open and slides the offending latex over my length. I hate using these with her. I'd give anything to feel her bare—skin to skin, her hot, wet heat. I groan out loud at the thought.

"No. But when my girlfriend is sexy as fuck, you never know when you're going to need one," I finally answer. Lifting her in my arms, I turn her back to the wall in the entryway. She squeals and laughs, wrapping her arms and legs around me.

"You know, we don't really need them." I freeze and look at her. "I'm on the pill."

"You tell me this now?"

She shrugs. "We've never talked about it. We probably should have. I know we talked about our past experiences, but we never really discussed birth control."

"I'm healthy. I used them out of respect for you. It's your choice."

"It's our choice. I'm healthy too, but this is something we decide together."

"And your vote?" I ask, trailing my lips down her neck.

"I don't want anything between us."

My heart pounds like a drum in my chest. "You sure about that?" I ask, pulling away to look her in the eye. "There is still a chance of pregnancy, right? I mean, nothing is a hundred percent effective."

"There's a chance, a small one."

"And you're willing to take that risk?" What I really want to say is that imagining her carrying a part of me inside her turns me on more than I ever imagined it would.

"With you," she says, her eyes boring into mine. "I'm willing to take the risk with you."

I slam my lips into hers, kissing her with all the passion and love that's coursing through my veins. She takes everything I give her. With her back against the wall, helping me hold her weight, I reach between us and pull the condom off, dropping it to the floor.

"You sure about this?" I ask against her lips.

"Positive."

Aligning myself at her entrance, I slowly push inside her and close my eyes to prevent them from rolling back in my head. Leaning forward, I bury my face in her neck as I adjust to feeling her with nothing between us. This is a first for me, and it's heaven. *She's* heaven.

"Baby, I'm going to need some help." I lift my head and lock eyes with her. "I've never felt anything this incredible, and I'm having trouble…" I swallow hard. "I'm having trouble holding on. I refuse to come before you do, but, babe, it's gotta be quick. I need you there."

A slow, sexy smile pulls at her lips. "We've got this, Taylor." She slides her hand between and begins to touch herself.

"Not helping," I growl.

She moans, tilting her head back against the wall. "What are you waiting on,

Taylor?" she asks, squeezing my cock. "You better catch up."

I don't try to hide my smile at her sass. Instead, I pull out and push back in, making us both moan. "Hold on, beautiful," I whisper, barely giving her time to brace her other arm around my neck before I begin to relentlessly pound into her. I bite down on my lip, trying to distract myself from the need to spill inside her. My hands grip the backs of her thighs. Her heels dig into my ass as I give us both what we need.

"Cam!" she screams, and I can feel her pussy going crazy, squeezing me like a vise. Both her arms are now around my neck, and she's hugging me tightly.

"Baby?" I pant. She doesn't answer, and I worry that I hurt her. That my need for her pushed her too far, and I was too rough. "Paisley?" My feet are moving when she doesn't answer. I carry us to the couch and sit with her still in my arms. "Talk to me."

She finally lifts her head, and there is a lazy, sexy smile staring back at me. "I think—I know that was the most intense orgasm I've ever had."

"Fuck, you scared the hell out of me. I thought I hurt you."

"What?" she asks, appalled. "No. In fact, we need to add another session like that to the to-do list." She chuckles.

"Anything you want, beautiful."

"I hate to say this, but we need to get cleaned up and get to my parents'."

"How am I supposed to face them knowing I was just inside you bare? It's all I'm going to be able to think about."

"You have a lifetime of facing them after being inside me bare, slugger. You're just going to have to figure it out." With that, she lifts off my cock, then my lap, and heads down the hall to clean up.

I stare after her, and yet again, I'm reminded how fucking incredible she is.

"THANKS FOR DINNER, MRS. MONROE," I SAY POLITELY AS I STAND TO HELP CLEAR THE

table.

"Larissa," she reminds me. "And you're welcome."

Everyone grabs their plate and carries it to the sink. We all take turns rinsing ours off and placing them in the dishwasher. With all six of us pitching in, the kitchen and dining room are cleaned up in no time.

"Cameron, you want to toss the ball?" Peyton asks me.

"Sure."

"Yes!" She pumps her hand in the air and stands from the couch.

"Lady, is your homework done?" Easton asks her.

"Aw, Dad," she whines. "I only have a chapter to read, and I'm done."

"Well, you better read it so you can toss the ball with Cameron."

"Fine," she grumbles but takes off, her feet pounding up the stairs to finish her homework.

"What about you, duchess?" Easton asks Parker.

"I'm done. I'll look over my notes for my history test again in the morning."

"Paisley, will you come upstairs with me? I want to show you the board I made for ideas for prom dresses," Parker asks her sister.

"Whoa. Hold up now. What's this talk about prom?" Easton leans forward, resting his elbows on his knees, giving his middle daughter a look that lets her and everyone else in the room know he's not impressed.

"Dad, come on. I'm a sophomore, and Tommy Holcomb is going to ask me."

"Who is this Tommy that you speak of, and how do you know he's going to ask you if he hasn't yet? And, exactly, you're a sophomore. It's a junior-senior prom," he reminds her.

"Yes, but underclassmen can get asked by an upperclassman."

"How old is he?"

"He's a junior. He's sixteen."

"Is he going to ask me for permission?" he asks.

"Dad." Parker rolls her eyes. "It's prom, not a wedding proposal." Parker turns to look at Paisley. "You'd think he would be ready for this. I'm number two."

"Duchess, a father is never ready to let his daughters go freely with a boy, no matter the age."

"Dad, not all guys are assholes," she challenges him.

"Duchess," he warns.

"Fine," she groans.

"Come on, Parker. Let's go look at those dresses." Standing from the couch, Paisley bends down and kisses me quickly. "I'll be right back," she tells me before letting Parker tug her upstairs to look at prom dresses.

"I guess this is what I have to look forward to," I say before I think better of it.

Easton's head whips toward mine. "Something you need to tell me?" he asks.

"I love her."

He stares at me, his gaze never wavering.

"One day, I'm going to marry her. And we'll have kids. I assume if we have a daughter or daughters, they'll be like Paisley and her sisters. At least I hope they are."

"Oh, my," Larissa says, coming into the room.

"Queen." One word and she goes to him, sitting on his lap.

"When is this happening?" Easton asks.

"I'll be sure to come to you before I do it." I'll ask for his permission. Not because I need it, but because I know it's important to him and to her. I want him to like me. If he doesn't give his blessing, it's not going to stop me from asking her.

"You want kids, Cameron?" Larissa asks.

"Yeah." I smile. "I grew up as an only child, so I'd like a few," I tell them honestly.

"Being a father and a husband are my two greatest accomplishments in life. My girls"—he smiles at his wife—"they're what's important."

"You're a lucky man, Easton."

He nods. "Damn right I am," he says as Paisley comes back into the room.

"She's really excited," Paisley says, sitting next to me on the couch. She leans over and places her head on my shoulder. "Dad, you should really let her go if she's asked."

"Princess." He sighs.

"Come on. You can't keep us all locked up in your tower forever."

"I think the fact that you no longer live here and that your boyfriend is sitting next to you on my couch means that statement is irrelevant."

"You know what I mean," she tells him. "We're growing up, Daddy." He nods but doesn't comment.

"I'd imagine it's hard to let go," I tell Paisley.

She lifts her head to look at me. "Not you too," she teases.

"I'm just saying. It's his job as your father to worry and to protect. That's part of the job description."

"Exactly," Easton chimes in.

I wink at my girl, and she rolls her eyes. I press my lips to the top of her head. I can see our future so clearly—a house full of kids and two parents. Something I didn't have, but she did. I glance over at her dad to see him looking at me. He nods once, and that's all the confirmation I need. He accepts what she means to me.

Chapter Twenty-Three

CAMERON

"FUCK YEAH!" HENDERSON SCREAMS AS HE LIFTS ME INTO THE AIR AND SPINS US AROUND. The crazy fucker drops me to my feet and rushes more of our teammates. We did it. We won our conference, and we're headed to the World Series.

World. Fucking. Series.

My eyes scan the dugout. There is only one person I want to celebrate with. I spot her standing with Dr. Thomas and another trainer. They're smiling wide, happy for their team. I push through the crowd of my teammates, their families, and reporters. I ignore the shouts that call out for me. I stalk toward the dugout, and I don't stop until she's in my arms and my lips are sealed with hers.

She wraps her legs around my waist and her arms around my neck and kisses me back. Neither one of us cares about who's watching. We're celebrating.

"Cam, I'm so fucking happy for you."

"My good luck charm," I whisper against her lips. "We did it, baby!"

"You're going to the World Series."

"I've dreamed of this. I never thought it would be possible. And to share it with you." I shake my head. "I love you. This game I love. It brought me you. Now, this—" I swallow back the emotion that clogs my throat.

"I love you too," she says softly before sliding down my body. I keep my hands on her even after she's found her footing. "You should go get changed. Your mom and Gerald, and my parents and little sisters, and Willow are all here, and we're celebrating!"

"They're all here?"

"They are. They wanted to be here to support you. This was either the last game of your season or your ticket to the World Series. Either way, they all wanted to be here."

I'm smiling so hard I fear my face might crack. "I'll be quick," I tell her.

"We're not going anywhere. Go, do what you need to do. I have a few people I need to check on."

"Love you." I kiss her again because I can. Because it's my first year in the majors, and my team is going to the fucking World Series. Because this is my team. My new agent negotiated my contract. Instead of three years at twenty-two million, he got me four years and thirty million.

Is this real life?

I look at my girl, who's smiling up at me, and I know that it is. This is our life, mine and Paisley's, and I can't wait to see what adventures it leads us to. After another kiss to her soft lips, I force myself to release her and head to the locker room.

My teammates are dancing and cheering and celebrating. It's so loud you can hear it coming down the hall. They earned it. *We* earned it. Pushing open the door, I'm hit by the sound. I make my way to my locker with slaps on the back and high fives. Henderson is buck-ass naked, dancing around the locker room. I just shake my head and laugh at his antics.

"Taylor!" he cheers, giving me his back and shaking his ass.

"Fuck off." I laugh.

"Come on, man. Shake what your momma gave ya."

"I need to get to my girl and our families," I tell him. "Oh, and Willow."

He stops dancing and stares at me. "She's here?"

"She is."

"Cool." He grabs a towel from his locker.

"You want to join us?" I ask him. What's one more in the grand scheme of things?

He smirks. "Damn fucking right I do," he says, heading for the showers.

Grabbing my phone, I text Paisley to let her know.

Me: Hey. Henderson is going to have dinner with us.

Paisley: Okay. I reserved a table for ten anyway to give us some breathing room.

Me: Something going on with him and Willow?

Paisley: ????

Me: He seemed awful interested once he found out she was here.

Me: That's why I invited him.

Paisley: Interesting. I'll see what I can find out.

Me: I'm headed to the shower. I'll be out soon.

Tossing my phone in my locker, I grab a towel and run through a quick shower. I know I have a lot of people waiting on me.

"So, where are we going?" Henderson asks.

"I'm not sure. Paisley took care of it."

"You didn't ask her?"

"No."

"What if you hate it?"

"Then I grab something on the way home, but my girl's not going to book a reservation for a place I hate."

"Pussy," he quips.

"Hey, you want to come tonight or not?" I goad. "I'm sure any one of these other jokers would be happy to sit next to Willow. Maybe Miller?"

"No." One word, which comes out like a growl, and I'm smirking. He's into her.

"You ready?" I ask.

"Born ready." He claps me on the shoulder. We grab our bags, tossing them over our shoulders, and make our way out of the locker room. Reporters are still swarming, and this is not something I've gotten used to yet.

"Henderson!" one calls out, and he stops and talks to them.

I keep moving, trying to get to my family. "Cameron!" one calls out, and I stop knowing I'm not getting out of this. I wasn't on the schedule for post-game interviews, and neither were these reporters. That's why they're here.

"Hi," I greet the reporter.

"Great game tonight."

"Thank you. The team is tight," I answer.

"Your first season in the majors, and you're going to the World Series. How does that feel?"

Fucking incredible. I clean it up. "Incredible." I smile at the camera.

"Congratulations on your contract," he says.

I nod. "Thank you. I'm honored to be sticking around for the next few years."

"Do you feel as though your contract had anything to do with your girlfriend, her dad, and their connections to the league?" the dickhead in front of me asks.

I keep a smile on my face. "No. I don't think that my girlfriend or her family had anything to do with my contract. I work hard on and off the field. The front office took notice."

"It had to have given you a leg up. You're dating the daughter of a Blaze great. Is that why you're dating her?" he asks.

What. The. Fuck? This dickhead has officially crossed the line. "No. I met the love of my life at a baseball game. We share a love of the game. Her family loves the game. My relationship with her is based on us, who we are together. It's based on the fact she's my world and has nothing to do with my career or hers. We love each other outside of and beyond the game."

Another reporter weasels his way in. "Do you think Easton Monroe thinks you're trying to take his life? His position, his daughter, his team?" the fuckwad asks.

Fuck. You. I'm trying to maintain my composure when I feel a hand on my shoulder. I look over to find Easton. "I'll take this one, Cameron," he says, wearing a camera-ready smile.

"I retired from the game several years ago. My time on the field is over. The Blaze is a great organization to work for, and I'm proud that both my daughter and her boyfriend are able to find gainful employment with the Blaze. As far as taking my daughter from me, well, that's not something that will ever happen. We both love her, and she's always going to be my princess." He glances over at me. "She's just going to be his now too." With that, he nods at me, and we burst through the crowd to find our group waiting on us.

Paisley runs to me and wraps her arms around me. When she pulls back, there are tears in her eyes. She doesn't say anything when she lets go and wraps her arms around her dad. "Thanks, Dad," she murmurs.

"I've got you, princess. Always."

She comes back to me, and I pull her close, kissing her temple. "Thank you." I hold my hand out for Easton.

"Family sticks together," he says, shaking my hand.

A quick glance at my mom, Larissa, Willow, Parker, and Peyton, and I'm surprised to see them all smiling at us with tears in their eyes as well. Gerald has a smile on his face and gives me a nod.

A throat clearing behind me has me turning to see Henderson standing there. With his hands shoved in his pockets, for the first time since I've met him, he's looking unsure of himself.

"Everyone, this is Travis Henderson. I hope you don't mind that he's joining us tonight," I tell them.

"Hi." Henderson waves to the group, and is he blushing? I make a mental note to use that as ammunition the next time he gets on me for being pussy whipped.

"I guess we should get going," Larissa says.

We file out of the stadium, and I move toward my truck. "Willow, you riding with us?" I call out to her.

She alters the route she was on and comes to the back passenger door of my truck. Henderson moves faster than he does on the field to pull the door open for her. *Interesting.* I raise my eyebrows at Paisley, and she just shrugs.

On the way to the restaurant, we all make small talk. Mostly about the game and the fact that the Blaze is going to the World Series.

Dinner goes the same way. Everyone is laughing and having a great time. Easton is recognized by almost everyone in the restaurant, and when they realize Henderson and I play too, lots of cell phones are turned our way. We just ignore them and enjoy our celebration.

We're all stuffed and full from dessert, but we're still here, talking and laughing and just enjoying each other's company. I'm sitting next to Easton with Paisley next to me. Henderson and Gerald are deep in conversation, and my mom and the rest of the girls are talking about some new salon in town they want to try.

"Thank you for earlier," I tell Easton.

He nods. "They're vultures—the worst part of the career. You'll learn how to handle them. Talk to Drew. The team has a coach you can work with who will help you with how to respond to the bloodsuckers."

"Yeah. I've taken a couple of their online courses. It's been crazy with the season, so he told me to just hold my tongue and that I could do the one-on-one with the coach in the off-season."

"Yeah, it's hard to work it in. Especially when you're on the road all the time."

The ladies burst out laughing, and the sound pulls our attention to them. My eyes are on Paisley as her head falls back. Her smile is wide, and her breasts shake with her laughter. "I can't believe she's mine." Easton reaches over and pats me on the shoulder, and I turn to look at him, and he's grinning. "I said that out loud, didn't I?" I ask him.

"You did. You're good for her."

"She's good for me."

He nods, and that ends that conversation. We end up staying way past closing and not even realizing it. Easton, Henderson, and I all leave a healthy tip, because hey, I can do that kind of thing now.

"Hey, Easton," I say as we make our way out of the restaurant. "Do you happen to have a financial advisor who you trust?"

"Yeah. Great guy. I've used him for years."

"Can you send me his number or maybe give him mine or Paisley's? I want to be smart about this. I know there's no guarantee in this kind of career, so I want to plan accordingly." Something that looks a lot like pride shines in his eyes.

"I'll text my princess the number."

"Thank you."

"Ready?" Paisley asks, sliding her arms around my waist and smiling up at me.

"Yes."

"We have to take Willow and Henderson back to the stadium."

I pull my keys out of my pocket. "I'm ready when you are."

Today is another day I will always remember. The day my team made it to the World Series and the celebration with friends and family. All the puzzle pieces of life seem to be falling into place, and I'm excited for even more to find their place and see what that big picture looks like.

Chapter Twenty-Four

CAMERON

I OPEN THE BATHROOM DOOR OF OUR HOTEL ROOM TO SEE PAISLEY SITTING ON THE EDGE of the bed with her phone in her hand. She's frowning at the screen.

"What's wrong?" I ask, stepping closer to her, a towel still tied around my waist.

"Have you seen this?" She holds up her phone to show me one of those online gossip sites with the headline, "Taylor rumors of a trade."

"Babe, you can't read that shit. They print whatever they have to in order to get sales and traffic to their sites." I don't tell her that I have indeed seen it. The vultures in the media went from showing clips of our kiss and the progression of our relationship to tearing it apart. Fuckers.

She tosses her phone on the nightstand. "So you haven't heard anything about being traded?"

"No. I just signed a new four year contract. I doubt they're looking to trade me. Besides, I think out of respect for you, Drew would tell us as soon as something like that was on the table." At least, I hope he would. My agent too. I texted him earlier, and he told me not to believe everything I read. I'm hoping that means this is false.

"You're probably right."

"Hey." Placing my index finger under her chin, I lift her eyes to mine. "It's just a gossip rag. Nothing to be worried about."

"It could happen, though. It's always a possibility." There's a storm in her eyes, and I know what she's thinking. The same thing I did when I read that article. If I get traded, I'll never see her.

I crouch down in front of her, where she still sits on the side of the bed. "It's a possibility, but if that happens, we'll figure it out."

"How? I work here for the Blaze, and if you get traded..." Her voice trails off.

"If that ever happens, I'm still going to be madly in love with you. You're still going to be the love of my life, and it's going to suck, but we'll make it work. I promise you that. There is no other option. We're spoiled right now," I continue. "The guys on the team, most of the time their wives and kids can't travel with them. I get you every day, no matter if I'm on the road or not."

"And what happens when we have kids?" Her eyes grow wide. "I didn't think about that when I picked this career. How are we both going to travel all the time and have kids?"

"Hey." I settle on my knees and move between her legs, wrapping my arms around her waist. "We will figure it out. We're not there yet. When we get there, it will be a choice we make together."

"Gah!" She closes her eyes. "I'm sorry. I don't know why I'm letting this get to me. I grew up with this. I know how it works."

"We talked it out. It's all good," I reassure her. "You hungry?"

"Starving."

"You want to go downstairs to the restaurant or order room service?"

"Room service. I'm not really in the mood to deal with all the fans tonight."

Reaching into the nightstand, I grab the menu and hand it to her. "I'm going to go change, and then I'll order us something."

I stand and make it maybe three steps before she calls, "Cameron." I turn to look at her. "Thank you."

"For what?" I tilt my head to the side.

"Calming me down, being patient with me. Loving me. I could go on and on."

"We're a team, Paisley. You and me. I've got you."

She nods and goes back to looking over the menu.

"I BET THE KITCHEN THINKS WE'RE HAVING A PARTY WITH ALL OF THIS FOOD," PAISLEY says, wiping her mouth and tossing her napkin on the table.

"It is a lot of food for two people, but I burn a lot of calories," I remind her.

"Yeah, well, I don't. My ass is going to start expanding if I keep eating like this."

"I like your ass."

"Yeah, I do too, at the size it is, but if I keep this up, I'm not so sure."

"I don't care how big or small your ass gets, or you are. What matters to me is what's in here." I tap my hand over my chest. "What matters to me is that you know without a shadow of a doubt that I love you. That I will always love you."

I watch her as she stands from the table and moves to the bed. She checks her phone that's plugged in on the nightstand and climbs under the covers. "Cam?"

"Yeah?" I ask, standing from the small table and making my way toward her.

"Are we allowed to talk about it?"

"Talk about what?" I ask, my feet carrying me to the bed. To her.

"The World Series," she whispers, like it's some super dark secret.

"Yes." I chuckle. "We can talk about it." I make my way to the bed and jump, falling next to her, making her laugh.

She turns in bed with a big smile on her face. "Two for two!" she says excitedly. "You think we can go for a—" She starts, and I clamp my hand over her mouth.

"We can't talk about *that.*"

She licks my palm, causing me to pull my hand from her mouth and drop it to her cheek. "Ew!"

She screeches as I start to tickle her. She squirms all over the bed, arms and legs flailing around. "Uncle!" she yells, and I stop my assault. Her breathing is labored, and her smile lights up her face. "Note to self: no talking about—"

I cut her off. "Paisley." It's a warning that makes her crack up laughing.

My voice may sound stern, but she and I both know when it comes to her, I'm all bark and no bite, well, unless I'm making love to her. She rolls over, resting her head on my chest, and I run my fingers through her hair. The silky strands are so damn soft. It's hard for me to keep my hands out of it.

Her breathing evens out, and I know she's fallen asleep. The lights are still on in our room, but I don't dare move for fear of waking her. Instead, I snuggle her closer, closing my eyes and letting sleep claim me too.

WE'RE IN THE BOTTOM OF THE NINTH WITH TWO OUTS, AND THE SCORE IS TIED. MARTY Harris, one of our power hitters, is up to bat. The bases are loaded. Everyone in the dugout is on their feet. And the crowd, they're on their feet as well. This is game four of the World Series, and if we win today, we win it all.

My heart pounds in my chest, my hands are sweating, and my knees hold a slight tremble as my eyes are glued on Harris. I can't imagine how Marty is feeling right now. This is his jam, and the bat is hot, but I imagine the nerves and the adrenaline are pounding in tandem through his veins.

"Bring it home." I send the words up to the universe and hopefully to Marty as he gets in position. The pitch is thrown, and my eyes follow every move as Marty swings. The crack of the bat echoes throughout the stadium, and the sound alone tells me all that I need to know. The ball is gone as it soars overhead and over the center field wall.

Grand. Fucking. Slam.

Harris takes his time jogging the bases, following our three other teammates. As they step across home plate, we're there to greet them. We're already jumping up and down and slapping one another on the back, celebrating the high that comes with this monumental occasion.

We won the World *fucking* Series!

Clean sweep!

Marty is lifted into the air, placed on shoulders as we all huddle together, jumping and screaming, laughing, and crying. It's a dream of every professional athlete to make it this far. To win it all. I can't believe I'm standing here at home plate with my teammates, celebrating our win of the World Series. This year has been a whirlwind of excitement, and I am here for it. For this. This moment, this entire year will be forever etched into my memory. My first year as a Blaze player, and this is what we do. I can't wait to see what we do in the next four years and the many years beyond that.

The Blaze, they're my home. I feel it deep in my bones. I don't know how long we're here, standing at home plate slapping backs and passing out hugs. I look around, my eyes searching for Paisley, and I find her standing just outside of the dugout with tears streaming down her face. If it weren't for the smile that joins it, I'd think something was wrong. Those are tears of joy. For me. For us.

I break away from my team and jog to her, lifting her in my arms and spinning us around. Her hands land on my face, and she kisses me. It's a bruising kiss, laced with the taste of her tears.

"I'm so fucking proud of you, Cameron."

"We did it, baby."

"You did it. The team did it. I was just lucky enough to be witness to it all."

"You are a part of this," I remind her. "You keep us healthy."

"The World Series, Cam!" she says, ignoring my plea that this is her win too.

"Clean fucking sweep!" I spin us again. When we stop spinning, her forehead rests against mine. It's on the tip of my tongue to ask her to marry me. I can't think of a better ending to this day than that, but she deserves better than some blurted request for her future to be entwined with mine. Besides, I promised her dad I'd let him know when I got to that point. I won't go back on that promise.

With my arm around her shoulders, we join my teammates once again in celebration. None of us are in a hurry to leave the field as we soak up this moment: the sounds, the smells, the emotions. I can guarantee that none of us ever want to forget this moment, from the veterans who have been here before to the rookies, like me, who are experiencing it for the first time. For so many of us, our dreams came true today. As I hold my girl in my arms, I realize that, yes, this was my dream. It's a moment I will never ever forget, but the woman in my arms? She's a dream I didn't know that I had, not until the moment I laid eyes on her. Having her here with me, at this exact moment, it's more than just a dream.

It's my future. My forever.

Chapter Twenty-Five

PAISLEY

IT'S BEEN A WEEK SINCE THE BLAZE WON THE WORLD SERIES, AND WE'RE STILL LIVING ON the high. Cam keeps dropping hints for me to move in with him, and it's getting harder and harder to ignore him. It's not just him that I'm ignoring. It's my need to be next to him too. No matter how much time I spend with him, it never seems to be enough.

"What's Cameron doing today?" Willow asks.

"He went with Henderson and some of the guys to the batting cages of all places."

"Do they not get the meaning of the off-season?" She laughs.

"They're machines. They still play, practice, and work out in the off-season. Not as vigorously as they do once the season starts, but they do it to stay on top of their game."

"Damn. Being a professional athlete is no joke. How did you get him to go without you?" she asks.

"I told him you took the day off work to spend with me, so he would be home alone anyway." I shrug.

"Aw, you missed me?"

"You know it."

"So, when are you moving out?" she asks casually.

"What?" My brow furrows at her question.

"Come on, Paisley. You stay most nights at his place. It makes sense." She nods.

"But we have this lease until the summer."

"And I make more than enough to cover this place on my own."

"I know." I nod. "I don't know what I want to do. He's been asking me to, and I keep putting him off."

"What does your heart tell you?" she asks.

"It tells me that I love him so much that it scares me." It's the first time I've ever admitted that out loud.

"I imagine that is scary," Willow agrees. "To hand your heart over to another person, expecting them to hold and cherish it. That's heavy stuff."

"Right?"

"I imagine that holding back is just as scary."

"What do you mean?"

"Think about it, P. The way you feel about him, and he you, if you keep holding back, you might never know the depth of the love that you share. I know you love him. He knows that you love him, but denying yourself what you really want and not giving it your all, think of what you could be missing out on. *That's* scary."

"When did you get all philosophical?" I ask.

She shrugs. "I'm on the outside looking in. It's easier for me to see it and to describe it than it is for you. I'm sure if I were in your shoes, I'd be feeling the same way, and I know without a shadow of a doubt that you'd be sitting right here telling me the same thing. To forget about my fears and take a leap into the unknown. If it doesn't work out, you know you have a place with me always."

"I feel like I'm just abandoning you."

"It's fine, Paisley. I know that neither of us had the expectations that we would be roommates for the rest of our lives. We both wanted to fall in love and one day start a family. Life comes at you when you least expect it, and sometimes you just have to take a leap of faith."

"Yeah," I agree. "I love him so much, Wil."

She reaches over and places her hand over mine, where I sit across from her on the couch. "I know you do. He loves you too. You'd be blind not to see it."

I let her words take root, and excitement bubbles up inside me. I want to take this next step with him. "I want to take the leap," I tell my best friend.

"Of course you do. And when he pisses you off, you can use your key to come stay with me."

"Like he would let that happen."

She laughs. "That man would go crazy not having you next to him."

I don't argue because she's right. I feel his love for me deep in my soul. I'll tell him tonight. "Maybe I'll take a few things over while he's gone," I tell her.

"I'm down to help." She smiles.

I know she is. Willow has been my best friend forever. She knows everything about me, and I her. I'll always be here for her, just like she's offered to be here for me. That's just what you do for your best friend.

"So, what's going on with you and Travis?" I ask.

She blushes. "I don't really know to be honest. Nothing? Something? He asked for my number that night we all had dinner, and he texts me all the time."

"Have you seen him again?"

"The first time since that night was during the World Series."

"What do you want to happen?" I ask.

"I don't know. The tabloids label him as a player."

"He is." I wink, making her laugh.

"You know what I mean. I don't play games."

"Do you feel like he's playing you?"

"No. I don't. That doesn't mean I'm not cautious."

"Well, it's the off-season, so you've got a few months of him being home to take some time to get to know him."

"We'll see," she says, not really committing to the idea as my phone rings.

"Hey, Mom," I greet.

"Hi. Are you busy?"

"No. Just sitting and catching up with Willow. What's up?"

"Well, I was supposed to pick Peyton up from school. It's an early dismissal day, and I just remembered. I'm at a fundraiser meeting across town, and there is no way I can get there in time. Your dad had a video conference scheduled for a commercial some deodorant company is trying to convince him to do."

"Sure, I'll head over now and pick her up."

"Thank you, Paisley."

"No problem. Love you," I say, waiting for her to reply before ending the call.

"Everything all right?" Willow asks.

"That was Mom. She's stuck across town and forgot Peyton has early dismissal from school today. I'm going to go pick her up and drop her off at home. You want to go with me?"

"Actually, I'm going to start on laundry. You coming back?"

"Yes. I'll bring us some lunch."

"I knew you were my best friend for a reason," she quips.

"I'll be back," I say as I stand and grab my purse, and head out.

"SO, WILL YOU COME?" PEYTON ASKS AS I PULL INTO MY PARENTS' DRIVEWAY.

"Of course I'll be there," I assure her.

"I'm so excited, and it's not going to interfere with softball. I'm going to be able to do both," she explains, talking about her play with the drama club where she was cast in the lead role.

"That's great, Peyton." Grabbing my keys from the ignition, I follow her up the steps. She's twelve so she can stay home alone, but Dad's supposed to be here.

I just want to check on things before leaving her. Otherwise, I can always bring her back to hang out with Willow and me for a couple of hours.

"You have homework?" I ask my little sister.

"Ugh. Not you too," she whines.

"Trust me. If you do it now and get it over with, you'll have the rest of the day to do whatever you want."

"Can I at least get a snack first?"

"Definitely," I tell her. "I'm going to go peek in and say hi to Dad."

I head toward the opposite side of the house to where Dad's office is. As I approach, I hear him talking.

"That's a tough call," Dad says. "I know we have a connection to the kid, but we can't let that influence this decision. And by we, I mean you." He chuckles.

"The relationship is an issue. I'm not sure where he's going to end up because of it." I hear my uncle Drew say, and my heart drops to the floor.

"He's a good kid and a hell of a ballplayer. I just don't know if all the drama is worth it," Dad replies.

I bite down on my cheek to keep the tears at bay. They have to be talking about Cameron. Who else would it be?

"I don't want the negative media distraction. Especially not after coming off a World Series win," Uncle Drew says.

I lose my battle with tears as one slips free, rolling down my cheek. Angrily, I swipe it away.

"You need to do what's best for business. You can't make this personal," Dad tells him.

How can he not think that this is personal? He knows what Cameron means to me. And what kind of media distraction are they talking about? The kiss? The media caught us on the field after the sweep, kissing, and they've been playing that clip as well as the kiss cam clip from the day we met over and over. I should have known that things weren't as easy as just letting them go. Now it sounds like our recklessness, not caring who saw us, is going to have Cam losing his job.

Holy shit! The trade rumors. They were true. Uncle Drew is going to trade Cameron. Because of me. The realization has my heart cracking wide open in my chest as pieces of love and hope break off. I can't let this happen. I have to stop them. My head spins as I think of how I can stop this from happening.

Unable to listen to another word of them deciding the future of the man I love, I turn and see Peyton standing there staring at me. I place my fingers to my lips, telling her to be quiet, as I make my way quietly down the hall. I slip into the half bath just off the kitchen.

Bracing my hands on the counter, I breathe in through my nose and out through my mouth. Over and over again, I repeat the process until I feel as though I can walk out of here and not freak my little sister out. I take a minute to splash some water on my face, wiping away the tracks of my tears. With my shoulders squared, I open the door to find her sitting on the floor waiting for me.

"What's wrong?" she asks.

"Nothing. I just realized I have something that I need to do." I open my arms, and she stands, coming to hug me. "I need to go. Dad's in his office."

"I know. I heard him talking."

"Peyton. Can we keep this between us?" I ask her. "Please?" She nods. "I love you, little sister," I say, pulling her into another hug.

By the time I make it back to my car, the tears are ready to fall again, but I choke them back. I have to fix this. I just don't know how. But I need to try. I'm almost back to the condo when I realize I forgot to grab some food. Turning around, I pull into the first drive-thru that I see and order Willow a burger and fries. I don't get anything for me. My stomach is in knots, and I know without a doubt, anything I eat will come back up.

As soon as I walk through the door of our condo, my phone pings with a message.

Cameron: I miss you. I hope you're having a good day with Willow.

That does it. A sob breaks free from my chest, and the tears I've been battling race down my cheeks.

"Paisley?" Willow asks. "What's wrong? What happened?"

I hand her the bag of food and fall into the chair, covering my face with my hands, and begin to sob. I feel her beside me as her hand rubs up and down my back.

"You're scaring me, P. Please tell me what's going on."

I nod, and take a breath and tell her what I heard. "I have to fix this."

"Are you sure they were talking about Cameron?" she asks.

"They had to be. The team was on point this season, Wil. No drama from the press, no scandals. Just me and Cameron. That stupid kiss cam and rumors that the only reason he got his contract was because he was dating me." It's because of me and our relationship that he could lose his dream of playing for the Blaze and have to move away from his mom. I can't let that happen. I can't be the reason his life is turned upside down.

"Maybe you should call Drew and talk to him."

"No. That won't fix this. My dad even told him that he has to make it business, not personal."

"What are you going to do?"

"The only thing that I can think of."

"What's that?" She eyes me warily.

"I have to break up with him."

Chapter Twenty-Six

CAMERON

I CHECK MY PHONE YET AGAIN, BUT THERE'S STILL NO REPLY FROM PAISLEY. THAT'S NOT like her. I try to tell myself that she and Willow are just lost in catching up, but something nags at me, telling me it's more than that. That's why when Miller says he's heading out, I use it as my chance to bail too.

"I'm heading out too," I tell them.

"You and Paisley have plans later?" Henderson asks.

"I'm not sure. She's with Willow now." He nods like he already knows. "Something going on there?" I ask.

"Not sure yet."

"But you want there to be?"

He gives me a slow, gradual nod. "Yeah, I think I might."

"Treat her right." I point at him.

"No other way, my man." He holds his hand out for a fist bump.

With a wave to the rest of my teammates, I head to my truck. It's taken me longer to get home than usual, due to traffic. There's a concert tonight, and the town is already packed. When I pull into my parking spot in front of my condo, I have a small sigh of relief when I see both Willow's and Paisley's cars parked in front of theirs.

I shake my head at my craziness, and all because she didn't text me back. I know she's been missing her best friend, and they're more than likely caught up in chatting each other's ears off. However, there is still this underlying sense that some things are not right. I know what will fix that. I just need to see her. I need to wrap my arms around her and breathe her in, and all will be well. I can go back to my place and wait for girls' day to be over.

That's what I need. I'm grabbing my phone from the cupholder and the keys from the ignition, and my legs carry me to their front door. My knuckles rap on the door three times, and I wait.

When the door opens, it's Willow who answers. "Hey, Willow. Is Paisley still here?" She gives me a sad nod and steps back.

"Hey," Paisley says. Her eyes are red and swollen, and my gut twists. I fucking knew it.

"What's wrong?" I step into their condo and pull her into my arms. She starts to sob, gripping my shirt. I look over her shoulder at Willow for guidance, and she, too, has tears in her eyes. "Baby?" I hold her tight, absorbing her tears and feeling her pain. I don't know how long we stand here, me holding her and her gripping my shirt as if her life depends on it while tears soak us both.

When she steps out of my hold, I run my eyes over her, looking to see if she's been hurt. "Paisley?"

"I need a minute," she says, not meeting my eyes. "Can you head on over to your place, and I'll be there soon?"

"What's wrong? Are you hurt?"

She holds her hand to her mouth and shakes her head. "I'm okay," she finally says.

"Is someone hurt? Anyone?"

"No. It's okay. I'll-I'll be over in a minute. I just need to talk to Willow quickly."

"I don't want to leave you."

She looks me dead in the eye. "I promise you I'll be right over. Five minutes tops."

My eyes flash from her to Willow and back again. "Okay. Five minutes, and I'm coming back."

"You won't have to," she assures me.

I nod, and against my better judgment, I give her the time she needs and walk out the door. My head is spinning, trying to figure out what could have her so upset. And Willow, she had tears in her eyes too. I pace back and forth in the living room. Pulling my phone out of my pocket, I check the gossip rags, but there are no new headlines about me or her or us. So it's not that. I'm at a loss. I don't know what caused her pain, but I know seeing her cry like that is like taking a knife to the gut. I hate seeing her so upset and in pain and not knowing why or how to fix it.

I look at the time on my phone, and it's been six minutes. "Time's up, baby," I mutter, stomping toward the door. When I pull it open, she's standing there. Her arms are hanging at her sides, and her face is streaked with tears. My heart shatters in my chest. I offer her my hand, and she hesitates for two heartbeats before placing her hand in mine and allowing me to lead her inside and shut the door.

I guide us to the couch and sit, pulling her gently into my lap. She curls up in a ball and cries softly. I don't know what to do. I can keep asking her what's wrong, but she's not going to tell me until she's ready. So, instead, I wrap my arms around her and hold her close. My hand runs up and down her back in an attempt to soothe her.

Eventually, she stops crying, but she doesn't move, so neither do I. I hold her, giving her my strength, if that's what she needs. Silently telling her that I'm here for her. Whatever this is, we'll get through it together. Hell, I may even be able to fix it if I knew what was causing her pain. If I knew what was causing her tears.

When she finally moves to sit up, the sun has long since dipped, and nightfall has set in. "Baby, I need you to talk to me."

She nods and scoots to the other end of the couch, pulling her legs under her. She reaches for a pillow and grips it tight against her chest, almost as if she's afraid she may reach for me or that I may reach for her.

"Paisley." My voice cracks.

"My mom called me today." I nod, not sure what to say to that. Did she give her a hard time about us? "She needed me to pick Peyton up from school. She was stuck on the other side of town, and Dad had a meeting too."

"Okay."

"When I dropped her off, I went to say hi to my dad." Her voice cracks, and I watch as she visibly swallows. "I heard him. He was on the phone." Her eyes find mine. "He was talking to Drew."

It doesn't escape me how she doesn't call him Uncle Drew. "What did you hear?"

"They were talking about you. About the media shit show that follows us."

"It's calmed down a lot," I defend, as panic grows in my gut.

"They're trading you," she says. "Unless—" She bites down on her lip.

"Unless what?" More tears race down her cheeks. "Unless what, Paisley?"

"Unless we're no longer together."

"No." I stand from the couch and begin to pace again. "Fuck that. No. Just no." I turn to look at her. "That's not happening."

"Cam, listen to me. We don't really have much of a choice on this. This is your career. It's doomed regardless. Either we end this or you get traded. Who knows where you will end up, and you know it won't be close, so you'll be further away from your mom and from me."

"We. Will. Figure. It. Out," I say through gritted teeth.

"Come on, Cam. You know long distance never works."

"Bullshit. That's an excuse, a cop-out." My heart is racing. No, it's thundering in my chest, similar to the storm that's going on in my head. I can't lose her. Fuck, I won't lose her. There's got to be another solution. Maybe she can get a job with the new team too, but then that moves her from her family as well.

"I can't let you get traded and moved away from your mom. You two are close, and you're all she has. I can't let that happen."

"No. What you can't let happen is you walking away from me. That's what you can't let happen." I beat my fist against my chest, over my heart that I swear feels as though it could stop beating at any moment. "You're right fucking here, Paisley. You own every inch of me, and living without you doesn't work for me."

"It's the only way," she says, her tears causing her to choke on her words.

I drop to my knees in front of her, where she still sits on the couch. "Listen to me." My hands cradle her face. "I love you. Not just for today, and not just for a little while. It's a soul-deep lifetime kind of love. Whatever happens, we can make this work." I'm pleading with her.

She shakes her head as more tears fall. "It's the only way. If the Blaze is talking about trading you for this, all the other teams will feel the same way. You've worked your entire life for this. Busted your ass to get where you are. I won't let you lose your dream for me."

"You are my fucking dream!" I yell, and she flinches. I drop my head in her lap, trying to get my temper in check. She's not fucking listening to me, and I don't know how to make her understand that I don't give a fuck about my career. I have a degree to fall back on. She's all I care about.

"Cameron." Her voice is soft. Broken. I lift my head to look at her. "I love you. I will always love you, but we can't do this anymore. There is no other option."

"That's not true. Fight, dammit. You and me, that's all that matters."

"I wish it were that simple. You have to think about your mom and all that you've worked for."

"Don't do this," I plead. I can see the resolve in her eyes. She's convinced this is the only way. "I can't lose you. I won't survive it." I'm not just being dramatic here. I know what life before Paisley is like, and I never want to go back.

"My heart is breaking too," she says sadly, calmer than she's been since Willow opened the door to their condo hours ago. "I'm not just breaking your heart, Cameron. I'm breaking my own too. There just isn't another way."

"So that's it then?" I climb back to my feet and stalk across the room. "Just like that, we're over?"

She doesn't answer, so I turn to look at her. She's standing now too. Her body is shaking from her tears, from her pain. "Y-Yes," she croaks.

"Fuck!" I roar, slamming my fist into the wall.

"I'm sorry. You'll see. Once you calm down, you'll see that this is the best way. The only way."

"I'll never see that us not being together is the best way. Never." Hot tears prick my eyes. Slamming my eyes close, I fight off the tears that threaten to fall. When I open them again, she's standing toe-to-toe with me.

Going up on her toes, she kisses the corner of my mouth. "I'll always love you," she says as she falls back to her feet and turns to leave.

Reaching out, I grab her wrist and pull her back to me. I wrap my arms around her and lose my battle with my tears. "Please don't do this."

"I-I'm sorry. It's the only way," she says, pulling out of my arms. This time I let her go, defeated. When the door slams, telling me that she's gone, I fall to my knees, bending over and slamming my fists against the floor. Tumbling back against the wall, I bury my face in my hands and let the tears fall.

What the fuck just happened? How did things turn from bad to worse? How in the hell am I going to live without her? How will I be able to play for the Blaze when I know they're the reason she left me? My mind races with how to fix this. How can I make this right? What do I have to do to prove to her that I need her? How do I convince her that there has to be another way?

Chapter Twenty-Seven

PAISLEY

I STUMBLED HOME YESTERDAY, BARELY ABLE TO SEE THROUGH MY TEARS. WILLOW JUMPED off the couch and held me. She guided me to my room, and that's where we are now. She slept in here with me. I had to pretend to be asleep in order for her to finally fall, but I didn't sleep a wink. I've been up all night. I couldn't stop thinking about Cameron and all the time we've spent together.

A sob catches in my throat as I stare out my bedroom window, watching as the sun rises, taking away the darkness of night. Too bad the sun can't take the darkness of my heart with it as well.

I've played yesterday over and over in my mind. From the conversation I overheard to my decision to end things with the only man I will ever love. I love him too much to let him give up his dream. I know both our hearts are breaking right now, but with time, it will get better. At least that's what I'm hoping for.

"Did you sleep at all?" Willow asks, covering a yawn.

"No."

"Hungry?" she asks.

"No."

"Come on, Paisley. You have to eat something."

"Not hungry."

"Well, tough shit. I'm going to make some coffee, and you have to at least eat some toast or something."

"Fine," I concede. I know my best friend, and she won't let it go until she sees me eat something.

"Coffee in five," she says, climbing out of my bed and leaving my room.

All I want to do is stay here and wallow in my pain, but I know I can't do that. I can't let the pain take over because it will consume me. Who am I kidding? It's already consuming me. I miss him, and it hasn't even been twenty-four hours.

Tossing off the covers, I force myself to get out of bed. I brush my teeth and wash my face. Not that it helps. My eyes are red and swollen from my crying. In my heart, I know I made the right decision. Prolonging it for a long-distance relationship that would have been doomed to fail, that would have taken Cameron away from his mom. I did the right thing.

I plan to keep telling myself that over and over, and maybe I'll believe it.

I made the right choice.

For Cameron.

For Grace.

For his career.

I made the right choice.

"Paisley?" Willow knocks on my bedroom door just as I'm coming out of my bathroom. I open the door, and she gives me a sad smile. "Come on, coffee and toast are waiting for you." I let her link her arm with mine and lead me to the couch. I sit, and she hands me a cup of coffee and a small plate with two pieces of buttered toast.

I'm midsip when there's a loud banging on the door. "Paisley," Cameron calls out. "Baby, open the door," he pleads.

His voice sounds broken. Lost.

"I know you're in there. Please, open the door." He bangs again, and I don't even bother to hide the tears that fall. "I love you, Paisley. I'm going to fix this. This is not the end for us," he calls through the door. "I love you," he says again, his voice cracking.

"You okay?" Willow asks once he's gone.

"No." There is no point in lying to my best friend. I know she can see right through me. "I don't know how to do this, Wil. I don't know how to be me without him."

"Maybe you should talk to him. Try the long-distance thing."

"I can't do that to Grace. You should have seen her when she was talking about how he was staying close to home. They are all that each other has. I can't be the reason he gets traded."

"What if they trade him anyway?"

"They won't."

"How do you know?"

"Because I'm going to quit my job."

"What? You love your job."

"I do. I love it, and I love the Blaze. But I can't go to work every day and see him. I can get a job with one of the bigger high schools or the football team. I'm going to ask Drew to help me. He owes me that."

"You'll ask him to help you find a new job, but you won't ask him not to trade Cameron?"

"You should have heard him, Wil. His mind was made up, and my dad, it's almost as if he encouraged it. He knew what this would do to me. Do to us. They both did, but that didn't come up in their conversation. It's business, not personal," I say with disgust.

"Tell me what you need."

"Cameron."

"Oh, sweetie." She sighs.

My phone vibrates in my hand, and I know it's him. I shouldn't look; I'm just torturing myself. He sent me a few texts last night, and I have yet to read them. I may as well get it over with. Let the knife in my heart twist a little deeper.

Cameron: Can we talk about this?

Cameron: Paisley.

Cameron: I'm going to fix this.

Cameron: I can't lose you.

Cameron: You are the love of my life.

Cameron: I can't sleep without you next to me.

Cameron: I can't handle this. I can't handle you not being in my life.

Cameron: How am I supposed to work there, knowing you're not mine?

Cameron: The sun's rising, and the last time I was up to watch that, you were in my arms.

Cameron: I know you were in there. That's okay. I'm going to fix this. I'm going to make it right, and then I'm coming to get you. I let you walk away from me once, Paisley Monroe. I will not make that same mistake twice. This isn't over.

Cameron: We are not over.

My hands shake as I read through his messages. He's hurting. I'm hurting, but there isn't another way. This is the only way to save his career and keep him close to his mom. He's not thinking about other teams and how they will see us being together. Once he has some time to think about this, he'll understand this truly is the only way.

It's going to take time for the pain to lessen. I'm not sure it will ever go away. No, I know it won't, but I'm hoping that with time it will get easier to hide it. I'm hoping it will be easier to pretend I didn't shatter both of our hearts for the greater good.

THIS DAY IS DRAGGING. CAMERON HASN'T TEXTED ME AGAIN, AND THAT CAUSES ME RELIEF and more pain. I'm well aware I'm an emotional basket case. It's going to take some time. When my phone rings, I jump and fumble to check the screen. My shoulders fall when I see my mom's face smiling back at me.

"Hey, Mom," I answer.

"Hey, kid. I just wanted to thank you for picking Peyton up for me yesterday."

"Anytime." What I don't say is me doing her a favor ripped my heart to shreds.

"What's wrong?"

Great. Her mom-dar is on. I may as well pull the plug and get this conversation over with. "Cameron and I broke up." I barely get the words out without bursting into tears.

"What? No."

"Last night."

"I never would have dreamed he would end things. He was so in love with you."

The knife twists deeper.

He was so in love with you.

Was.

"I broke it off."

"What? No way. What's going on, Paisley?"

"Nothing. It just wasn't going to work out."

"I'm not buying that."

"I'm sorry, Mom. I don't know what else to tell you. It was time."

"What are you not telling me?" she asks.

"I don't want to talk about it."

"When you're ready, you know my number. Do you need anything? Ice cream?"

I give her a light chuckle. "No. Willow is here with me. We've been watching movies all day."

"It helps to talk, and I have a hard time believing that the two of you are over. Things will work out."

"Not this time."

"Did he do something?"

"No. No, he's… everything."

"Paisley," she says with pain in her voice. "I hate that you're hurting. What can I do?"

"Nothing, Mom. I just need some time. Listen, I'm missing the movie. I need to go. I'll call you in a few days. Love you."

"Love you too." I don't wait for her to say more. I hit end and toss my phone beside me on the couch.

"You good?" Willow asks.

"I will be." *I hope.*

"Why don't we grab a hotel room for the night?" Willow suggests. "That way when he comes back, you won't have to listen…" Her voice trails off.

"You know what? I love that idea. How soon can you be ready?" I ask.

"Give me five." We both scurry from the couch to pack a bag.

Eight minutes later, we're leaving our condo, overnight bags in hand. "I'll drive," I tell her.

"We should both drive. That way, he's not beating on our door all night. He'll know that neither of us is home."

"Good plan." I nod.

"Follow me." Willow gives me a sad smile before climbing into her car. I do the same, following her all the way to the other side of town. Away from our condo and away from the stadium.

Away from Cameron.

Chapter Twenty-Eight

CAMERON

THE DRIVE TO THE STADIUM DIDN'T TAKE LONG. THAT COULD HAVE SOMETHING TO DO WITH my urgency to get there and my lead foot. I might have broken some speed limit laws, but this is of utter importance. I have to do this now. Today. I can't go another night without her in my arms. It just can't happen.

Pulling into the players' lot, I park my truck and head inside. As soon as I hit the button to call the elevator, the door slides open. I should have called, but I know he's here. He's got at least one trade to take care of.

Mine.

The doors slide open, and his secretary smiles. "He in?" I ask her, not bothering to stop.

She nods as her smile drops. Apparently, I look as bad as I feel. I keep moving past her desk, my stride long and full of purpose as I reach his office door. I don't knock. Instead, I walk on in like I own the place. Drew looks up from his computer and smiles.

"Cameron," he says. His face drops when he takes in my appearance. "You okay?"

"No." I take the seat in front of his desk. The same one I was in a few weeks ago when I signed my contract. The same seat where I believed my life was working out. I had everything I ever wanted and some of it in part to the man sitting across from me, and now, he wants to take it all away.

"Tell me what I can do?"

"You can start by tearing up my contract. I don't care what I have to do. I'll pay whatever I have to pay to get out of it. It may take me some time to make it happen, but I'll do it."

"What?" He seems surprised.

"She told me. Paisley, she told me you were trading me, and I can't leave her."

"Where did she hear that?" he asks, sitting forward, resting his elbows on his desk. His gaze is passive, not giving anything away.

"She heard you!" I yell. "She heard you, and she thinks that if she leaves me that you won't trade me. She doesn't think we can work long distance, and I can't fucking breathe without her," I say, gripping my hair. I look up to find his brow furrowed.

"Look, I know you're just doing what you need to do. I get it. It's business, not personal. Either way, I lose her. She doesn't want a long-distance relationship. Neither do I, but I would do it for her. She also thinks that no other team will want me if we're still together, so I lose her either way. This is the only solution."

"I need to make sure I understand you. Paisley heard me saying you were getting traded. She's afraid of long distance and claims other teams won't want you either. How am I doing so far?" he asks.

"That's it."

"And you're here to get out of your contract? Your four-year thirty-million-dollar contract you just signed?"

"Yes."

"Explain that to me."

"I told you." I sigh. "I can't do life without her." I tap my fist over my chest. "She's here," I tell him.

"Cameron, we can't just rip up your contract."

"Do whatever you have to do. Just make sure by the end of the day I no longer play for the Blaze."

"Just like that?"

"I don't see any other way. And even if you agree not to trade me, she's going to stand behind this ridiculous 'we need to break up' ruse. She thinks she's saving my career."

"Isn't she?"

"Yes, but that's just it. I'm in a position where I have to choose."

"You could take the trade and move on."

"Fuck that. No. This is the only way."

"I'm going to need to hear you say it, Cameron."

"I choose her. Every fucking time. I choose Paisley. So, I need out. I don't care what we have to do to make it happen. I just need it to happen." I take a deep breath and sit back in my chair, waiting for him to tell me what we need to do to make this happen.

He stares at me for several long minutes. "You're awful calm for a man who's here to toss away a major league contract and thirty million dollars."

"Easiest decision I've ever made."

He tilts his head to the side. "You mean that, don't you?"

"Yes." There is no hesitation in my reply.

"I'm going to need some time."

"No. Were you not listening to me? I don't have time. I need this done. I need her back in my arms, Drew. I can't fucking breathe when she's not. So, no, I don't have time."

"It's not as easy as you think that it is. You're just going to have to suffer a few more days. I'll start the process on my end and get back to you."

"What can I do to help? Call my agent? Attorney? What can I do to make this go away?" I ask, my voice cracking.

"I need twenty-four hours. In the meantime, you don't say a word of this to anyone. Not your teammates, not Paisley, no one. You understand?"

"Done."

Drew nods. "Come back in tomorrow. We'll talk more."

"Tomorrow," I repeat, hating I'll have to spend another night without her. "Fine. I'll see you tomorrow." I'll take what I can get. I know this kind of thing doesn't just happen, but we're going to need to do whatever it takes so that it does. I need her.

Stalking out of his office, I get back on the elevator in a daze. The doors slide open, and in front of me stands Easton Monroe and his youngest daughter, Peyton.

"Hi, Cameron." Peyton waves.

"Hi, Peyton." I try to smile for her, but from the look on her face and her dad's, I fall short.

"Everything all right, son?" Easton asks.

My heart stalls in my chest. "Not really, no."

"Anything we can do?" he asks.

"Talk some sense into your daughter." The words are out of my mouth before I can stop them.

"What's going on?"

"She ended things."

"Why?" Easton truly seems to be surprised by this knowledge.

I have to bite my tongue to keep from lashing out at him. He's a smart man. He should be able to put two and two together. "Doesn't matter. I'm taking care of it."

"What does that mean exactly?" His eyes narrow.

"It means I will do whatever I need to do to keep her in my life."

"Cameron—"

I hold my hand up to stop him. "It's done. Look, I need to go. I'll see you soon." I reach out and tap Peyton on the nose with my index finger and walk around them. Once I'm in my truck, I pull out my phone and send her another message. Not that I expect to get a reply.

Me: I'm fixing this. The wheels are already in motion. Can we talk? I can

tell you about it?

I wait far longer than I should, hoping like hell she replies, but it never comes. Starting my truck, I point it toward home. Maybe this time, when I knock on her door, she'll let me in.

IT'S MIDNIGHT, AND SHE'S STILL NOT HOME. WHEN I GOT BACK FROM THE STADIUM, HER car and Willow's were both gone. They're still gone, and I don't know what to do with that. I don't know where she is, and according to her, she's no longer mine to worry about. She's wrong. Dead wrong. I read over my messages again.

Me: Where are you?

Me: Paisley, it's getting late. I'm worried.

Me: It's late. Please, at least let me know you're all right.

Paisley: I'm fine. I'm with Willow. I'm no longer yours to worry about.

That last message had me gripping my phone so tight I'm surprised the screen didn't crumble to pieces. She's mine. She will always be mine.

Me: You will always be mine.

I hit send and toss my phone onto the couch. I move to look out the window again, and the spots where their cars usually sit are still vacant. How am I supposed to sleep, not knowing where she is? I've considered calling her parents, but I know that would land me in more hot water, making them worry. She's with Willow, and I'm smart enough to see this for what it is. She's avoiding me.

I've considered scouring the city looking for them, but it's the equivalent of finding a needle in a haystack. I have no choice but to stay put and wait for her to come home. She has to come home, and when she does, I'm going to be here waiting for her.

I meant what I told her. I let her walk away once. It's not going to happen again.

Chapter Twenty-Nine

PEYTON

MY BELLY IS TWISTING AS I STEP ONTO THE ELEVATOR BESIDE DAD. PAISLEY ASKED ME NOT to tell, but this feels like it's a big deal. Like maybe I should tell even though I promised my big sister that I wouldn't.

I think about the tears that day and what I heard my dad say. I didn't know what to think, but I didn't think she would break up with Cameron. I know I'm only twelve, but even I can tell that she's important to him. They remind me a lot of our parents, and they're the real deal.

The elevator's doors slide open, and I step off beside my dad, following him to my uncle Drew's office. "Easton," Uncle Drew says. He sounds upset.

"I just ran into Cameron. What the hell is going on?" Dad asks.

"You're going to want to sit for this," he tells him. Dad sits, and I take the seat next to his. "He came in here telling me he wants out. He wants his contract destroyed."

"What?" Dad asks in disbelief.

Uncle Drew goes on to tell him how my sister overheard a conversation between the two of them and that she's convinced that they were talking about Cameron. "How could she have overheard, and did you set him straight?" Dad asks.

"I don't know, man. No, I didn't set him straight. There was no talking him down. He's convinced this is the only way to keep her in his life. The only way that Paisley will be happy."

"Son of a bitch," Dad mumbles.

"Daddy?"

He turns to look at me. He must see the guilt written all over my face. "Peyton, what do you know?"

He very rarely uses my real name unless he's mad or it's very serious. "I was there. When she heard you."

"Go on," he urges softly.

"She picked me up from school yesterday. She was going to your office to say hi to you, and she heard you talking about her and Cameron. I heard you too," I confess.

Dad leans over and gives me a one-armed hug. "Thank you for telling me. You do realize that eavesdropping is wrong, right?" he asks.

"I know. I didn't mean to. I went to find Paisley, and she was in the hallway listening, and it was hard not to hear," I say, as a tear rolls down my cheek.

"It's okay, lady," he says gently. "You're not in trouble. Thank you for telling us. Now we know what we're dealing with and how to handle it."

"I'm really sorry," I say, the tears continuing to fall.

"Peyton," Uncle Drew says. I turn to face him. "You did good, sweetheart. Thank you."

"What do we do?" Dad asks.

"I need to have a talk with my niece."

"I'm going to call her," Dad says, reaching for his phone in his pocket.

"No." Uncle Drew holds his hands up. "Let me do this. She needs to understand what he's doing for her. I'm afraid if it comes from you that she's going to get defensive. If she knows he came to me and what he asked for, she's going to take that seriously."

"Fine," Dad grumbles, sliding his phone back in his pocket. "You have twenty-four hours, and I'm stepping in."

"Won't need that much time as long as my niece is cooperative and answers her phone."

"Let me know what you need," Dad says, standing. He holds his hand out for me, and I take it. He doesn't speak until we are on the elevator again.

"Love you, lady," he says, pulling me into a hug.

"I love you too, Daddy."

I know he's not mad at me, but Paisley, she's going to be, and that still makes my belly upset. I hope she doesn't hate me.

Chapter Thirty

PAISLEY

THE HOTEL STAY WAS A GOOD IDEA. WE STOPPED ON THE WAY AND LOADED UP ON JUNK food, and spent the night watching TV and snacking. We didn't once bring up his name, and I'm grateful. However, even though I was exhausted, I couldn't fall asleep when it was time for bed. My phone mocked me from its place on the nightstand. It's been turned off since we left our condo. I reached for it several times through the night, only to put it back in its spot without turning it on. That's an accomplishment.

However, my willpower is waning. The clock on my nightstand shows 6:00 a.m. on the dot. I know that Willow will be up soon, and we have a 10:00 a.m. checkout. I can no longer hide from my reality.

Glancing at the bed across from mine, I see Willow is still sound asleep. Grabbing my phone, I turn it on and wait for it to power up. Sure enough, there is an onslaught of missed calls and messages. Most of them are from Cameron, but there are three missed calls from my uncle Drew and a message. I go straight to the message.

Uncle Drew: Call me when you get time. I need to ask you something.

He's not just my uncle. He's my boss. I know I wasn't supposed to be at work this week, but tension still builds as I wonder what he wants. Forgetting that it's the ass crack of dawn, I find his contact in my phone and hit call.

"Paisley," he answers immediately.

"Hi," I say meekly.

"Where are you?"

"Why?"

"I went by your place last night. I couldn't get you on the phone, and I need to talk to you about something. Your car wasn't there, and Cameron came out of his place to tell me you'd been gone all day."

"Yeah. Willow and I had a girls' night. We rented a hotel room, ate junk food, watched trash TV, that kind of thing." I blow it off like it's no big deal.

"He told me you called it off."

And there it is. The one thing I hoped I wouldn't have to talk about. "I did, but that's not why I called. What's up? Your text said you needed to ask me something."

"I do. I was hoping you could meet me at the stadium so we could talk."

"Talk about what?" My stomach drops at his request.

"Changes in the training room. Not staffing wise." He's quick to say. "Organization and layout. I thought it would be nice to see it through fresh eyes. As our newest trainer, that defaults to you."

"When?"

"Today if possible. I… need to get on this."

I'm not really ready to face him and any conversations he may want to have about Cameron. However, I do need to talk to him. To turn in my resignation. Bile rises in my throat when I think about it, but it's what I have to do. "Okay. I have to run home for a few, but I can stop by after." I need to print my resignation letter.

"That's perfect. I'm getting ready to head there now."

"The sun is barely up," I tease, hoping to expel some of the tension I feel. I don't know how he'll take me quitting, and I'm sure that will put a strain on our relationship.

"Just because the season is over doesn't mean my work is done. Now's the time to plan next year, the roster, the layout, and so much more."

"I know you have a lot on your plate. If there is ever anything I can do to help, just let me know." The words are out of my mouth before I can think better of them. He's not going to need me or even ask me for help once I quit. He'll be mad, and I understand, but this is what I have to do. Cam is… my heart. I can't let him lose everything he's worked for over me. I can find another job locally. He, however, can't.

"Thanks, sweetheart. I'll see you soon." The line goes dead, and I drop my phone beside me on the bed.

"Who was that?" Willow asks groggily.

"Uncle Drew. He wants my help with some reorganizing and layout of the training room."

"Does the man sleep?" she asks.

I chuckle. "He does. My guess is he wants to get the ball rolling and delegate so he can take some time off."

"Maybe," she mumbles.

"Anyway, you probably heard, but I'm going to head there after I stop at our place and print my resignation letter."

"We need breakfast."

"We ate our weight in junk food last night," I remind her.

"Don't care. We need breakfast."

"Well, get moving, lazybones. We can hit the hotel restaurant on our way out."

"Good plan. You shower first," she says, snuggling back into her pillow. "Hey, P?"

"Yeah?"

"You sure this is what you want to do? Put in your resignation?"

"It's what I have to do for him. It's the right thing."

"Then why break up with him?"

"I need to shower," I say, ignoring her. I don't really know what I'm doing. It feels as though my heart has been ripped out of my chest. Maybe once this all blows over, he'll forgive me and we can find our way back to each other? If not, well, at least I know that I did what was right.

I toss my pillow at her and throw the covers off, climbing out of bed—my body protests from exhaustion. Maybe, just maybe, when I get home, I'll be tired enough to at least take a nap. I can't keep running on fumes. Something has to give. It's just hard to sleep without him.

I WAVE TO THE SECURITY GUARD, FLASHING MY BADGE AS I MAKE MY WAY INTO THE stadium. The sounds of my footsteps echo off the walls. It's a complete contrast from game days. Then this place is busting at the seams with excited fans. I like it both ways. Loud and boisterous, as well as quiet and calm.

Stepping on the elevator, I hit the button to take me to the top floor, where all the offices and conference rooms are located. When the doors slide open, I'm not surprised to see that the desk where Uncle Drew's secretary usually sits is empty. It is Saturday, after all. Making my way down the hall, I stop outside his office and knock on the open door.

"There she is." Uncle Drew smiles. He stands from his desk and walks toward me. My feet carry me into his office, meeting him halfway. He wraps his strong arms around me in a hug and ushers me to sit at one of the chairs across from his desk. "How are you?" he asks, concern lacing his voice. I see the worry in his eyes.

I shrug. "Don't really want to talk about it."

"Talking helps," he counters.

"Please? Don't make me do this." It's a plea that I shouldn't be asking for. I know that tucked in my purse sits a plain white envelope with my resignation letter. My hands tremble, so I grip them into fists to keep him from noticing. "Actually, I do need to talk to you. I have something to tell you." I reach down to my purse, and freeze when my name is called.

"Paisley." I hear my name called from the door, and I close my eyes. This can't be happening.

Snapping my eyes open, I glare at Uncle Drew. "Did you set me up?" I accuse.

"No."

"He and I are meeting today. I was just stopping in before hitting the gym," Cameron says, his voice now closer than before.

I keep my eyes locked on my uncle. "You didn't think that was important to tell me?" I ask through gritted teeth.

"I didn't anticipate an issue," he defends.

A hand lands on my shoulder, and my body instantly relaxes. His touch has always been able to do that for me. "I'll go," Cameron says softly. "But can we maybe talk later? When you're done here?"

"Cam." I sigh. "I don't think that's a good idea," I say, staring down at my lap.

His hand rests under my chin, and he lifts my head to look at him. His eyes are red as if he hasn't been sleeping, and he's a wreck. His hair looks as if he's been constantly running his fingers through it, and the sadness I see in his eyes has tears welling up in mine. "I can't do this, baby. I can't sleep. I can't eat. I can't do life without you."

I slap my hand over my mouth to keep a sob from breaking free as I shake my head. "Why are you doing this? I know you, Paisley. I can see it on you too. You're exhausted, and you're fighting me at every turn. I told you I would fix this, and I did."

"Cameron," Uncle Drew speaks up. "Why don't you give us some time? I'll text you when I'm ready for you."

Cameron nods. He leans in, placing a kiss on my cheek as he whispers, "I love you," before walking out the door.

I'm able to hold it in maybe a solid ten seconds before a sob breaks free and the tears that I was holding back begin to fall. A box of tissues appears in front of me, and I yank out a handful. Uncle Drew takes the seat next to me. He rubs his hand gently up and down my back, trying to soothe me.

"Paisley, I need you to tell me why you broke things off with him."

"I d-don't want to t-talk about it," I say through my tears.

"I know you don't, but we need to."

"Why?"

"I lied to you. I don't need your help with the training room. However, I do need to ask you a question."

"What?" I ask, confused. The letter in my purse is long forgotten.

"Why didn't you come to us, your dad and me, when you overheard our conversation?"

"How do you know about that?" I ask.

"Answer my question, and I'll answer yours."

"Because I knew. I knew you were talking about us." I take a deep breath. "I did what I had to do to save his career. He loves this team, he's close to his mom, and if he's traded, that's all taken away from him."

He holds my stare. "And you felt calling things off was your only option?"

"Yes. Other teams are not going to want the drama, just like you don't," I explain. "And long distance, it will never work. I need him too much." My voice cracks. "I just—This was the only way."

"That's funny because I had a meeting with my new first baseman yesterday morning. He came to tell me he wanted out of his contract. He wanted me to rip it up. He didn't care about the repercussions."

"What?" I whisper.

"Cameron." He gives me a pointed look. "He wants out of his contract. He claims that's the only way he can have you because you're stubborn as hell."

"No. You can't do that. He's worked too hard for this. Please. You have to just let him stay."

"And how is that going to work out for you? Seeing him every day?"

"I've been looking for other positions."

"Since when?"

"Yesterday."

"No." He stands and walks back around his desk. "You're not quitting."

"You can't tear up his contract. He'll be fined, and just… no."

Uncle Drew shrugs. "It's what he wants."

"No. It's not what he wants. He's being stubborn. He's not thinking clearly. He can't just throw away his career."

"It's his choice, Paisley."

"No. He can't do that." I stand from my chair. "I can talk some sense into him," I tell him.

"Yeah?" he asks.

"Just… don't do anything. Not yet." I turn and storm out of his office and to the elevator.

I can't believe Cameron did that. I'm trying to save his career while he's trying to ruin it. He's fighting against me, and I don't understand it. When the elevator doors open, I rush off, heading toward the workout room. The closer I get, the madder I get at him. I did this for him, and he still makes moves to ruin his career. What the hell is he thinking?

Pushing through the door of the gym, it's eerily quiet except for the low hum of the treadmill. I glance that way and see Cameron with his headphones on, staring straight ahead as his feet pound away on the belt.

Seeing him here, working out in his first week into the off-season, I see his dedication to the sport he loves and to his career. I don't know why he told Drew to end his contract, but that's not happening. Not on my watch.

I stomp toward him and stop in his line of sight, planting my hands on my hips. He stops the machine and rips the headphones off his ears, grabbing a towel and stepping off the machine.

"Paisley." He breathes my name like a caress. One that I force myself and my body to ignore.

"What in the hell do you think you're doing?" I yell at him.

He glances at the treadmill. "Working out."

"Don't play dumb with me, Cameron Taylor." I step forward and poke his chest. "Why are you trying to get out of your contract? Why did you tell Drew to rip it up? You're throwing away your career."

He nods.

"Speak!" I yell again. "Use your fucking words, Cameron. I want to know why. Why are you doing this? You're fighting against me. I'm trying to save your career while you're trying to ruin it. Tell me why."

"Why?" He huffs out a laugh. "You just don't get it, do you?" He shakes his head. "You want to know why? I'll tell you why. Because I fucking love you, Paisley." I open my mouth to speak, but he talks before I have a chance. "We're talking soul-deep never-recover kind of love." His voice softens. "I love you beyond the game, baby. You are the most important person in my life. There is nothing I wouldn't do, nothing I wouldn't give up to be with you." His eyes bore into mine.

My heart stalls in my chest as I process what he's saying. He loves me enough to give it all up. Not just a trade but all of it. Just like I was willing to do for him. I've never felt this kind of love. Never imagined what it would feel like to be equally loved heart and soul. Standing here before him, I know he's my future. Before I can reply, clapping starts behind us. I turn to see my uncle Drew and my dad standing a few feet away.

"What are you doing here?" I ask them. My voice cracks, and I feel as though I could shatter from relief and from the stress of the past few days. Cameron, always in tune with me, wraps his arms around me from behind, holding me close. I can feel the steady beat of his heart against my back, and I take a full deep breath. It's going to be okay. Everything is going to be okay.

"We need to talk," my dad says. His voice is stern, and his eyes are hard as they land on me.

"My office," Drew grits out before both men turn on their heels and walk away.

I look over at Cameron for guidance. "We better get in there," he says, grabbing his gym bag, shoving his headphones inside, and walking toward me. He lifts his hand as if he's going to place it on the small of my back but then drops it, thinking better of it. Instead, he jogs ahead of me and opens the door.

We walk in silence to the elevator. We remain silent on the ride up, and when the doors slide open, he nods for me to walk out first. My feet feel as though they are filled with lead with each step. When we reach Drew's door, I don't bother knocking. He's expecting us.

He and my dad are both leaning back against his desk. Drew has his hands braced on the desk behind him while Dad has his arms crossed over his chest. Both men look pissed.

"Sit," Drew orders.

We do as we're told and take the two chairs across from them.

"Paisley, we're aware that you overheard our phone conversation," Dad says.

"Yes."

He shakes his head in disappointment. "Princess, what you heard, we weren't talking about you and Cameron."

"What?" I ask, my heart dropping.

"A guy we used to play with, his son is an up-and-comer, and his dad called. He was trying to pull some strings to get him on the active roster," Drew explains. "He's into partying, and he couldn't care less what the media prints about him. He's a hell of a ballplayer, but the shitstorm of the media circus that follows him isn't something I want for this team."

"Oh, no," I breathe. I cover my face with my hands as more tears begin to fall. I can't look at Cameron. I can't look at any of them. I assumed the conversation was about us, and I caused a mess.

Two strong arms wrap around me, and I know it's him. His hold is tight, and he buries his face in my neck. Not able to resist, I move to wrap my arms around him, and he sighs, causing more tears to fall.

"I'm sorry," I tell him. "I'm so sorry."

He doesn't reply, and that scares me. He's holding me, but for how long? I put us in this position, tore us apart from eavesdropping and jumping to conclusions. When he finally pulls back, he moves to stand in front of me, dropping to his knees. I realize my dad and Drew are now standing on the other side of the room.

When Cameron's hands palm my cheeks, I pull my attention back to him. "You're mine, Paisley Gray. Nothing will ever change that. I don't care what I have to give up to have you in my life. Every sacrifice will be worth having you in my arms every night." He leans in and kisses me softly.

"I love you. I'm so sorry," I say against his lips.

He reaches out and smooths my hair back from my eyes. "Never do that to me again," he says, his voice solid. "Never. You hear me. I can't live without you."

"Promise," I whisper. I've learned my lesson.

"I hope you've learned your lesson," Dad says, making me laugh.

"I just thought those exact words," I say, turning to look at him.

"You should have come to me."

"I know. I'm sorry. All I could think was that Cameron was going to lose everything he'd worked for because of his relationship with me."

"Even so, relationships are a two-way street. You need to be able to listen to the other person. Their wants and their needs. It's not just about you and what you think is best." Dad gives me his stern dad look. "It's work, princess. Every day, you have to work at it. It doesn't matter how much you love each other if you don't put in the work. This is what you get." He points at Cameron and me.

"I know. I messed up. I'm sorry. To all of you, I'm sorry." I make eye contact with each one of them.

Uncle Drew gives me a soft smile. "You almost lost me one of my best players. Let's not do this again, yeah?" he asks.

"Deal." I stand and give him a tight hug, then move to my dad. "I'm sorry." He wraps me in his strong arms and presses his lips to the top of my head.

"Love you, princess," he murmurs. "He's waiting for you," he says, only for me to hear. I pull back and meet his eyes. He gives me a subtle nod as he releases me.

I turn to look at Cameron. He smiles and opens his arms. I rush toward him and hug him as tightly as I can. I love this man. To be in his arms again, when I thought I never would be again, it's soothing. Tilting my head back so I can see his face, I ask, "Can we go home?"

His eyes soften. "Yeah, baby, we can go home." We say our goodbyes, and we're quiet all the way home. He holds my hand firmly in his, never letting go.

"Your place or mine?" he asks as we walk up the sidewalk.

I turn to look at him. Exhaustion is written all over his face, and I'm sure he sees the same thing staring back at him. "Ours." It's what I had planned the afternoon that I heard my dad talking to Uncle Drew, and I let my eavesdropping prevent it from happening.

"Ours." He nods, a smile tilting his lips as he leads me to our condo. Once inside, we kick off our shoes, strip down to nothing, and climb into bed. He sighs when his body wraps around mine. "Mine."

I close my eyes and whisper, "Yours," before sleep claims me.

Epilogue

PAISLEY

THREE YEARS LATER

"I CAN'T BELIEVE YOU'VE GRADUATED," I TELL PARKER. WE'RE SITTING OUTSIDE ON THE deck at my parents' place, watching as all of our friends and family mill about at her graduation party.

"I can't believe you're married," she fires back.

I look down at my left hand, where my engagement ring and diamond wedding band stare back at me. Cameron and I were married a year ago this month. We decided on a destination wedding with our closest friends and family. It was a gorgeous day and one I will never forget.

"You excited for college?" I ask her.

"Definitely. Freedom." She grins.

"Just remember to call me anytime. No questions asked. I don't care what time, night or day. You need me. You call me."

"Thanks, Paisley."

"Be prepared for Dad to call you every day in the beginning. Mom too, but she slacks off way before he does. Lucky for you, they still have Peyton at home to keep them occupied. She's the one who's going to struggle the most. When she leaves for college, they're going to have an empty nest, and I already know that's going to be hard for them."

"Let's not tell her that. Not yet." Parker laughs.

"Good plan. You decided on a major yet?"

"Not yet. It's a big decision."

"It is. One I didn't think through so well," I say under my breath.

"What's that?" she asks.

"Nothing."

"Come on, Paisley. What's up?"

I glance over at my middle sister. She's now eighteen and all grown up. It's hard to believe, and it makes me feel old. We've grown closer the last couple of years, and I hope that the same thing happens with Peyton. I may be a lot older than both of them, but they are still my sisters. "Cam's been asking about starting a family."

Her eyes light up. "You want that, right?"

I nod. "More than anything."

"So, what's the issue?"

"We both travel so much. How are we going to raise a baby when we're both on the road?"

"Ah." She nods.

"Yeah. I didn't think about that when I chose my career. I was so dead set on staying a part of the sport that I loved that I didn't look past the career and to the future and what my life might look like."

"You're married to a millionaire."

"And?"

"And money isn't an issue. You could quit." She says the words so simply.

"I could, but I love my job and what I do."

"Yeah, but what is it Dad's always saying? Always speak from your heart?" she asks, and I nod. "What is your heart telling you? If I know anything, it's that life likes to toss out curveballs. I know you're Miss Independent, and you wanted a career where you didn't have to depend on anyone else to support you.

There are other jobs you can get as an athletic trainer. It doesn't have to be with a professional baseball team."

"I know, but then I'm giving up all that time with him."

"But you'll be with your babies," she says softly.

She's right. "When did you get so smart?"

"I learned it all from you," she says.

"What's going on over here?" Willow asks. She's holding her hand over her baby bump.

"You mean your husband let you out of his sight?" I ask.

"Nope. My worrywart of a husband pleaded with me to stay put while he ran inside to the restroom, and here I am." She grins. She'd been sitting on a lounge chair with her feet propped up. "I'm pregnant, not made of glass. Besides, I need in on the girl talk."

"How are you feeling, Momma?" Parker asks, rubbing her baby bump.

"Like I'm ready to pop."

"You're glowing," I tell my best friend.

"Yeah, well, you need to work on your glow. I want our kids to grow up together," she tells me.

Parker's eyes find mine, and she grins, shrugging.

"I'll see what I can do," I tell Willow.

"Uh-oh." Parker laughs. "You've been spotted."

We follow her gaze to see Travis Henderson, Willow's husband, and my husband headed in our direction.

CAMERON

I'VE BEEN SITTING HERE WATCHING MY WIFE AND MY SISTER-IN-LAW FOR THE PAST twenty minutes. The party is going strong, and no one seems to mind that I'm sitting here being antisocial. It's not that I don't want to socialize. It's that I can't take my eyes off my wife. We've been married for a year, and I'm still not used to calling her that.

"Hey. Have you seen my wife?" Henderson asks, his gaze scanning the crowd.

That's something else too. Willow and my teammate Travis Henderson hit it off. They were engaged a couple of years ago and married three months later. They're expecting their first baby, something I'm trying really hard not to be jealous over. Henderson is like a watchdog when it comes to his wife and unborn child.

I stand from my chair, already knowing he's going to want to go to her. Not that I can blame him. The season is in full swing, and he soaks up as much time with her as he can. I get it. If my wife wasn't with me when we travel, I'd be the same way. I make a mental note to talk to Easton, my father-in-law, about how he handled being away from Larissa and the girls when he traveled. I know they made adjustments, like today, for instance. Parker graduated over a month ago, but they held off on her party so Paisley and I could be here. There are lots of concessions you have to make when you're a professional athlete.

"She's with mine." I point to where the girls are sitting, and just as I thought, he begins to move, with me hot on his heels. I'll never pass up a chance to be near my wife.

When I reach Paisley, she stands, and I take her seat, then pull her onto my lap. We are so in tune with each other it's as if she's in my head.

"Baby, I thought I asked you to stay put?" Henderson asks Willow.

She stands with his help, and he sits, gently placing her on his lap as well.

"I'm out." Parker pushes back on her chair, waves, and walks away.

"Hard to believe she's leaving for college," I comment.

"Right?" Paisley and Willow say at the same time.

"Ugh," Willow groans, standing.

"What? What is it? Are you in labor?" Henderson asks her. The panic in his voice would be comical if it were not so endearing. He's a papa bear, and protective of his wife and unborn child. I get it. I imagine I'll be the same way.

"I have to pee."

"I'll walk with you," he says, immediately standing, placing his hand on the small of her back to lead her inside the house.

"Can you imagine how bad he's going to be when the baby gets here?" Paisley asks, turning and draping her legs over the chair so she can see my face.

"Yeah. I can, actually. Think about it. Growing inside of her is a piece of him."

"Aw, are you getting all sentimental on me, Taylor?"

"Always when it comes to you," I say, leaning forward and pressing my lips to hers.

"You ready for that? For babies and diapers and late-night feedings."

"Yes." I don't even hesitate. "Are you?"

"Yeah. It's a good thing too." There's a light in her eyes, along with a glimmer of tears. "I only have about seven and a half months to get prepared if I wasn't."

My hand slides over her still flat belly. "We're pregnant?" I whisper.

"According to my doctor, six weeks."

Sliding my hand behind her neck, I press my forehead to hers. "I love you so fucking much, Paisley Gray Taylor."

"I love you too. I'm going to put in my notice. This is my last season with the Blaze," she tells me.

"What? No. You love your job. It's your dream job."

"I do love it. And it was my dream job, but something more important has come up." She places her hand over mine that still rests on her belly. "You and this baby, that's my dream now."

"Paisley—" I start, but she stops me.

"Beyond the game, Taylor."

My heart is so full of love for this amazing woman. My wife. The mother of my unborn child. Those three words have deep meaning for us, and I know she didn't come to this decision lightly. I'll support her with whatever she decides. I told her we would figure it out, and we can. Together.

Acknowledgments

To my family:

You are the glue that holds me together. Thank you for always being there for me. We've had a rough year, but we're still standing. I love you.

Sara Eirew:

I bought this one years ago and I have been holding on to it. I'm glad to finally write a story for this image. Thank you for doing what you do.

Jersery Girl Design:

Thank you for making the paperbacks beautiful. You're amazing and I cannot thank you enough for all that you do.

Sommer Stein:

I love the cover design for this series. Thank you for working with me in making Beyond the Bases and the design a series. I can't wait to reveal the remaining two covers.

Lacey Black:

My dear friend. Thank you for always being there with life, and work. I value our friendship, and our working relationship more than you will ever know. I can't wait to see what our co-writing journey takes us.

My beta team:

Jamie, Stacy, Lauren, Erica, and Franci I would be lost without you. You read my words as much as I do, and I can't tell you what your input and all the time you give means to me. Countless messages and bouncing idea, you ladies keep me sane with the characters are being anything but. Thank you from the bottom of my heart for taking this wild ride with me.

Give Me Books:

With every release, your team works diligently to get my book in the hands of bloggers. I cannot tell you how thankful I am for your services.

Tempting Illustrations:

Thank you for everything. I would be lost without you.

Julie Deaton:

Thank you for giving this book a set of fresh final eyes.

Jenny Sims:

Thank you for helping polish this book to be the best than it can be.

Becky Johnson:

I could not do this without you. Thank you for pushing me, and making me work for it.

Marisa Corvisiero:

Thank you for all that you do. I know I'm not the easiest client. I'm blessed to have you on this journey with me.

Brittany Holland:

Thank you for your assistance with the blurb. You saved me!

Chasidy Renee:

Our working relationship is new to both of us, but I'm so grateful for you. Thank you for everything you do!

Erica Caudill & Kaitie Reister:

Thank you both for your baseball expertise. You helped me so much with this book!

Bloggers:

Thank you, doesn't seem like enough. You don't get paid to do what you do. It's from the kindness of your heart and your love of reading that fuels you. Without you, without your pages, your voice, your reviews, spreading the word it would be so much harder if not impossible to get my words in reader's hands. I can't tell you how much your never-ending support means to me. Thank you for being you, thank you for all that you do.

To my reader group, Kaylee's Crew:

You are my people. I love all of the messages and emails you send me. I love the little book community we've created. You are my family. Thank you for all of your love and support not just with books, but with life. Thank you for being on this wild ride with me.

Much love,

Kaylee Ryan
AUTHOR

Made in the USA
Monee, IL
28 February 2022